The Daughter-in-Law Society

This is a work of fiction. All of the main characters and events portrayed in this novel are products of the author's imagination.

For information, email Patricia@PatriciaWeber.com

ISBN 978-0-615-62759-5

Edition June 2012

Daughter-in-law, you are not alone. We welcome you with open arms at www.Motherinlawhell.com

To my Mother and Eric

If it was not for your unconditional love and guidance, I wouldn't be the person I am today. You have always been my biggest fans.

Acknowledgements

Before all others, I must thank my genius editor, Kerry Zukus who guided me through this scary and sometimes defeating process. You believed in me as a writer and helped to turn my words into something more. You are an honorary DIL now. I put your badge in the mail.

This book is dedicated to the real women of our ever-growing web community. Through your own stories, you have helped so many women realize that they are not alone in this struggle. To my SIL Robin, the website would be nothing without you. To my brothers Bruce, Eric and Joel, I am finally happy that I wasn't an only child. And to my best friend Debbie Johnson for sitting down next to me in 5th grade when no one else would. Even then, you saw something in me that others did not. As much as you think you owe me, I really owe you for always believing in me and my crazy ideas. To mother-in-law, father-in-law and sister-in-law, thank you for welcoming me into your life with open arms. And to Tom, Shalini, Brandon, Melina, Joey, Tyler, and Tricia. I could not have picked a better family if I tried. To my second parents Gus and Druann, the Olsen, Johnson, and Greenwood families, Skylar and Payton, I love you all. To E'Schell for giving me a lifetime of laughter. Cathy, Tami, Jared, Bari, Michelle K, and to all of my friends, I hope I bring you as much happiness as you bring me.

Dad, I know how proud you are of your Goo Goo Chicken. And to Robert, you will always be my Man of Honor. I know you are taking care of my Chloe and Skeemo. I love and miss you all so much.

And to my husband Ray and little Suki Bean, I love you with all of my heart and then some.

The Daughter-in-Law Society

A novel

By Patricia Bachkoff Weber

Chapter One

What am I doing here?

It's the sort of thing a person thinks when they're about to enter a crackhouse or the temple of a Kool-Aid-drinking cult. For all I know, I might just be at the doorstep of either.

Let me explain.

I hate my mother-in-law. Check that; *she* hates *me*. Inversely, when one is hated, one is often compelled to hate back. I wish it weren't the case, but it's like the punch and the "Ouch!" One reactively follows the other, regardless of lack of forethought or premeditation.

How do I know I am hated? No single event. It's simply cumulative. There have been, in fact, hundreds of events; enough to fill a book. But along with those living nightmares, there is simply the day in, day out beating down of my soul. For instance, just once I want my mother-in-law to smile when she sees me instead of looking like she just ate a piece of dog poop. I want her to make it through just one meal without making some wiseass remark about my cooking. I want her to say, "Hello," when she calls our house instead of snapping, "Can I speak with my son?" I want her to respect that I shall make babies if and when it is appropriate according to *my* personal timetable. She does *not* own my uterus.

My mother-in-law is my Achilles Heel. I can handle any boss, any co-worker, any client, any anything it seems. But I love my husband and I want our marriage to work. I want it to be like my own parents' marriage, which is wonderful, and that's what is making this all so hard.

Boys love their mothers; at least most of the boys I have known. You can have every kind of fight with a man, but leave his mother out of it. That must be why they invented those "Yo Momma" jokes. The object of the game is not only to be the funniest, but to incite your opponent to violent anger. I can say just about anything to my husband, Kyle, so long as I don't diss his mom. When I do, his entire disposition changes. It's the one time I *really* don't like him when he's angry. After an argument about his mother, there is definitely no make-up sex.

I'm rambling. Sorry.

I'm sitting in my car, getting up the nerve to enter what appears to be the antithesis of a crackhouse—a gigantic, faux-English country manor mansion in Beverly Hills, to be exact — yet my North Carolinian paranoid anxiety has me imagining I may be breathing my last breaths, agonizing my last agonies. Devil-may-care I am not.

How did I get here? How does anyone get anywhere these days? The Internet. That series of tubes which allows us to send much-needed funds to temporarily inconvenienced Nigerian princes. After six years of trying damn near everything else, I finally went onto the 'net and instead of illegally downloading movies or songs, I started looking up "mother-in-law." Too broad. I narrowed that to, "want to kill my mother-in-law." Too violent. It could cause a stir over at Homeland Security if they were looking in on me.

This went on and on until I found a site where women like me were trying to survive hubby mama drama. A place where everybody knows your shame, but not your name. I admit, the ones from Third World nations where phrases like "honor killing" were common, had me beat by a long shot. As for the others, their stories were different yet similar to mine. I was easily able to add some of my own greatest hits.

I made friends with women who understood my angst. I got suggestions. I tried them. They didn't work. Finally, I got what will either be a lifeline or an invitation to star in a snuff film, which is what has brought me here today. My husband thinks I'm at work; cute, lovable fool that he is. Where other women might be slipping out for some hot midday slap and tickle with Chad the college intern, I'm about to attend my first meeting of the Daughter-in-Law Society. Pray for my soul.

Chapter Two

Flurries of anxiety bubble in my belly as I anticipate walking into a room full of people I don't know and discussing my mother-in-law problems. Even more frightening is the possibility I might know someone in there. Los Angeles is big, but gossip spreads faster than wildfires around here — and we know all about wildfires. What if one of my mother-in-law's friends is at the meeting? It's possible they too may hate their own mother-in-law, but it probably won't make them any more understanding of my own feelings toward their dear friend. She can be human in front of others; I've seen her do it. Her fangs shrink but I've never been sure what she does with her tail. She probably has her slacks tailor-made to hide the damn thing.

"Welcome!" the smiling, gorgeous, late-thirties blonde greets me, holding her arms open like some starlet on a game show. She all but blows me air kisses. "Come in, come in!"

Did Entertainment Tonight's camera crew just arrive? I look behind me and see no one else—no cameras, no reporters, so she must be talking to me. She's very enthusiastic. I'm politely ushered in. So lavish is the home that when I hear music in the background, I wonder briefly if Sir Elton is sitting at a white grand piano somewhere off stage. Two tiny designer dogs, Chi-Poos I think, run in from another room and bounce around my feet like little battery-operated toys. One wears a *Miss All That* shirt and the other one is sporting a tee that kindly proclaims *Drama Queen*. Nice. These mutant dogs are a staple now in LA and have replaced the passé purebreds. For me, give me some pound hounds like my mutts Skeemo and Chloe any day.

The home and the hostess, who introduces herself as Claudia, are both quite magnificent in appearance. Then again, what is not magnificent in Beverly Hills? Claudia must be a model or something that requires her to be beautiful. I'll get the 4-1-1 on her later. She takes me and the bouncing yappers down a long dimly lit corridor. Claudia casually looks behind her and smiles at me every few seconds, her blonde mane swinging over her shoulders. It's as though she's checking to make sure I'm still there and haven't second-guessed myself and run out the door. But no, I'm in for now, unless I see a pentagram painted on the floor in blood.

We cross through the main living areas of the home. We make a right, then a left, passing other lavish rooms that look like decorator showcases. I catch a glimpse of myself in a mirror and immediately feel the burn of humiliation heat my face. Who is that loser walking meekly behind the confident platinum covergirl? The truth is suddenly right there in the ten thousand dollar gilded mirror. I've lost my mojo, at least when it comes to my relationship with my mother-in-law, and probably even with my husband. He married me because he said I was funny, pretty, good... wait... actually *fantastic* in bed, and smart. Where did the smart go?

Professional speaking, I am an unstoppable powerhouse. At a young twenty-nine years old, I have worked my way up the corporate ladder to my stressful yet cushy job as Senior VP for a Fortune 500 Internet Technology firm. And there were no horizontal interviews either. I worked hard to perfect my skills as a master negotiator and learned that the way to win a deal is with honesty, sincerity, and product knowledge. I live my personal and professional life this way, or at least I used to. Yet here I am, unbeknownst to my husband, in a stranger's home, maybe risking my life, and humiliating myself because I cannot get my mother-in-law to be civil towards me.

After what seems like an eternity, and about the time I am wishing I had worn track shoes instead of heels, we reach the end of a hallway and approach a closed door. I notice a Louis XIV table piled high with stacks of folders and stapled papers. Before I can ask if we have finally arrived at our destination, Claudia abruptly stops and turns, folding her arms across her cleavage like a school crossing guard. Her tone is sweet yet stern when she says, "Honey, before we go in, I will need you to sign a non-disclosure agreement stating you will not speak about what we do or discuss at our meetings. Everything that goes on is to be held in the strictest of confidence."

Claudia rifles through the papers trying to find the right forms to secure my complicity and silence in whatever the hell is going on here. The long walk has served to calm my nerves ever so slightly, but now this talk of silence and secrecy has my skin crawling and my heart thumping anew. Looking at Claudia's dramatic black leather leggings and six inch Christian Louboutin pumps, I wonder if I'd read her email and her website wrong. Perhaps it was just a front for a kinky S&M club. Jesus, what have I gotten myself into? Of course, I can't just turn and run like a scared little girl. The curiosity bug has bitten me. I must know what is going on behind these paneled mahogany doors.

I try to hide my confusion and terror. I scout out the other exits just in case I need to make a mad dash out of here. If I walk in and see anything other than a group of women pouring their hearts out about their mothers-in-law, I'm sure I'm a goner. Claudia hands me a three-page agreement, which I scan and sign. Nothing scary. The only thing unique is the glossary: Mother-in-law — "MIL". Daughter-in-law — "DIL". I could add a few more of my own. "PS" — Personal Satan. "MBH" — Momma's Boy Husband. What is it with every topic, every hobby, and every job in the world? They all have their crazy acronyms and jargon. Pimps must defend calling their women "ho's" because it really stands for "Hourly Operators." I hand the papers back to Claudia and smile.

"Let's go!" Claudia grins and opens the door.

Behind the previously closed doors is not just a ballroom or dining room as I'd expected. It appears to be a darkened Regal Cinema-sized movie theater, not merely some jacked up home theater with a couch. Other than the screen, the only thing throwing off light is a wall with a commercial-sized refreshment bar complete with cappuccino machines and popcorn makers. Lest one thinks the size and scope of this theater shocks me, let it be said I live in an area of California where the idea of taking a vacation includes renting a private yacht and chillin' in St. Tropez with a personal wait staff of half a dozen or so. More so, the founders of the tech company I work for are worth billions of dollars, and I personally made a few million from the stock I was given as a sign-on bonus. Not exactly liquid, but an asset nevertheless. Still, I am impressed.

I can only see the tops of the heads of the people watching the flick so I'm not entirely sure if the audience is women, men, or a combination. I recognize a famous face on the giant screen. Then another. They're A-listers and I've seen all their films, yet I can't recall them ever appearing in anything together before. Then it hits me. Yes! I've seen the previews for this movie, but it's not even in theaters yet.

Claudia must have been reading my mind because she informs me her husband is a bigwig movie producer and gets to pre-screen movies before they hit theaters. She likes to share them with her "close friends." Wow, I guess I'm a close friend now. As I am about to say what a cool gig that is, Claudia floats away. She is heading back down the hallway from where we just came. I stand alone in the dark theater, my eyes gradually adjusting to the room.

Do I just stand here and wait for the meeting to start, do I grab a seat, and if I do, do I attempt to initiate a conversation with someone? I hear some people talking — sounds like women — yet it's unnatural for me to talk during a movie. Just one of those things from childhood. My mom was a "shusher." Feeling a bit out of place, my chest starts to tighten from stress. You would think I'd have some Xanax or Valium handy for occasions like this. Doctors around here give them out like candy.

"Hi! I'm Julia," says a woman with the lean, lithe body of a teenage gymnast. Julia sports a perfect toothpaste commercial grin, something one doesn't see enough of in La-La Land. That's a little secret in Hollywood. You can smile, but don't stretch the smile lest you invite the dreaded laugh lines. It's a city full of women with every reason in the world to be insanely happy, yet big-ass loopy smiles cannot be found anywhere.

"I'm Katherine," I say. My tension travels from my chest to my stomach, which growls as I grit my teeth in an effort not to break wind — a poor way to make a first impression. "But you can call me Kat." I reach for Tinkerbelle's, I mean Julia's, hand but she isn't having it. Before I have time to protest we are embracing like the best of friends.

"Welcome to your new family, Kat. I promise, things are going to get better for you starting today."

Oddly enough, I am not creeped out by her forwardness or by her little arms that make it only a quarter of the way around my body, which I have to say, makes me feel huge. In fact, her sincerity almost seems sincere, something I am no longer accustomed to 'round these parts. Afraid to leave the hug one-sided, I squeeze her back and risk snapping the frail little thing like a potato chip.

"That's the best hug I've had in a long time," I say, and I mean it. Really. We both laugh.

"I give great hug," Julia says, winking slyly, then giggling at her own joke.

I laugh, too, in spite of myself. "You're sweet." I give her back my trademark vampy wink. I do it more for myself than for her and I admit, I'm being somewhat insincere. Fake it 'til you make it, as they say. I'm still feeling out of my element here, so to compensate, I pretend I'm at work. At work, I am a power goddess. I used to be one outside of work as well, but no more. Now I step out of my office and the specter of my "MIL" (still gotta get used to the acronym) turns me into a wimpy whiner.

The "new family" phrase lingers in my brain, making me wonder if this is all a front for the Scientologists or some New Age self-improvement operation. This is LA, land of the Me Movement. Anyone can become a guru.

Julia and I make small talk when Claudia walks back into the theater with two more women. I can instantly tell they are first timers like me by the "holy crap" astonished looks on their faces. I'm pretty sure I had the same expression when I walked through the doors but I'm old school now, part of the in-crowd. Well not the in-crowd yet… just Julia's crowd.

"Kat, I would like to introduce you to Debbie and Ashley," says Claudia. Both women nervously smile at me and I reciprocate. I wonder if I should go in for the hug like Julia did with me; it felt really great. Nah. You're either a hugger or you're not. If you have to think too much about it, it's simply not your thing.

With my eyes fully adjusted, I see that instead of regular movie theater seats, this room is filled with lush leather recliners and sofas. Nice. The credits roll across the screen. The film has finished and the other women are slowly making their way over to us. Yes, it's all women here, just as I'd expected. A society, a sisterhood… or a witch's coven; take your pick. Several of them are holding wine glasses. Movies and wine… two of my favorite pastimes.

Now that the group is together and the ADHD-ers no longer have the film to distract them, Claudia herds us over to another comfortable sitting area with white satin sofas grouped in a U-shaped arrangement. In the center, a gorgeous burled wood table holds several wine decanters and a silver tray of goblets fit for royalty.

We select our seats; the newbies naturally sticking together like sorority pledges. "I want to welcome you all again to our group and into my home, particularly those of you who are with us for the first time," Claudia begins. In the dim mood lighting she looks even prettier than she had at the front door. "This is where we meet every Thursday afternoon at three. I am very happy you have found us and I am one hundred percent certain you will feel that same gratitude soon. And please don't get me wrong; we wish you didn't have the need to search for this type of help at all. However, you are obviously having mother-in-law issues and that is what brought you to our support group. We hope you find comfort in knowing you are not alone. I would like to give you a brief overview of how this group came to be, our global reach, as well as our mission statement and goals."

Claudia turns toward Debbie, Ashley, and me for the rest of her speech. "The mission of the Daughter-in-law Society—you'll find we shorten it to 'DILS' and refer to ourselves as "Sisters"—is to protect and empower women who have sought refuge in our organization and eliminate injustices brought upon our sisters by overbearing and oftentimes cruel mothers-in-law. Our commitment is to provide you with a safe haven where you are free to express your frustrations without being judged, blamed, or ridiculed. Over time, you will find your own inner strength. Until then, we are now your backbone and we will support you."

Debbie loses it. She puts her head on her knees and starts sobbing, crying so hard it sounds like she is drowning. Claudia's speech has struck a real chord with her. Since I am sitting closest to her, I scooch over a bit and put my arm around her shoulder. For some reason unbeknown to me, I feel totally natural in the role of her comforter. I am usually pretty shielded when it comes to strangers, but I feel a connection with her and I want to make her feel like everything is going to okay. Perhaps it is, because I really hope everything is going to get better now that we are part of something larger than ourselves. My arm is still around her shoulder and as I am stroking her, I can feel her trembling subside. I lean down towards her and ask if she is alright. She lifts her head and her tear-stained face sports a small, tentative smile. I gave her a little reassuring "you're not alone" squeeze and move back over to my seat. I glance over at Ashley, who is sitting on the other side of Debbie, and can't help but notice she doesn't seem the least bit concerned and appears almost bored. Ice Queen. I know the type.

Claudia walks over to Debbie and takes both her hands into her own. "I swear to you on my own children that if you commit yourself to this group, your mother-in-law issues will eventually disappear."

While her attention is focused on Debbie, I silently repeat part of Claudia's Mission Statement in my head—the part about eliminating "injustices brought upon our sisters by overbearing and many-times cruel mothers-in-law," and how she swore our mother-in-law problems would soon be gone. Before today, I imagined the only way my mother-in-law problems would go away is if one of us is dead or I am divorced. Even then, I fear the undead and I know she would find a way to come back and haunt me from her grave. That just leaves divorce, and MIL issues seem like a tragic reason to end an otherwise storybook marriage.

Claudia continues. "As you have just witnessed, we will be your strength when you don't have the power to stand on your own." She pauses again and I wonder if we should applaud. Before I begin the classic, solitary, slow clap and make an ass of myself, Claudia clears her throat and asks if we would like another glass of wine before she moves onward.

Before we even have a chance to respond, Tinkerbelle flies off into the kitchen and is back in seconds with an uncorked bottle of California Cab Sav. As Julia is passing around glasses, Ashley puts her hand up and says, "I don't drink red. Unless you have a nice dry white, don't bother." The comment is incredibly rude. When you're a guest in someone's home, just take it and don't drink it, right? Julia looks a bit taken aback but just smiles sweetly and moves on. Ashley reminds me of my mother-in-law right now and I have such an urge to tell her so. However, I have to remind myself this isn't my home. I'm a newcomer and I need to bite my tongue. For now. Claudia pretends not to notice and resumes her speech.

"Three weeks from today, ladies, the DILS will proudly celebrate our fifth anniversary. For five years, we have been helping women all over the world rectify their mother-in-law problems, while at the same time forming life-long friendships. I founded this organization out of my own desperation. Years of being told I wasn't a good wife or a good mother took its toll on me, too. My mother-in-law had virtually crushed my self-esteem. I hated her and I resented my husband for not protecting me from a monster who was destroying me. I went online and searched for information on how to deal with an abusive mother-in-law. Yes, there were bits of information here and there, mostly articles written by pseudo-psychologists, but nothing that helped me. Then I went to an online women's community and posted my first mother-in-law story. I kept it brief and just gave one example of what a terror she was. Within three hours, over twenty women had responded to my post. Some shared their own horror stories while others poured out anonymous hatred and anguish. By the next morning, more than hundred women had replied. They all said the same thing: They were relieved to know they were not the only ones out there dealing with this issue.

"This told me something. There was a gaping hole demanding to be filled and I attempted to fill it. I started the website you all joined. Some of you have been with us for years, while others maybe only a few weeks. If you haven't spent a lot of time on the site, please do. For us, it has become a sanctuary, a place of sanity to know there are tens of thousands of women who are all dealing with the same issues as you, just on different levels of severity."

I must admit, Claudia's website has become almost addictive for me. It goes on for page after page and if I stayed on it long enough, I could become like one of those social network junkies who forgets to bathe, eat, shave, or clip their toenails. During the day, I take quick breaks and chat with my new "sisters" from around the world. Guys may have their porn; me, I've got my DILS.

"Many of you have only put your toes in the water, swapping or reading stories, but it's much deeper than that. It's 'instant advice' from women who understand you. You post your dilemma and women respond immediately.

These are real posts from real women. It's an organic movement, not something we ever had to puff up with phony postings. We're proud of that. We've prevented break-ups and blowups and above all else, we are brutally honest. If a DIL is in the wrong, we say it. It's not all pro-DIL—we are pro-sanity!"

"You see ladies, once you discover how many women can relate to you, you can stop blaming yourself. Although we are spread out across the globe, we all have or had something in common—a mother-in-law from hell. Through our communications, we are able to provide one another with a different perspective on the problems at hand. My problems with my mother-in-law didn't magically disappear overnight. However, with the advice I received, I was able to handle her in a different way. Even though my new friends weren't always standing next to me, I felt stronger against her. It was as though I was now part of an army!

"Eventually, many of us decided to end our cyber-anonymity and began meeting in person. We now have chapters such as this one in sixteen different cities around the globe. We meet, we talk, we socialize, and we help each other in an even more direct and active manner. To you newcomers, I hope you enjoy our session today and decide to formally join us on a regular basis. If you do, I assure you, your life will forever change for the better."

Debbie has become deeply engrossed in Claudia's tale. Ashley is applying lip-gloss, lost in her own world. Me, I'm simply amazed that Claudia's tale so closely resembles my own. Receiving an invitation from her to come here today, I was skeptical, and remain so. I'm not much of a joiner, and I take a little while to warm up to strangers.

I would never have the nerve to invite one to my home, sight unseen. But Claudia did that with me and so far, so good.

Claudia clasps her hands together, looks around the room, takes a deep breath and sighs. "Well, I think I've lectured enough for one day. We have a guest speaker today, one of our greatest DILS success stories. I'm sure you'll learn a lot from her. Meanwhile, ladies, let's enjoy some wine."

Chapter Three

I love my Kyle, but we've been together long enough that we've both developed little tricks to get over on one another. Kyle, for example, knows I've been struggling with his mother and so he gives me fait accomplis, delivered electronically and in a manner to which I cannot respond. Example: Today, a few days after my first DILS meeting, I return home from work to find a message on our answering machine. "Honey, Mom is joining us for dinner tonight around eight. See you then!"

The bastard. He communicates with me all day long at work (and vice versa). I have a cell phone, a Blackberry, a PC, a web cam, and a secretary, but when it comes to his mother, he either leaves me post-it notes on the refrigerator or messages like these at home, knowing I've been at work all day long and can't respond until it's far too late. Sometimes I think I should treat him similarly. Call him at work and ask his secretary to interrupt whatever meeting he's in — the larger the better — to announce, "Mr. Embers, your wife just called. She wants you to know she's banging her tennis instructor and would you mind not coming home for another few hours unless you want to watch."

My stomach knots up. I deal with captains of industry all day long — CEOs, billionaires, actors/actresses, and your everyday playboy who wants to start his own e-business, but the idea of having to provide a meal for my MIL (I've now begun to use my new DILS acronym jibber-jargon), is more nerve-wracking to me than having to lose my virginity all over again.

What did I learn at my first meeting? Oh yes… call my sponsor. Damn, this is just like AA. Why *can't* it be AA and not DILS? I enjoy drinking far more than having a mother-in-law. Couldn't I trade in one problem for another?

But I'm still so new; I don't yet have a sponsor. I go to my Blackberry. Julia. Julia, the little waif. I felt a connection with her; I can't quite explain it. Part of me wants to call Claudia, the Grande Dame, but that's bad office politics. Too needy and too presumptuous to be the new person who throws off the vibe she can only deal with the top dog. Naw, I'll start farther down the food chain.

I hear the line ringing and the most pixyish voice says, "Hello?"

"Julia, this is Kat. We met…"

"Oh, I remember you," she says with warmth in her voice. I like this girl; I really do. "What can I do for you?"

I hadn't quite thought through my speech, but I wing it anyway. "You wanna be my sponsor? I'm in a dilemma and I need someone to talk to… right now!"

There's a dead silence on the other end that I don't like. Finally, Julia squeaks, "Well, I'm not on the level of some of the other girls, but I'll do my best. I've been attending meetings for about six months now." She pauses. "You're the first person who ever sought me out!"

I do a quick mental inventory. Not a pro, but six months into the program. Well, that's six months my elder, so she's way ahead of me. What have I got to lose?

"Here's the deal. My husband — soon to be ex-husband if he does something like this again — left me a message telling me his mother's coming over for dinner in two hours. There is no single thing that batters me down worse than having this woman in my house, eating my food. I would rather get waterboarded with rat blood. What do I do?"

"Hmmm…" Julia muses. "As it so happens, that's one of the more common issues we talk about in group."

We talk about in group. God, how I hate the way that sounds. I am not a mental patient. When she says it like that, I envision myself sitting in an assless hospital gown in some dank basement with walls painted Institutional Green, surrounded by greasy-haired girls with cuts up and down their arms.

"Here's the first question: What would you do if *I* were coming over for dinner?"

Odd, but I'll play along. "I'd pull out a recipe I've had success with before and I'd send the housekeeper out for provisions. Why?"

"Okay, so you're one of those types," Julia replies.

"One of *what* types?" Suddenly I'm a type?

"No, no, it's a good thing. I'd say it indicates you're a very nice person who cares a lot about her guests and wants to extend herself in order to make them feel special when they come to visit her."

"You mean, as opposed to seeing whatever leftovers I have that haven't turned green or blue yet from homicidal fungus?"

"Right!" she responds in that perpetually bubbly soprano cheerleader voice of hers. It really should irritate me, but she pulls it off so organically that, for her, it works. "So, go and do just that. Treat your MIL just like you would treat me. The key is, you need to pretend tonight is a new beginning. I'm sure you've had her over for dinner before…"

"Oh, don't let me get started…"

"Right, but we're not going there now." Without missing a beat, little Julia is taking over and I must say, I respect that. That kind of behavior motivates me to give promotions and raises to my minions at work.

"You must put yourself in a state of mind, Kat. You must pretend this is a new day. You're going to first try the high road, no matter what has gone down before. You'll make a really nice dinner and pretend you're doing it for someone who will appreciate it."

I pause for a second or two before letting out the biggest guffaw of my life. Even Julia finds it infectious enough to join in.

"No, no, listen to me; this works. Trust me. This one is tried and true. If it doesn't work, it will still establish a premise from which you can move forward. Are you still with me?"

"Aye, aye, Sergeant," I reply, still giggling a wee bit.

"Pretend, pretend, pretend. Fake it 'til you make it; that's the key."

"But I thought the group was all about backbone and standing up for what's right?"

"It is. You have to work through these things, Kat. The answer is not in making everything a battle royal. You have to try to out-think her, not out-scream her.

"The issue with MILs is we're vying for the love of the same man — our husband and their son. We, as logical women, know there's no reason we can't both share and get what we want, which makes us the sane ones here. They, on the other hand, do not believe this. So in order to win, we must sometimes utilize non-violent civil disobedience."

She has me laughing again, which I like. It's taking my mind off my nausea, which would have floored me by now, but is instead but a freckle in my mind's eye. I guess this is what that whole "sister or sisterhood" thing is about, which Claudia prattled on about so much at the meeting. Talking to Julia, I feel I'm part of a team, not standing all alone in a kitchen, waiting for my MIL to come along to slice and dice me with her ginsu knife of a tongue.

"You want me to be like Gandhi?" I jokingly respond, chuckling at the visual.

"Think about it," she says. "If Gandhi punched out a British commander, would we still be talking about him today? By letting himself get beaten and imprisoned, we empathized with him. He won our hearts."

"I certainly feel beaten and imprisoned, so I'm halfway there already."

"Fine, but remember… new day. High road. You're going to make that great dinner and you're going to do it to the best of your ability. If you screw it up, you'll apologize graciously, just like you would with me. But that probably won't happen anyway…"

"No, I cook a pretty mean Chicken Kiev."

"Fabulous! Just make sure you know your guest's likes and dislikes — food allergies and stuff. Please, don't battle her from the outset. I can tell from the way you're breathing, you want to slip her a roofie and carve your initials into her forehead while she's unconscious, but resist the urge."

She's got me laughing out loud again, like some long-lost twisted sister. Even her sense of humor is as sick as mine. "But we've been down this road before. No matter what I do, she will put me down and belittle me. And worse than that, she will get me off my game and get my husband to take her side."

"Yes!" she explains. "I'm sure that's exactly what she does. And you're erudite enough to have already figured that out. That's half the battle. So what you have to do now is turn the tables. She knows how to be rude in a way that pushes your buttons. In fact, she's probably done it enough times that half your buttons are already pushed before she steps inside your door. That's what I mean about 'new day, high road.' We get you off on the right foot by having you pretend it's me who's coming to dinner, not her. Next, when she inevitably says something rude, play the victim."

"Play the victim?" I repeat.

"Yes. Remember, your husband has somehow become blinded to how rude his mother is to you, but suddenly gets his sight and hearing back when you try to deal with it. That's when *she* plays the victim; am I right?"

"How did you know? Do you have hidden cameras in my place?"

"No, I don't have to. I don't want to say this in the wrong way, but I've heard this one before. Like I said, it's a group favorite. Kind of like 'DILS Greatest Hits, Volume 1.'"

"So you've tried this and it works?" I ask.

After getting into an easy flow with my new best friend,

I get a hesitant silence once more. "Sorta," she stammers. "With my MIL, things are a little more insidious. For example, to my face, she would never say a word. Incredibly gracious to my face."

"I could live with that," I reply.

"No, you don't understand. It's all behind my back. It's horrible. My husband talks to me in bed and tells me after she's been so nice to me, she calls him on his cell and blasts me like I'm the plague or something. It's really horrendous." She pauses for a second, then quickly recovers, "But that's not what we're here about. Tonight is about you."

"Hey, I'm a two-way street kind of person. I'm happy to be your sounding board."

"Thanks," she says. "I appreciate that. But I've got a job to do now and that's to help out my sister, Kat."

Sister Kat. I like that. Kyle's tried to talk me into converting to Judaism for a while now, but maybe I could offer up a switch to Catholicism as an alternative — some religion to which neither of us belongs. It could help in the bedroom. Catholic schoolgirl uniforms. Nun's habits with Victoria's Secret naughties on underneath. Judaism's fine, but there's nothing potentially kinky about it sexually.

Julia continues. "When she puts you down or says something rude, look like you've just been slapped, and physically turn inwards toward your husband. Shrink and wordlessly allow him to comfort you."

"Oh God, that is *so* not me."

"It's a game; play it. And yes, it has to be physical as well as verbal. That's what will make it believable.

"Most likely, it won't work immediately. So let her throw a few more punches. By around the third nasty comment, say something like, 'That's really hurtful. I wish

31

you wouldn't say things like that to me.' You may have to say it a few times and when you do, vary it, but whatever you do, do not respond in kind. Do not lose your cool. Each time she verbally slaps you, say something about how it makes you feel and then physically retreat into the arms of your husband. And whatever you do, don't call her names. Don't call her 'mean' or a bitch or anything like that. And don't bring up anything from the past. She'll try that, but don't buy into it. Ignore her and pretend she didn't say it. Deal in the here and now and nothing else.

"Keep all your speeches short and to the point. If you drone on, you'll accidentally say something she will latch onto and play Ju-Jitsu with your words. And finally, two mental images: You are serving me, not her, and you are Gandhi."

"Got it. Serve the Julia; be the Gandhi."

"Right!"

I'm about to hang up when a thought or two occurs to me. "But didn't you say this doesn't work for you?"

If I could see her over cellular space, Julia would have her shoulders hunched down right now; I can just feel it in the quiet. "Try it," she perks back up. "I'm not telling you it will work miraculously and your troubles will be over. Think of this as a battle and not the entire war. Occasionally, you have to incur a strategic loss in order to win big later."

"I do that at work plenty of times."

"Precisely! Think of your MIL as a business problem you have to solve or else be out on the street, looking for a new job. If that works for you, use it. But don't give up, at least not yet. And if this doesn't work, or even if it does, call me and we'll discuss what to do next."

"There's going to be a next? Can't it be like a game show where if she loses, I get all the money and she goes away forever with nothing but a year's supply of processed cheese and a copy of the home game?"

Julia laughs. "Concentrate. Get your game face on. Focus. This is war."

Chapter Four

"Hello Mom, come on in!" I say cheerfully. God, this really is acting. It does have the slight affect of catching her off-guard though, since I haven't been this blissfully cheerful to her face in years. Still, she replies silently with that "just had a root canal" look to which I've grown accustomed.

"Why is it always so cold in here? I have to bring a sweater every time I come over."

I put on a look of concern which, like the cheerful greeting, is as fake as all get-out. *Serve the Julia; be the Gandhi.* If Julia indicated she was cold — though God knows, she would be nicer about it—I would adjust my temperature controls and so, even though Kyle's mother did not say it nicely, I do as I would with Julia. It's too soon and not quite the right setting for me to pull the "You hurt me by the way you said that" bit. Grrr…

As I walk to the thermostat, I try not muttering under my breath, but it's hard, oh so hard. She's hurt me so often, I resent every single thing about this woman. I even resent having to call her "Mom." Kyle's brothers' wives — the ones with children — have to call her "Momma Lana" to differentiate between their own mothers and her so the grandkids won't get confused. If I ever have children, that will be worse. "Momma Lana," sounds like "Momma Lana Ding Dong" like bad doo-wop karaoke.

"I hope you brought your appetite. I'm cooking Chicken Kiev. Nothing spicy; I know you don't like spicy." Shit, I'm not in the "here and now" as Julia would tell me. I'm ruminating over the thousands of times she told me everything I made was too spicy. How do you make banana pudding too spicy? Momma Lana could claim my mashed po-fucking-tatoes were too spicy. But I digress; I digress into my own private hell where she rents space in my head — and it's a rent-controlled apartment she has no intention of leaving.

She harrumphs and plops down on my sofa. "Jesus, how is a person supposed to get up from this thing? It's not substantial enough — it's too soft and too low."

She is referring to my Antonio Citterio sofa, the one that cost the equivalent of an entire mortgage payment — maybe several. It is, perhaps, the most comfortable, fashion-forward piece of furniture in all of mankind. The Pope would be lucky to have his tushy cradled by one of these babies.

"Well, I can imagine with your…" I was about to say, "short, stubby legs," but think better of it. Julia is short, too, but I would never insult her twig-like bronzed gams in such a manner and so I, again, let this one go. But don't I owe it to Antonio to defend his furniture? Sometimes I feel she's not just insulting me; she's insulting artisans of all sort all over the world. Who the hell does she think she is to do that? What did *she* ever create except Kyle and his brothers

— and I have a laundry list of things that are imperfect about *them*, yet I know better than to read it to her face. "I have some higher, firmer chairs if you'd like. Please, sit anywhere," I smile through gritted teeth.

"I'll stay here. I can't get up anyhow," she growls.

Kyle, meanwhile, is upstairs ostensibly getting ready, which in Kyle-speak means he's cruising the Internet and making business calls while forcing me to entertain his Holy Mother. If he loves her so much, why does he leave me alone with her so often? Still, without him here, I can't do the victim thing, yet I also can't snap back at her because she'd snitch on me once he came downstairs and I'd spend the rest of the evening defending myself and that would certainly not be the plan I'd laid out with Julia. So for now, I just take my punishment. Double grrr…

I escape into the kitchen to put the finishing touches on the meal, knowing full well once Kyle and his mother come to the dinner table the first thing she'll say is something about how I left her all alone in the living room. After a while, these things all become predictable. Perhaps this works to my advantage. It's like going to a Red Hot Chili Peppers concert. You know if you wait long enough, they'll eventually do "Under the Bridge."

Kyle joins us, makes chit-chat, and we retreat into the main dining area. He pulls out his mother's chair while I, of course, have to seat myself. She's soooo fragile. With those ham hock arms of hers, she could probably knock my ass into the ocean if she wanted to. Kyle and I make "How was your day?" type banal small-talk — me, afraid to speak of anything of greater importance for fear Lana will insert some suggestion that could only be classified as both insulting and stupefying. Coupons. Her answer to everything is "coupons." I gave up trying to tell her, "Mom, my company developed an Internet search engine. It's free. They're all free. What's a coupon going to do?" Her response is just to shake her head in a tsk-tsk manner like *I'm* the stupid one, followed by her story about her Uncle Lewis who "invented off-price clothing for men in Philadelphia." I could repeat her "Uncle Lewis" stories verbatim, for she only has about half a dozen stories to her name and I know them all by heart. She manages to recite them on cue even if no such cue exists. I could probably tell her I was just diagnosed with Lou Gehrig's Disease and she'd somehow find a correlation between that and men's off-price clothing.

I bring out the salad.

"Don't you use dressing?"

"It's right here on the table. Six different choices; all good." If I had put it on for her, she would have complained.

She fusses with the bottles, "Don't you have fat-free?"

"They're all fat-free. See…" and I point out the words "fat-free" in letters large as the Hollywood sign.

Still, she looks exasperated. "I don't see anything I like." She then turns her attention to the naked salad before her, as if waiting for it to dress itself by some miracle of nature.

I smile serenely. "Just tell me what brand and flavor of salad dressing you like and I promise, the next time you come over here, I'll have it for you." This is killing me, it really is, but it's what I might say to Julia and it's definitely how Gandhi would speak to a colonialist asshole.

Later, I bring out my Chicken Kiev. I love my Chicken Kiev. Everyone loves my Chicken Kiev. I usually put more fresh garlic in it, but for my MILzilla, I've learned to cut back but…

"What's in this sauce?" she asks, looking quite offended.

She knows damn well what's in the sauce; I've made this for her before. And sure, she's hated it before, but she's hated everything I've ever made her. I simply decided this time to put my best foot forward and make it to the very best of my ability, damn the torpedoes. But I smile anyway and answer as if it was Julia and she had never been to my house before and never had Chicken Kiev before. "Butter, parsley, chives, and a little hint of fresh garlic. You'll love it!" I say, channeling a smiling Martha Stewart on Ecstasy.

"Butter will clog my arteries. What are you trying to do; kill me?"

Slap. Time to do another Gandhi bit. "Actually, I've been reading that most commercial margarines are hydrogenated, which makes them worse for the heart than butter. Besides, in Chicken Kiev, butter brings out the flavor just right. Think of it as a guilty pleasure," I practically purr, looking at her turd-face and imagining it's Julia or some other human.

"There's no pleasure in being dead."

Oh, I beg to differ. If she were dead, I would have more pleasure than a 15-year-old girl stranded on a desert island with Taylor Lautner and Robert Pattinson. But I ignore her and bring out the rest of the meal.

"Is this asparagus? I hate asparagus. It gives me gas."

"Oh, go ahead and let loose. We're family here; we won't mind," I laugh. Julia didn't say anything about humor and I gots to have my humor or I'll go crazy.

I keep my shit-eating grin on while consuming my fabulous meal, smiling from time to time at Kyle, who sort of smiles back, although I can tell my behavior is striking him as odd and out of character. Better I mess with his head by being incredibly nice to his mother-monster than by conking her with a dinner plate.

From time to time I glance over at Momma Lana, who has even found a way of dealing with the food on her plate that is bound to offend. First, she scrapes the breading off the chicken. Then she cuts into the center and proceeds to squeeze out all the buttery sauce. Next, having expectorated the sauce, she pulls the chicken away from it so she can eat it dry and tasteless, leaving behind a pool of butter sauce that looks for all intentions like a puddle of pee, after which she exclaims…

"There's not much taste to this."

Of course there's no taste to it! You removed *all the taste from it!* I want to scream, but I can't; I'm Gandhi. Gandhi don't scream. Instead, I slowly turn to her, smile like Miss USA, and say, "What can I add to it to make it more to your liking? Anything, anything at all. I've got a spice cabinet that has everything from A to Z; from allspice to…" and for the life of me I can't think of a spice that starts with the letter "Z" until I blurt out, "…zesame zeed!"

They say a trial lawyer should never ask a witness a question to which she doesn't already know the answer. I know exactly how Momma Lana will answer and here it comes:

"Nothing," she grumbles. "Some people just can't cook," she says as she pushes her plate away.

Gotcha! Now for phase two, courtesy of my new "sponsor." My shoulders visibly droop, which requires less acting than all this nicey-nice gobble-dee-goop I've been putting on for nearly half an hour now. I shrink in my seat, my chin drops, my head turns in towards Kyle, I reach my hand across my chest so it braces itself against his and I say, "That hurts me so much! I try so hard to be a good hostess and to cook you the best meals I know how. I have never served anyone who ever spoke to me in such a way. I have never eaten a meal in anyone's home and said such a thing…" By this time I have my head buried in Kyle's chest, my shoulders shudder, my breasts heave, and although I have no formal acting training, I have no trouble at all going to my "sad place." I *am* in my sad place. My sad place is right here, in my own home, with my own husband, who time and again favors his own hateful mother against me. In a matter of seconds I have Kyle's shirt wet with my tears. Real tears.

"Well, I never! I have never been talked to in such a manner in my entire life! I cook for *you*, I open up my home to *you*, and you treat *me* this way? You've hated me from the start. There has not been a moment you did not want to break up my family. My family! My children are my family and you don't want me to have a family anymore! I can't take it…"

I have no idea what the hell she just said. I have no idea how one could string together those words or those sentences and still be taken seriously. She did not respond to a single word I actually said or a single thing going on in the here and now, but it doesn't matter. It doesn't matter because no matter how much I am crying, she is now wailing as if someone has cut off her arms without anesthesia. She is making sounds I imagine coming from a truckload of puppies being shoved into a Cuisinart.

I feel something strange against the top of my head. I lift my face from Kyle's chest to see what I think I'm feeling and when I see it, I can't believe it, but there it is — a head full of teased red hair coated in Aqua Net appearing to be nursing at his *other* breast, crying into the *other* side of his shirt! We look like twin babies playing "Battle for the Breast," with Kyle as our frustrated suckled mother.

Little did I know but from the moment I raised my head, I lost the battle, like the kid who ran out of air while bobbing for the last apple on Halloween. Kyle's head swerves back and forth between me and his mother, me and his mother, and finally, his astonished, bugged-out eyes come to rest upon the Last Head Standing — his mother's. I'm still crying, but it doesn't matter. He instinctively begins to cradle her weeping head and shoulders, giving her a tentative and uncomfortable "there, there" pat, trying not to mess up her 'doo — or get his fingers stuck in it.

I am in a state of shock. This is it; this is a turning point. I made sense and she did not. I bent over backwards for her and she did nothing but complain and insult me from the moment she entered my house. And now that I am expressing my victimization in a way any neutral observer would find sympathetic, my husband has chosen her over me —again.

I stare at Kyle still holding onto her. I admit, he does look torn — torn and confused. Totally uncomfortable, but then, men frequently have that "uncomfortable" look on their faces, like when you ask them not to go to the ballgame but take you to the ballet instead. "Uncomfortable" means at least they have a soul of some sort, a part of them that loves us. But it's not enough, not this time.

I toss my napkin on the table and silently go upstairs. Before I had to force out my tears, now I can't even see straight because they are just pouring out of me.

I may have to leave him.

Chapter Five

"Do you want me to talk to her?"

"Mmmoooooommmmm…" I drag the word out like a whiny child, irritated yet in need of help.

"Well, what else are you going to do?"

Silence, then a peep so soft I can barely be heard. "I don't know."

"I wish you were back here." She doesn't have to explain why. Home heals. There's no need to debate the phenomena; it just does.

She continues anyway. "I know you love the travel and the excitement, but your roots are here. Why did you always feel you had to be away? Couldn't you just take vacations? Why did you have to go to college so far away? Why did you move so far away?"

Her voice is the thing that seems so far away. Her voice with that distinctive North Carolinian accent. The voice that always soothed, even when it reprimanded me. She always had a way of doing it that never made me feel unloved. I feel unloved now, not by her, but by everyone else in my life.

"Do you have trouble getting along with Tami and E'Schell?" Tami and E'Schell married my two brothers, and all four live within an hour of my mom.

"No," which would have been "Hell no," had she not been in such a soothing, motherly mood with me, her adult daughter, crying on her shoulder long-distance. "We get together all the time. We go shopping, we have lunch; I watch the kids."

"Are they perfect?"

"The kids?"

"No, Tami and E'Schell. Are they perfect wives and mothers?"

I hear a chuckle so softly. "Nobody's perfect, least of all me."

"I'm sure they do things differently than you. What do you do when that happens?"

"I do what everyone should do. I keep my damn mouth shut. Unless someone is struggling so mightily they could hurt themselves, you let them figure life out. We all do things differently. I could run through their houses remaking their beds, rearranging their kitchens, reading different books to their kids. What'd be the point, though? As soon as I'd leave, they'd just go back to doing it their way. And who's to say I was right in the first place? The older you get, the more you learn to let go. You become more tolerant. When I was a young mother, I was a wreck with you kids. I'm calmer now. For all the mistakes I made— and I felt at the time everything I did was a mistake—you all turned out all right. I managed not to kill any of you."

"But she's not that way. She's the opposite."

"I know, you've told me. And you can tell me anytime you want. I'm always here for you. Besides, the upside of

43

her making you miserable is it gets you to call me more," she giggles sweetly and I can't be mad at her for that. "But I have to put in a commercial for myself and tell you if you moved back here, you'd have none of that nonsense from me. And you can tell Kyle as well. He's a good boy. I'd stay out of his hair."

I try to imagine coming back home. The good scenes come rushing back into my mind—the Sunday dinners, the family fun in the backyard, and even just hanging around watching TV with nobody talking, yet the mood oh so placid. No worries. No stress. Then reality sets in and I remember why I left in the first place: No worries. No stress. No challenges. Bored out of my skull, using only a small portion of my potential.

I know she wants to push it, but I also know she's aware it's never going to happen. I'm the rolling stone, the child always destined to be the one she bragged about to her neighbors. "Kat's living in Los Angeles now. Yes. She's got a big job with one of those computer companies. No, she doesn't fix computers; it's something else; I can't remember how to describe it. But it's a big job. She bought Dave a new fishing boat for Christmas."

I'd have bought my dad an entire island if I knew he'd accept it. But it's never been about me trying to buy their affection. If I knew it would work, I'd buy Momma Lana the island. I just want the love, peace, and the serenity of family to wrap around me like a soft old blanket. I used to have it. Now I only have it over the phone.

To my mother, Los Angeles might as well be Moscow or Tibet. So exotic. So far away. I actually could have a job in some little storefront fixing computers and it would still sound rich, fast, sexy, and exciting to her. That's why she knows I'm never coming back. But the offer isn't about what's on the surface; it's about what she's saying between the lines: "I love you. I'll always love you. You can fail or you can succeed, but you'll always know where to go for love. Its right here, right here with me," and it makes me want to cry tears of gratitude.

In the end, she has no answers, but she gives me love and that's the greatest gift of all. If I live to be a thousand, I'll never be able to show her how much that means to me or adequately show her how much I love her back—how I'd do anything for her. That's the real love. That's the good stuff.

Chapter Six

In a one-industry town, it was a pleasure for Julia Rader to befriend someone like Kat, who did not fall all over her, did not, in fact, even seem to acknowledge who she was. In that sense, Kat made her feel as if she were living somewhere else, somewhere far, far away, like the far-away places she writes about in her books. In LA, aspiring whatevers dropped their waiter pads and raced up to stunt men and location caterers to fawn over them and slip them either a script or a headshot and resume. When you're the author of an entire hit book series, the first volume of which is already in post-production for a major film release, you literally have to sneak out of your home incognito in a burqa simply to take your dog to be groomed. Only once she'd moved to LA had Julia wished she had written under a pseudonym, but alas, it was far too late for that. The best she could do was limit her personal celebrity, happy instead to continue to write her stories and do all the things she could never afford to do growing up in an alcoholic and dysfunctional home — travel, shop, and simply experience pleasure anywhere and anyhow she pleased. The *Dream Song* series had taken off like nothing she had ever imagined, making her the idol of book-hungry teenage girls the world over. Had she stayed in Colorado, where she spent her formative years, it would have been more manageable, but LA was the sort of place she'd always dreamed of, a place to spread her creative wings, happy to discuss story ideas and creative interpretations with agents, editors, screenwriters, and directors. Also, LA meant Mark, who had grown up here and whom she met on her second book tour.

Mark was not a fanboy, thank God, nor was he simply tolerating the hour-long wait in line for her to sign *Starlight Princess* for the benefit of some whining daughter or niece he had in tow. No, Mark said he saw her on *Book TV*, one of the few television venues on which she agreed to appear, and thought she was cute, sexy, refreshing, unpretentious and had somehow managed to find a way to make money writing books. Last but not least, Mark was the only guy that made her heart flutter since Jason, the friend she was not-so-secretly in love with but who never saw her as more than a friend. Pieces of Jason could always be found in the characters of her books.

Mark was her first "fan" who did not want to drone on and on about elves and fantasy lit in general, hoping to cop a feel at some point so he could brag about it on his blog. No, he was a handsome, intelligent, serious writer who wanted to discuss the art as well as the commerce, while at the same time gazing deeply into her eyes in a way that said, "Frankly my dear, I want to ravish you right here on this white tablecloth even if I were to discover you did nothing more than work as a janitress at a Bob's Big Boy." It was an intoxicating combination, so much so that they were married less than a year later.

It was a hazy, sunny day, with light streaming in through the fourteen-foot floor-to-ceiling windows of the gorgeous modern pleasure pad Julia bought with her movie advances. Although she had no idea how many more *Dream Song* books were inside of her, she had already been paid handsomely for the film rights to the three that had already been published, while she toiled away on the still-untitled book four.

Chesh, chesh, chesh. Julia bounced up and down on her mini-trampoline, one of the many ways she tried to mentally drift away to plot out a scene. Chesh, chesh, chesh. "God," she thought to herself, self-conscious for a moment, "quite a difference from the old days." Back then, in order to find solitude away from her perpetually drunken and dramatic single mother, she would stroll in the woods outside her small town for untold hours, discovering special places among the trees and brush, places she would delude herself into believing she'd been the first to discover, places that were put there just for her and her thoughts. That's where she did the first draft of *Children of the Forest*, her first book, prior to moving in with her Aunt Lucy once her mother threw her out of the house for the final time. Aunt Lucy was a notable freelance journalist with books published here and there by independent presses. Aunt Lucy helped her hone her craft, assisted her with rewrites, and eventually opened the door for her with a literary agent with which she had once worked. The rest, as they say, is history. Now Julia dreamed her fairy dreams in a home office larger than any entire house she'd ever lived in, bouncing up and down on a trampoline instead of picking moss from the bottoms of pretty trees she found among the scraggly brush.

It must have been while she was in mid-air, in-between the sounds of the rustling tramp springs, when she heard Mark let out a loud sigh, as if designed to get her attention. She turned around and braced herself in order to slow down her elevations. "What?"

Mark's lips looked like someone had drawn a perfectly straight line where his mouth should be. He appeared neither happy nor sad, angry nor pleased. It was an odd sort of "forced neutral."

"What?" she repeated, a little more intensely.

He pursed his lips and shrugged his shoulders as he dug his hands deeply into the pockets of his jeans. God, he looked good. He could model those jeans, she thought, and his cotton shirt was just so right, so crisp on him that one wondered if he ever sat down or did anything in order to wrinkle it or anything else he wore. He was just so… perfect. The kind of man the girls who bought her books dreamed of finding someday. In fact, by her third book, *Moon Motes*, Prince Jeunard, her male lead, had begun to resemble her real-life Mark more and more in so many ways.

Mark let out another sigh, then finally said, "Did anyone ever plant a thought into your head and for as much as you initially disagreed with it, you couldn't stop thinking about it?" He looked downright uncomfortable as he spoke, as if he were trying to cover up a wrinkled attitude.

"What's on your mind?" she asked, now worried and upset. Julia was the emotional/emoting one, like Princess Lily Lilac, her fairy heroine.

"You know how Mother always said these back-to-back offices wouldn't work?"

"I wanted us to share one *big* office. I told you I thought that would be cool," Julia answered.

"Yeah, I know, but that wouldn't work either." He paused. "I mean, Mother said that idea was preposterous. She can be so opinionated sometimes."

Julia's face lost its spirit as she stepped off the mini-tramp. Mark inhaled as if to begin his next thought, then visibly paused again as if he were catching himself, editing himself before he committed. "Mother says most writers tuck themselves away in small rooms, not 'gymnasiums' like this. Lots of privacy. And she's never heard of two writers working in such close proximity. The way this place is laid out, there's not even a hallway between us; there's not even a door."

"Do you want a door?" Julia asked.

Mark took his hands out of his pockets and began to gently rub his temples. "I don't know what I want. I want… I want this pressure to stop. I just want to write, okay? I'm not that fussy. I'm easy to get along with; you know that. But I've been blocked and I can't tell my mother about it because every time I do, she just blames it on you and we have a fight."

Julia turned from concerned and glum to looking like she'd just had an icicle stuck between her shoulder blades. "Why?" she stammered. "How?" she continued to sputter.

"A master of the English language as always," Mark replied quickly, almost slapping his hand over his mouth once he said it. "I'm sorry. That wasn't me; that was my mother; you *know* that. I would never even think such a thing."

"She's poisoning you against me, isn't she? Mark, I can't

stand this. I've tried to talk to her, confront her as maturely and diplomatically as possible…"

"I really wish you wouldn't do that. We're Russian. We're pretty stoic and don't discuss our feelings. Look…" and again, he searched for words, a battle raging inside his own head. "You and me, we're good. I love you; I always will, but I feel like I'm at a taffy pull and I'm the taffy. I just want to write and make love and have everything be fine. I don't need the drama. I despise drama."

"Who's bringing the drama?!" Julia screeched.

"Uh, you did just there. See, I'm talking low, slowly, and calmly, and you just hit a high C an octave above Pavarotti."

Mark, what do you want me to do? What? Just say the word and… and we'll work on it." Damned if she was going to volunteer the world on a string. She wanted this relationship to work, but she'd also become quite empowered over the past six months going to DILS meetings. The idea was to be reasonable, not a doormat. There was a fine line between the two.

"Jules, there is nothing you can say to her to make her a different person than she is. I'm her only child — it's a 'thing' with her. She wants what's best for me — in her opinion — and she always will."

"And this has to do with our house how?"

Mark paused again. "*Your* house. It's your house."

"Our house," she corrected him. "You're my husband; that makes it our house."

"My mother emasculates me, and the thing she emasculates me about is she thinks *you* emasculate me. It's your house. I didn't pay for it. She burdens me with that, but furthermore, she resents you for creating the situation."

Julia balled up her fists and strode across the room, then took Mark's hands in hers. "Let's stop speaking in generalities and broad strokes. What do *you* want? You, Mark, not your mother. What do you want?" Her intensity made him look away, but she would not let him escape her gaze.

"I want…" he started haltingly. "I want world peace." Julia chuckled for just a moment. He continued, "What I mean is, seriously, I want peace in *my* world. I think if things started to go my way, it might change the whole dynamic."

"Between you and me?" Julia asked.

"No, no, that's all fine; I keep telling you that. I mean the dynamic between you and my mother, and between me and my mother. It would be easy for me to just tell her to screw off and cut her out of my life, but I can't do that. I know you did that to your mother, but that's not for me."

Julia reeled back once more. "I did not cut my mother out of my life. You know it didn't go down that way. She didn't want to be a mother anymore and she gave me two choices: Move in with her sister or live on the streets. She abandoned me, not the other way around."

"We're getting way off-topic."

"Hey, you brought it up. It's hurtful and insulting."

"See, that's my mother again."

"Mark!" Julia practically screamed. "Mark, which part of this is you and which part is her? When I see her, when we have her over here or when I ask to take her shopping or out for coffee, she's pleasant as punch to me. I bring all this stuff up and she denies it. Frankly, she looks hurt that I even bring it up."

"So you think this is me? Is that it?" Mark pulled away,

insulted.

Julia threw up her hands. "I don't know what to do. What do you want? What does she want? What do either of you want of me? Just get it out into the open so I can deal with it. I can't take the mystery and the intrigue anymore. I've tried everything. If you've got a suggestion, just toss it on the table and I'll tell you what I think of it. God, I can't take this anymore."

Mark looked out the wall of windows as he spoke, not meeting Julia's eyes. "She's bitter. She feels you're... a hack. She doesn't respect the writing you do. She looks at all the money she and my father invested in sending me to all the best schools, sending me to Stanford, and here you are, this kid with barely a public high school education, and you're making millions and I can't even get an agent. I can't even get my stuff read.

"And this dribbles down to me, too. She keeps asking me, 'Why aren't you writing more? Why aren't you getting published?' And all this stress, it's blocking me. I wander around and everything I see, everything I hear, it sets me off. I hear you bouncing on a trampoline and I can't think straight. I hear her voice in my head saying, 'your wife can write her trash on a trampoline, but you can't even get a story printed in *The New Yorker*.'"

Julia stood silently, feeling like she used to feel when her own mother invaded her thoughts, making her feel useless and worthless. Now she had it all, but it was not enough. Her mother's ghost haunted her and now even her husband and her mother-in-law tramped down on the great things that surrounded her. Who wouldn't want her life? By the time the *Dream Song* movies come out and the series is finished being written, she could have J.K.

Rowling money, Stephen King money. But what did it matter if she didn't have the basics — a loving home and a man who could give himself to her unconditionally?

"Mark, I can't not be who I am. I write what I write. I'm sorry your mother thinks its garbage. That hurts, it really does, but there's not much I can do about it. It is what it is. And it's made money and outside of giving it all away to charity, I don't know what I'm supposed to do about that either. And as for you…" Mark was still staring out the window and despite all the hurt and the anger she was feeling, nothing he had said made her think he looked any less handsome than when she first laid eyes on him, "…would it help your concentration if I stopped using the trampoline?"

Chapter Seven

I don't exactly consider myself new in town anymore, but when someone suggests meeting at a restaurant, I still get a tinge of panic if its not somewhere I've already eaten or passed by a thousand times. Restaurants in LA are like teen idols — blink and you'll miss the latest one and before you know it, they're on some "Where Are They Now?" type show and you realize not only do you not know who they were, you *really* don't know where they are now, nor do you care. Personally, I can't be that involved in transitory culture, with the exception of fashion and for that, sue me, go ahead and do me.

My high school Spanish tells me that "Casa De Tellez" means House of… Tellez; so what the hell is "Tellez" anyway? People who work in a Mexican bank? Thank God for setting aside His eighth day in order to create the GPS, for otherwise I'd never find this place. Tossing my keys to the valet, it looks like every other conspicuous-for-looking-totally-inconspicuous hot LA lunch spot. Of course, it bears no signage at all, for if you need a sign to tell you you're here, you must not belong here, so go away,

Tourista!

Today is neither the day nor time of our regular DILS meeting and I only heard about it from a personal call I'd received from Julia, my new BFF and sponsor. She, in turn, said she got the call directly from Claudia herself, who must be acting as *her* sponsor. Outside of that, the only thing either of us knows is that it's for a small sub-group personally selected because, although we have been loyal DILS attendees, we have demonstrated little to no progress with our MILs. In short, one could look on the bright side and consider this a VIP meeting or else figure we've been remanded to summer school for remedial reading.

As usual, I am fashionably late as I stride across the threshold. While the entertainment biz holds only marginal allure for me, I can't help but notice two former Academy Award nominees sitting at different tables, each deeply involved in pitching or being pitched something or other. Folks at the tables around them attempt not to notice, just as I do, but we all seem to be failing at the task. Oh well.

A beaded curtain is pulled aside for me and I enter a private room where Claudia and Julia are already seated — well, semi-private, considering the only thing separating us from the TV and movie folk is a damn set of glass beads. Julia jumps up and gives me a great big hug, or as big a hug as the little thing can manage, pulling me over to the seat next to her. Plopping down, I notice some other woman I don't know and… Ashley, Ice Queen of the Hills.

Actually, Ashley seems to have defrosted a tiny bit as of late. I have this habit of pigeonholing people from the moment I meet them and I must learn to stop that, but nevertheless, Ashley will never be someone I would describe as warm and fuzzy. In the meetings since we first met, I've heard her speak about her personal situation with her MIL and truth be told, it was compelling.

"When I met Marshall, it was instant 'Wow!' We clicked in a way I've never felt before. My knees buckled and once we got to talking — once I was *able* to talk — I realized I had also found my soul mate.

"The thing was, his father died a number of years before and left him a lot of money. I'd never been with a Trust Fund Kid before, but Marshall wasn't like any of the clichés. He was nice, and he wasn't spoiled at all. In fact, he lived downright frugally.

"Soon after we got involved, I discovered a lot of that non-materialistic behavior was just Marshall coping with his personal situation. His dad set up his trust so Marshall's mother controls it. I mean, we're not talking a little kid here. Most kids with trusts, they get to manage all the money themselves by the time they turn eighteen or twenty-one, or at the worst, twenty-five. But Marshall's dad, even though Marshall never gave him any reason to distrust him, set it up so the mother held all the purse strings for as long as she lived. Every single year, Marshall has to literally get down on his hands and knees to beg for pennies from the table. That money is his! His mother already has her own money. The old man was loaded. I don't know what she's doing with it. Marshall doesn't even get regular statements. He practically has to sue in order to get a look at where the money is and what's happening with it. And even what we see, I don't necessarily trust to be accurate. His mother is so evil, I wouldn't be surprised if there were two sets of books and she was skimming off the top. My fear is that when she croaks, there won't be a dime left for us.

"It's easy to say, 'it's not all about the money,' but in this case, the money is at the root of it all. So long as she controls Marshall's trust fund, she controls Marshall, and since Marshall is my husband, she controls me. I can't stand it. I've spent my life as an individual, as an independent person, and now I'm some sort of indentured slave. Marshall and I, we live like paupers."

"What does Marshall do?" asked one of our fellow Sisters.

"He's a dentist, but what does *that* pay? I mean, he doesn't have that big a practice. And he does the whole, 'fix the rotten teeth on the Third World child for free' thing, too, which eats up time and brings in no money.

"It's expensive to live in this town. I'm not asking for Spelling's mansion; I just want to live a nice, comfortable lifestyle. If Marshall got his money — the money *he* inherited that's rightfully ours — he could continue to tinker around with teeth and we could live right."

"What do *you* do?" asked another Sister. "Do you work?"

"Of course I do," Ashley said with more than a hint of irritation. "I have my real estate license. Do you know one out of three Californians has a real estate license? That means there are two customers for each of us! How can you make a living that way? How many of you here have your real estate license?" Hands all over the room rose meekly skyward. "I rest my case."

If I had to depend on Momma Lana Ding Dong for my grocery money I would have to murder the woman, which jumped to the forefront of my mind as I thought, *of all the women here, this is the one who might be best served by hiring a hitman. I wonder if Claudia offers that as a value-added service.*

My eyes wander to the other woman at our lunch table, a stranger to me. She looks exotic — Latina, I would presume — and is so stunning. I peg her for a model-actress, although one who is over thirty and thus already playing more mature roles — not that there's anything wrong with that. Claudia turns to me and says, "Katherine, this is Gabriella." Gabriella takes my hand and makes eye contact, yet at the same time has some sort of communications device in her other hand and something stuck in her ear and never ceases to keep working them both. Me, I'm in the tech industry and I keep up on these things, but Gabriella's got some sort of new Apple Blackberry Mochachino Half-Caf Blue Tooth Green-Eyed iMonster thing-a-ma-jiggy that even I've never seen before. And this chick is giving me the firm handshake, the straight eye, talking to Tokyo via Iceland on conference, while texting Bermuda in Italian and she's got it all covered, all at once. I have met the fembot cyborg of the future and she has the power to destroy us all.

In our private dining room we have our own private stealth waiter, the kind who magically appears and disappears as needed and never interrupts a single conversation, and he's pouring sparkling water that never goes flat and never fluctuates from a perfect temperature. Ah, the good life.

Claudia runs the soiree with the sort of effortless, elegant, yet unquestionable control known only to ancient Egyptian queens. "Ladies, for those of you who do not know my great, great friend Gabriella, she, too, is a member of our organization, one who has also trodden down the same road all of us have landed upon. Gab… well, perhaps, I would fall short were I to attempt to bring Gabriella's own unique story to life anywhere near as well as she herself can, and so I give her the floor."

All eyes swivel towards Gabriella, who I swear is still having at least three different telephone conversations at the same time in four or five different languages, while continuing to text message at two hundred ninety words per minute. I don't even need to hear this chica's story; I'm already impressed beyond words.

Without missing a beat, the brunette stunner taps half a dozen buttons and discretely whispers what I can only assume is "good-bye" in Japanese or Hindi and is immediately focused on the rest of us staring at her from around the table. "It's a pleasure to meet you all. What Claudia says is true — what brought us together was her website, a life raft I found amidst a sea of misery I could not continue to live within.

"I was born in Argentina. My father was an attorney and my mother was a stay-at-home mom. They each had very different plans for me. My mother had a dream of living in the US and saw me as her ticket out. Although they had what appeared to be a good marriage, my mother's drive for glitz and glamour far exceeded her desire to keep our family together. She left my dad and headed to LA to get me into show biz. I got plenty of modeling work as a child and in my teens. I managed to keep in touch with my father and visited him once a year in Argentina. I loved my father; I always will. To me, he was real and honorable at a time when all I found around me was damage and lies.

"My mother was my manager and she worked me like a dog. My interest in being professional eye candy began to waiver because, unlike the other bimbettes, I really enjoyed school. When my mother tried to force me to drop out to dedicate more time to modeling and acting, it was obvious she no longer had my best interests in mind, so I hired a lawyer to help me get emancipation from her. Through the emancipation process, I found a true love for the law. For me, it became something to cling to when I felt powerless, and I never wanted to feel powerless ever again.

"After graduating high school with the highest honors, I plowed through undergrad and then pursued a law degree from UCLA. My father helped pay my tuition and I had plenty of money saved from acting and modeling. I graduated in the top 5% of my class and was offered a job at a prestigious entertainment law firm. They hired me on the spot because I had experience in the industry, which meant I wouldn't get star-struck by their clientele, plus I understood the importance of confidentiality.

"Then I met Scott, a Formula One driver. Instant electricity. He's a mechanical engineer, so he's no redneck dummy, and he travels the world, which appeals to me greatly. Last but not least, he's not in the entertainment industry, which, given the way this town is laid out, was like finding a living, crystal unicorn.

"The problem, though, the problem we all share, was his mother. Scott's mother did not like that her son was marrying a spic. Yes, I said it. I said it because she said it — verbatim. At our wedding, she drank too much and told everyone she hated the thought of Mexican grandchildren."

"But you're Argentinean," I quickly add, engrossed in her tale.

"Yeah," she responds curtly, yet obviously still stinging from the incident. "But when you're a bigot, you don't make distinctions. It only got worse from that point forward. Every holiday, my mother-in-law would 'accidentally' forget to set a place for me at the dinner table. One time she served me tacos when everyone else was having Cornish game hens. She would constantly make insults to my face. Scott would try to stand up to her but his mother would start crying and Scott would back down. I've seen Scott ream out everyone from mechanics to team owners to sponsors to the owners of major car companies. He's fearless, in a controlled, professional way, but with his mother…"

"We know what you mean," says Julia.

"His father died a few years back, so he feels even more protective of her, and she used to use that to her advantage any time she could. When our children were born, she started insulting them, calling them little spics, and that's when even my husband couldn't take it any more. He cut off all communication with his mother."

"Sounds like 'problem solved' to me," sniffs Ashley, empathetic as usual.

"Not really. 'Drama delayed' is not the same as 'problem solved.' You have to figure at some point the woman will get sick, or else our kids will start crying for their grandmother and then what? All we would have done is deliver her the victim card to play and damn it, I knew she would play it as often as possible. No, tossing her completely to the curb was not a viable option, especially once there were grandkids involved."

"I can second that one," says Claudia.

"Besides," Gabriella continues, "I'd done that already to my own mother and it took me a few years to patch that up. Granted, she didn't give Scott the hard time Scott's mother gave me. On the contrary, my own mother tried to cozy up to Scott in order to get him to side with her against me, but that's a story for another day.

"Anyway, the way I'm wired — and yes, I'm sure having kids contributed heavily to this —I didn't want to have such a disconnect and I wanted my children to know their grandmothers, so there I was, back where I started, trying to figure out how to work through the issues I had with my MIL."

"I can't help but notice," says Julia quietly and respectfully, "that you told a lot of your story in the past tense. Any particular reason for that?"

"Julia, you're a step ahead of us all," says Claudia. "Yes, Gabriella talks about her problems in the past tense because she is one of our foremost success stories. She's been right where you three are today and she knows your pain, as I'm sure you can tell."

"So what can we do? Where can we go from here?" I say. "I mean, no disrespect…"

"None taken," says Claudia, smiling like a Cheshire cat.

"…But we've been going to meetings for quite a while now. I think I speak for the three of us when I say, we've been trying and trying the strategies we've been given to work with and… well, either we're not doing it right or else they don't work for everyone." At work, I'm much less afraid of hurting anyone's feelings, but at work, I feel like I'm succeeding, even when faced with an acute crisis. But in my marriage, in this situation with my MIL, I have yet to score a single victory so I am loathe to piss off any of these women for fear I will have nowhere else to turn except to a divorce attorney. I wonder if Gabriella does that sort of work.

"I don't go home with each of you at night, so I can only take you at your word that you've been earnestly trying all we've shared with you at our regular meetings," says Claudia. "I wouldn't have invited you here today if I felt you were hopeless cases. The fact is, hopelessness is not as much in the situation, but rather in how the situation is handled."

"You're saying our mother-monsters can still be handled?" asks Julia.

"I've heard nothing to make me feel otherwise, and as I said, you three appear to have been dedicated in your efforts, as well as consistent in your attendance."

"So what now? Get to the point of why we're here," says Ashley.

Claudia stares at her for just a second, as if to say, "I'm here to help you, ingrate; step off!" Letting silence rule the moment, she finally continues. "Right now is about what Gabriella brings to the table. She's too modest, so I'll say it for her. Gabriella Eastbrooks is possibly the best friend any of you could ever have if you found yourself in a court of law — or wanted to avoid stepping into one. She's a take-no-prisoners fighter who never loses."

I see Ashley about to open her mouth and say something snide, but this time both Julia and I glare at her in unison and she thinks better of it and keeps her yap shut.

"Ladies, Gabriella is Level Two. Level Two is for once you've tried everything else and you still have a MIL who cannot be dealt with and who is destroying your marriage and your home life."

"I can take it from here," says Gabriella firmly yet politely, and Claudia graciously gives her back the floor.

"Ladies, most people have secrets. Check that; *everyone* has secrets. Part of what I do as an attorney is help my clients hide their dirty little secrets so no one can find them… unless they're parceling them out in order to get sensationalistic press, but that's another thing entirely. I also help them dig up dirt on others when they need to change the power dynamic. For this, I have at my disposal some of the best and most discreet private investigators alive. And from working with them, I've picked up quite a few of their tricks myself, so when I really want to fly under the radar, I can do quite a bit without having to farm out the work."

I turn my head slightly and see that Awful Ashley is actually enthralled for once, as opposed to looking for her next zinger.

"Level Two is more than a strategy. It's a decision for each of you to make. It comes at a cost; I won't lie to you about that. But unlike shopping around for it on the open market, dealing with me you'll be dealing with a sister-in-arms. You won't have to over-explain or have someone play amateur psychoanalyst, trying to talk you out of it or whatever. I know what your problems are, by and large. The only things unique are the specifics. I'm not here to judge you.

"By, perhaps, having certain bits of sensitive information on your MIL, you will gain the upper hand in your dealings with her. What if you were to discover she'd had an affair a few years back? Think of the power that would give you in the relationship."

"It's not merely the information itself and you waving it in front of her," adds Claudia. "It's the self-confidence you'll regain knowing you have something on her. Imagine every time she gives you grief, in your mind you'll be able to flash to that dirty little secret of hers. It will empower you. Watch, you'll see."

"Yes," says Gabriella, "and there's always the possibility of using it outright. For that, we have special sessions with Claudia and me. Juicy information, used improperly, can be like setting your house on fire to shoo a fly."

"You can do this? How much? How quickly can you get results?" Ashley is literally jumping out of her chair. Me, I find it interesting, maybe even a bit more than interesting. I can't fathom what a private dick would ever dredge up on ol' Lana. She appears to lead the world's most boring life. I think insulting me is her only entertainment.

I'm here because I'm getting more and more desperate, when by now I imagined I'd be feeling somewhat better. I'm pulling farther and farther away from Kyle; I know I am. We're having sex less and less. I tell him I'm tired from work and he buys it. He even said something the other night about us "getting older" and made some lame joke about how the sex drops off the longer a couple is married, but none of that is true in my case. I don't want to have sex with him because I can't get out of my head that he's sleeping with the enemy — his own mother.

Level Two. In for a dime, in for a dollar. Let loose the dogs of war.

Chapter Eight

No matter how old you are, there are still those phone calls; the ones where your sense memory flashes back to the first time you ever called a boy, or the first time you asked a college professor to write you a recommendation. You sweat, your intestines clench up — or over-loosen, which can be even worse—your face gets flush, and you spend half the day mumbling to yourself, practicing what you're going to say. Me, I make important phone calls every day, all day long, and still, at least once a year or so, the thought of making one call or another takes me back to that horrible, horrible place. Today is one of those days.

The phone rings on the other end and I know the first thing that will happen is that I will have to get through the Call Screener From Hell. This, I am used to. Hell, I have one of my own. This usually does not faze me, for most people I call think they've died and gone to heaven because I am on the phone to them. A call from me could land millions of dollars in their lap, so you're damn right I can get past their meager little gatekeeper. Someone asking, "And what is this regarding?" could be on a short path to a pink slip and they know it, or they ought to know it. But then there are the exceptions.

"And what is this regarding?"

"She knows me. We belong to an organization together."

"What organization might that be?"

I was afraid she might ask that. The way I figure it, Gabriella Eastbrooks's secretary most likely does not know about DILS, just as *my* call screener does not know about me and my MIL troubles. I would sooner discuss my period with her than that. Some things, no matter how embarrassing, are universal. Other things, while one might regard them as rather common, still depict one as weak, and weakness is not something I can project, not in my line of work. Sure, I can say to anyone in my office, "Kyle's mother is such a pain!" But there's a world of difference between saying that and adding, "… and she's turning my whole world upside down. She makes me want to cry." Big executives don't cry. There's no crying in Corporate America.

"D.I.L.S." I reply. I don't say "dills," as we usually do, for fear she'll think I'm with a pickle company. I also don't volunteer to explain what the acronym means, but…

"And what does that stand for?"

I want to kill this woman. My mind races and I try to make something up on the spot, but all I can think of is, "Debutantes In Love with Satan," and that won't do unless I'm starting a death metal band. D.I.L.S. also sounds a lot like some international shipping service (Deliveries In Lower Siberia?), but I can't quickly come up with anything plausible about packages, so I'm stuck stammering like an idiot, sweat poring out of me despite the coolness of my air-conditioned corner office.

"This is a personal call. I met her through Claudia Steadman. Could you please do me a favor and let her know I'm on hold. I'll guarantee she'll ask you to put me through, if she's not too busy."

There's a slight pause, followed by a condescending sigh that makes me want to throttle her disembodied voice, but finally, she sees things my way and puts me on hold. I wait. And wait. And wait. In my mind, I fantasize the call screener has merely left me on hold and is staring at the little flashing green light, thinking, "I'll leave her there for about fifteen minutes. If she goes away, she goes away. If she stays on, I'll ask to take her number, but won't write it down. I am the Call Screener and I control the world!" But only a minute and a half goes by and suddenly I hear a familiar voice.

"Kat, how are you?" Gabriella's voice is pleasant, yet not overly effusive. From seeing her live performance a week ago, I imagine she's juggling her call to me with one to James Cameron, another to Johnny Depp, and yet another to Matt Damon. This makes me feel extra special, and yet I wonder about her level of concentration. I mean, if she starts switching back and forth, back and forth, will she offer me the lead in the newest "Bourne" movie?

"Fine, thanks for asking. I was wondering; I don't want to sound overly desperate…" What a lie. I *am* overly desperate. "… But I wanted to know if you've been able to dig up anything on my mother-in-law yet. Lana Embers."

"Hold on a second," she says, and I suppose she's either gone into her desk to find what she has on Momma Lana, or else she's deemed my call too frivolous and has gone back to a call with some famous producer, discussing a lesbian remake of "Casablanca" starring Megan Fox and Jessica Alba.

A minute or two goes by and she's back, still using her robotically precise voice that still leads me to believe she is setting world records in multi-tasking. "I'm not quite finished, which is why I haven't called you…" Okay, that's a subtle dig, but I can take it. "… But it seems our Ms. Lana Embers has some drinking issues."

Drinking issues? Momma Lana? "Really?" I say.

"It appears she attends AA and Al-Anon meetings nearly every night of the week. Quite the dedicated member. Were you aware of this?"

I stumble and bumble and finally manage to blurt out, "No," and nothing more. So verbose of me.

"Well, as I said, that's all so far. I wouldn't act on it at this point. I'll wrap it up in a little bit. I promise, I'll get to the bottom of it. In the meantime, sit tight and continue to do all the other steps in the program. Keep going to meetings…" She pauses. "That's funny. 'Keep going to meetings.' Makes us sound just like AA people." Gabriella may have thought it was funny, but still, her voice never betrays emotion, just takin' care of business all the way.

Momma Lana an alchy. Come to think of it, I can't quite recall having ever seen her take a drink in my presence. It causes me to sit and philosophically ponder. Lana an alchy. Kyle never mentioned it. *She* never mentioned it, God forbid. All the fault she finds with me and *she's* the one with an addiction problem. Maybe that's why she's so nasty. Nasty drunk. It's an official two-word phrase, like "dirty liar," and "flaming asshole." Momma Lana is a flaming asshole and a dirty liar for coving up she's a nasty drunk.

Sweet.

Chapter Nine

Back when I was a senior at the University of Chicago, a boy stood me up. Every man and woman gets stood up some time or another, but this was our fourth date. You stand up a first date, perhaps, because it's a blind date and once you see the other person, you vomit a little into your mouth and quickly run the other way, hoping they didn't see you. You stand up a second date because you realize you only agreed to the second date because you are way too nice, but the truth is, you hated the first date and you know you had absolutely no attraction to this person whatsoever. But you do not stand up a fourth date. These are the rules.

Needless to say, I was pissed. Pissed and a little crazy. It was a Saturday night and I was looking forward to this all week long. I'd been working like mad and I needed some release, and now here I was, left high and dry.

I managed to find out this little weasel was out, out on the town. I suppose he didn't want to be in his dorm room where I could easily find him, so he split. Normally, this is where the story would end, but that night, no.

The unofficial motto of U of C is "Where Fun Goes to Die," so I knew he was nowhere on campus. Chicago is a city of vibrant nightlife and once I realized I'd been officially stood up, I picked myself up and decided to head into town as well, to blow off some steam and see what mysteries the night held for me. But still, the whole thing nagged at me and so I did something I have never done before or since. I stalked him. No, I did not stalk him the way a typical desperate man or woman would, hoping to see him so I could patter up to him and say, sheepishly and pathetically, "Did you forget about me? Was it something I said? Was it something I did?" No, I was going to track his ass down and ream it out sideways with a chainsaw.

I became a woman obsessed. I went from bar to bar, hitting every nightspot I knew and every one I had ever heard of. I rode the train and I hoofed it 'til my ankles were sore and my nose was so cold I thought it would fall off my face, but I was going to find that shitheel and bring him to justice. How dare he! Fourth date! Fourth date! The nerve!

That entire embarrassing yet cathartic episode came zooming back into my mind as I set about looking to catch Momma Lana in the act. There are 3.8 million people living in Los Angeles and there are about 3.7 million AA chapters. I exaggerate only slightly; the 3.7 million figure takes into account things like Marijuana Anonymous, Crystal Meth Anonymous, Overeaters Anonymous, Sexaholics Anonymous, and Anything That Feels Too Good To Be Legal Anonymous.

The reason I flash back to that cold night in Chicago is today I am doing the very same thing, albeit in a much sunnier clime. I have my list of AA and Al-Anon meetings and I'm trolling like a horny teenage boy with his first phony ID trying to get into strip clubs. In many cases, I arrive in the middle of a meeting and poke my head in, look around, and sheepishly say, "Is this the 'Make Millions Breeding Chinchillas' seminar?" then leave before being officially asked to. That might embarrass some people, but this week, not me. Like them, I'm all about turning my life around, just in a different way, so who cares what they think?

Another reason that night in Chicago revisits my memory is when I got to certain bars, I couldn't manage a subtle hit and run. A woman looks kind of crazy racing around a really large disco, obviously in search of someone or something. I may have been on a mission from God, but I still had my pride, so often I would order a drink. Standing at the bar, waiting for my drink order, I looked normal, not crazed, maybe even alluring to other men there, being that I was alone and, if I may say so myself, looking attractive. Holding a drink in one's hand is always been a neat social crutch. You immediately look like you fit in, even as you do laps around the club. You have a purpose and you're giving off the vibe you're the sane, sociable type.

At AA meetings there is no bar, but there is a coffeemaker. And standing and holding a drink still makes one look normal so if I arrive at the beginning of a meeting, I imbibe in order to fit in. I want to ask if anyone there knows Momma Lana, but I'm smart enough to remember the second "A" in AA is for "anonymous," so I don't bother.

I rarely stick around for the same reason I didn't hang out long in any of those Chicago bars. I am on a mission. Time spent in a place where my prey is not is time wasted. The trouble, though, is akin to the problems I had that evening in the Windy City — drinking all night long takes its toll. This means introducing myself to at least forty different ladies' rooms, which is not a pleasant experience. Public restrooms are the burden of civilized man. Everyone needs them but no one likes them, except for closeted gay guys and frequent fliers who want to brag about belonging to the Mile High Club. The other problem is the effect of the beverage in question. I got bombed out of my skull that night in Chicago and wound up with the worst hangover of my life. And I still never found the guy who stood me up, although by the next day I could care less, my righteous indignation replaced with a splitting headache and trench mouth.

I am now on my third consecutive day of support group crashing and I have used up all the toilet paper in California, spreading it out as I do on foreign public toilet seats in various church basements across the City of Angels. I have also not slept a wink, as I despise the taste of decaf and I now have enough caffeine buzz to light up all of Mongolia. Despite my issues with Kyle, I have literally raped him every night this week, figuring he was in my bed for some purpose or another. Usually he would appreciate this, but jumping on top of him at 3AM when both of us have work in the morning doesn't seem to be his hottest fantasy, but I am up and I figure he should be, too. Thank God at that hour he doesn't need consciousness or will to perform or I might rupture him.

The constant caffeine high helps me at work, after a fashion, as I have the energy of a hummingbird on crack, although people are starting to look at me funny and at least two or three have tapped their index finger to their nose, the universal sign of, "Got coke?" I've also lost my temper umpteen times and I may be getting a bad reputation with the underling class, but such are the sacrifices one makes for one's home life.

When I never found the Chicago guy, I often wondered if it were less an issue of location than of timing. I pictured him going to the same places I had been, only behind me instead of ahead of me. Chasing someone is a positive mental visual — it keeps you moving forward, ever onward. Considering the possibility you are actually moving aimlessly and cluelessly while your target goes on his merry way is depressing as hell and makes you frequently stop and wonder, "Why the hell am I doing this again?" That is what I am feeling now about finding Lana at an AA meeting just so I can shout, "J'accuse!"

I skip into my sixth consecutive AA meeting in a row, vibrating like a pair of Ben-Wa balls filled with microscopic agitated Chihuahuas. Crashing AA meetings has turned me into a caffeine addict. The irony.

This place is nicer than most — a large conference room belonging to a major non-profit in a new high-rise office building. I'm late, since I just came from another meeting that started elsewhere at the very same time, so I'm prepared to do my stick my head in/looky-loo thing. At this point I've practically given up any hope of ever finding her. It's become more like an obligation to myself, like constantly going to the gym while facing the fact those pesky last three pounds are never ever, never ever coming off no matter what I do.

And there she is. Not only do I see her, but my impeccable timing is such that it appears she's just finished speaking and is heading back to her chair to a round of polite applause. The moderator — what does the person leading these meetings call his or herself, the head drunk?

— sees me, since I am agape, staring at Lana as I stand in the doorway. "Hello. Are you in the right place?"

Yes and no, but I can't say that. Instead, I jitter some more, which only causes the crowd to look empathetically at me, as if to say, "Of course she's in the right place. She's even going through DTs as we speak."

"Yeah, yes," I stutter. Since I have finally found the white, fake-auburn-haired, short, middle-aged, Jewish whale I have been pursuing for what seems like a lifetime, I have been reduced to frozen amazement. This is why Stanley was so ridiculously understated when he said, "Dr. Livingston, I presume?"

"Have a seat. Is this your first meeting?"

Well, yes and no, but I can't quite bring myself to say that. It's too late for me to run out, yet I don't exactly know how I'm going to handle the confrontation with Lana. The caffeine has thrown me off my game, as does the presence of other alcoholics, obvious as it should be that there would be some here.

"First time at this one," I say, opting for the truth. I shake and bake my way to an empty seat as eyes follow me, each set offering sympathy, possibly wondering if I actually belong at the Crystal Meth meeting. As I sit, I look up and see Lana staring right at me. It's a moment I've been waiting for, ever since I began this Quixotic journey, but if looks could kill, I'd be dead ten times. These are looks that make her normal crinkle-mouth frowns appear downright cordial by comparison. Her eyes are like slits and I can tell she's wondering, "What is she up to *now*?"

"Would you care to introduce yourself?" asks the moderator.

No, but I don't know a polite way to say that. If Lana

weren't here I could use an alias like "Peaches Daiquiri", but she'd only call me on it and blow my cover.

I rise. "I'm Kat, and I've been sober for…" How the hell long have I been sober? I'm not a drunk. I'm caught between trying to remember when I last had a drink, which is what these people usually mean when they make that statement, and when the last time was when I was actually drunk. Amidst these two mental challenges, I'm also thinking, "Who cares? I could make up anything. Do they have a way of testing to see if I'm telling the truth? And if so, why don't the cops use it on DWI stops?"

"… Three weeks." I'm buzzing too much to come up with an honest answer so I pick a number and go with it.

"Congratulations, Kat!" says the moderator, and I get the same semi-enthusiastic applause Lana got when I first entered the room. "Would you like to share anything with us this evening?"

I'm dying to get up and say, "Yes, Jim Beam, or whatever the hell your name is. I'd like to share the story of my mother-in-law. She's right over there. She's been constantly putting me down and trying to break up my marriage. Now it turns out she's a dirty, stinking, hypocritical drunk — present company accepted." But I can't. I'm outnumbered. This room is filled with her peeps, not mine. They could shiv me in the alley with cheap corkscrews and I'd bleed to death slowly, with a slightly oaken nose and a cherry aftertaste that ages to perfection the longer I stay out in the open air.

"No thank you," I reply, tamping down my lesser urges.

I sit there, trying to melt into the cheap metal folding chair. I'm bored as hell, perhaps more so because the caffeine makes me want to jump up and shout, "Hey everybody, let's play dodgeball!" I look across the room from time to time and Lana is still staring at me, glaring at me. It is a death threat look. It is the kind of look I should be doling out to her, and after about ten minutes — or about three and a half hours OSST (Over-Stimulated Standard Time) — I finally crack, returning her ugly stare with an exaggerated, bug-eyed, forced frown that makes me look like a mocking four-year-old. It's the most overtly rude thing I have ever done to her, but I've had it. It is topic-neutral. It merely says, "I hate your guts, so there!" I'm done. I'm outty. I don't know if this is how I truly feel or if it's the Starbucks talking, but I'm full-out belligerent now.

The meeting ends and I stomp across the room to where Lana is sitting, stopping directly in front of her and folding my arms across my chest, my face in hers like two boxers about to get it on. In my daydreams, I expect her to be contrite, apologetic, and embarrassed. Instead, she's giving as good as she's getting from me and I haven't gotten a good hold of my quivering mind to ask myself why that might be.

"So, you're a lush," I finally say. "That might explain a few things."

Her jaw drops and her tongue practically falls out of her mouth. "Me?! You're the one who's only been sober for three weeks! No wonder my Kyle is so embarrassed by you."

"Embar..." I can't even mouth the word. "Embarrassed?"

By this time, Jack Daniels, the moderator, has run over to try to break up our tiff. "Ladies, can I help you?"

"This is my mother-in-law," I say, pointing at Lana as if

78

I were telling a pit bull whom to bite. "She's trying to ruin my marriage and now I understand it's because she's an alcoholic, a fact she's managed to keep from my husband and I." I turn slightly to Lana and lay into her, the thing I've been dying to do ever since Gabriella told me about her. "You are a hypocrite, a liar, an evil, evil woman, and now I understand why — you're a drunk."

"Uh, this may not be my place, but Lana is not an alcoholic," says the guy playing referee. "She was our guest speaker this evening. She started four Al-Anon chapters in the greater Los Angeles area. Those are support groups for families of alcoholics. If you had been here at the beginning of our meeting, you would have known that. She's been one of the most coveted guests of all of the chapters in Southern California. Her story is very inspiring. But she's not an alcoholic; are you Lana?"

I look over and Lana has tears streaming down her cheeks. I feel like I've just killed a basket of kittens.

"I think," says the moderator, "you should be a little less judgmental in this process. As it is, you've come to us as well. We don't judge others here. This is a safe place." As he speaks, he comforts Lana and I am suddenly reliving the scene from when she last came over for dinner at my house. She's in the wrong and still, she's the one getting comforted.

"But she criticized me for only being sober three weeks and that's a crock because I'm not even an alcoholic…"

"Kat, denial isn't just the name of a river," says the platitude-spewing leader of the recovering lounge lizards.

"I am not a drunk! I lied to get into this meeting. I came looking for her," I say, pointing at Momma Lana, enacting in my mind the moment in my daydreams when

I have broken her down by being right, right, right, and now I am using my accusatory finger as a weapon, saying, 'Bad dog! No bone for you!' But instead, I've just blown my entire cover.

"You came looking for me?" she says, sniffling her tears to a slow trickle and looking at me oddly, like I suddenly have three heads. "How did you know I was here?"

"I… I just knew. I thought I heard… I thought you had a drinking problem."

Lana's waterworks have about ended and she stiffens slowly. "Kyle's *father* had a drinking problem. If it weren't for AA, I don't know what we would have done. AA doesn't accept large donations, so I give them my time. I go to meetings and I speak. I serve on boards. I set up Al-Anon chapters. This is what I do to give back."

The guy next to her nods his head. "It's true. I've known this lady for years. She's wonderful."

"But Kyle…"

"Kyle was too young. He never knew. It wasn't necessary," she responds, her voice a low, Darth Vader growl.

The deal is to me, but I've got deuces high and so I fold. Both of them are staring at me, but I have nothing more to say, nor do they. I've never been more trumped in my life.

I cannot even manage an audible apology or a good-bye. The moderator drifts away and Lana picks up her purse, all the while continuing to stare at me, while I simply gaze at the floor. She brushes past me and the last thing I hear her say is the thing I say about her every time she's out of earshot of me.

"Bitch."

Chapter Ten

We're dining al fresco and as much as I enjoy lunch out with the girls, I approach today with trepidation far more severe than when I usually go to a new eatery for the first time. I've been tiptoeing around my house like a cat burglar ever since the AA episode with Momma Lana. There is indeed something worse than knowing you're about to die — it's knowing you're about to die, but not having a clue in the world when it will happen. That's the situation Lana has put me in — check that; that's the situation I have put myself in, for Lana did not set a trap for me; I conjured one up for myself while she went about her life blissfully unaware her daughter-in-law was teetering on the edge of insanity.

I have been horribly sweet to Kyle of late; what, with the late night sex attacks followed now with the simpering behavior of someone hoping not to get rightfully blasted for doing a terrible, terrible thing. Over the last few days I've felt like Lucy Ricardo, hoping Ricky won't blow a gasket after learning about one of my crazy schemes, telling me I've got some "'splainin' to do." Kyle, for his part, doesn't know what to make of me, but being a man, he is a simple creature. He got some sex, now he's getting some inexplicably contrite and geisha-like behavior, so he's a happy camper. Confused, but happy, and when a man is happy, he usually just goes with it. Ah, to be so uncomplicated. Men are like machines with only half as many moving parts, particularly between the ears.

But Lana now has it all over me. Karmic irony. I set out to frame her and instead she holds all the cards over me. She's toying with me; I know it. The only reason she didn't call Kyle the moment she got out of that AA meeting is because she feels no good reason to destroy whatever illusions he had of his father, but she will tell him, eventually, I just know it. When you've got an ace up your sleeve, why play it just to beat a deuce? No, slit my throat when the stakes are as high as possible, whenever that may be. Why, why, why did I give her all this power over me?

Julia is the only one there when I arrive. She gets up and hugs me as she always does, though this time I feel like I'm being comforted at my own funeral. There's that lingering feeling, the soulfullness one usually doesn't get with a mere "Hiya!" hug, followed by a whispered wordless look that says, "Is there anything I can do for you? Should I stop by later with a deli platter?"

"I'm so sorry," she says, and yes, I do feel like someone has died. I called Julia the moment I got in my car, outside of the AA meeting. I had to talk to someone. That or go get drunk which, considering I'd been trolling AA meetings, was just way too ironic for my own good. She was sympathetic, but of course, she raised the issue of the elephant in the room: "Gabriella told you not to act on it yet; that she was still gathering information. Why didn't you listen to her?" Granted, she said it as empathetically as humanly possible, but she would have been remiss to not say it and I respect her for doing so. Today, though, we're being joined by Claudia and Gabriella and I know I'm going to get that same message thumped into me in quadraphonic stereo. It raises the issue: how many times must a person hear the obvious?

Settling in with Julia, I try to change the subject slightly, attempting to take the focus off myself. "Have *you* heard from Gabriella? Has she been any help in your situation?"

Julia smiles pleasantly, as is her natural state of being, but does not get as excited as she is apt to do when something is really great. "I called her when I hadn't heard anything, just like you did. So far, nothing. Darla, Mark's mom, leads a pretty dull life. Gabriella is wild. She ran credit checks and background checks of all sorts. Amazing.

"I mean, Darla isn't perfect — who is? — but being thirty days late on your Nordstrom's bill five years ago doesn't really give you the hammer of the Gods; you know what I mean? I probably have a few of those black marks myself."

"What else does Gabriella do? How else does she dig? Do you know?"

"Oh yes, Claudia was telling me. Gabriella finds all of the MIL's friends and associates. She or a colleague hook up with those people, befriend them under some guise, and pump them for info. Just wild stuff."

"I'm impressed. Low tech as well as high tech. Gabriella should work for the NSA."

"I think the NSA wishes they could break half the laws Gabriella does and get away with it," Julia chuckles.

Just then, Claudia rounds the corner and heads toward us. Impulsively, I drop my head in shame. I can't recall every word of every form I filled out and signed when I joined DILS, but somehow I figure I must have violated something or other and perhaps this is actually my exit interview. "We have to terminate you, but as you're cleaning out your desk, is there anything you can tell us so we can better accommodate our future Sisters?"

Claudia smiles pleasantly, but I would expect nothing less. She is the least likely person to have a screaming fit out here in public in the middle of the day. We exchange hellos and she glides into her chair and orders an iced green tea. "So, rough week I hear," she says as she looks at me sanguinely. I think if aliens landed right now and began shooting ray guns at everyone, Claudia would casually invite them to join our table and they probably would. She has this unflappable, poised manner that makes me wonder how on earth she ever got to the end of her rope with *her* MIL, let alone with or about anyone or anything at all. Claudia Steadman is who I want to be when I grow up.

"Yes," I say, afraid to add much more. My head is still down, as if I am waiting to be punished. Claudia and Gabriella are in a similar position as my MIL, each of them holding the same embarrassing thing over my head, along with the ability to use it against me in a horrible way that could jeopardize my marriage.

It's strange, but since I joined DILS, my enthusiasm for finding kindred souls and feeling I am taking a positive step in accepting responsibility for my own happiness has been tempered with a slight feeling of guilt, as if I were cheating on my husband. I've never been a cheater, but this must be what it feels like. I'm loyal to a fault, not just to my husband as well as to the many men in my life before I found him, but also to my employer, my girlfriends, and my family. But here I am, sneaking around behind Kyle's back, and it doesn't feel good. Right now it feels downright shitty.

"It happens. I can say to you, with all honesty, that I *do* know how you feel, Kat," says Claudia, leaning across the table toward me.

"You mean you screwed up this badly when you were trying to fix your situation with *your* MIL?" I ask.

"Ha, ha," she chuckles politely, rolling her head back wistfully, as if remembering the past. "Kat, I did just about every hair-brained, crazy thing one could imagine. I was desperate. I threatened the woman. I bought her gifts. I withheld sex from my husband. I *bombarded* my husband with sex. I threw her out of my house. I asked her to move in with us. I was completely bi-polar. You name it; I did it. And embarrassing? God, you have no idea! They could make a sitcom out of half the things I did."

Her words pore over me and I begin to believe I might actually not be getting the ax. She honestly doesn't seem pissed at all. But perhaps that's just Claudia. Wait 'til Gabriella gets here.

And then she does. I really don't study other women that closely, but watching Gabriella Eastbrooks walking towards you is a rare treat no matter what your gender or sexual persuasion. In its raw and unadorned state, she and I probably have the same hair color — plain ol' brown — but her colorist belongs in some hall of fame. Her highlights look like someone took every individual strand and said, "Okay, you do this, you do that, a little blond for you, a little caramel for you, and when it's all done, voila!" It's like a Seurat pointillist painting. If you were staring right at her scalp from three inches away, none of it would make any sense, but from a comfortable distant, it is magnificent. Beyond that, her walk is more like a sensual dance, her hourglass shape undulating with every step. All this, while she continues to talk and text like a human switchboard. Amazing.

"Hello, ladies," she says with a professional smile, bipping and bopping off her electronic devices so they do not disturb us. As she sits, I again drop my head, losing whatever relaxed confidence I'd been regaining from talking to Claudia. I feel I'm about to get blasted for not following orders, so here goes. But instead, the chatter that follows is just that — how's the weather, what's good to eat, yadda-ya. This only drags out the pressure.

"Kat," says Claudia, "what's the matter?"

"Huh?" I reply.

"Kat, I don't know you all that well, but is this you?"

"What do you mean?" I respond.

"Kat," she says, as she reaches her hand across the table and puts it on top of mine, "Who are you? When we first met, you told us you were a tech executive; that you had a top position with one of the biggest firms in the country; that you had hundreds of employees answering to you. Honey, I'm sitting across the table from you and I can't picture you getting hired to be someone's entry-level secretary. I'm not saying that to hurt your feelings, quite on the contrary, but what's going on?"

I flop back in my chair, my legs outstretched, and bringing my hand up to cover my eyes like a washcloth thrown on the face of someone who's just fainted. My head tilted towards the sky, I mumble, "I've never lost before."

It wasn't meant to be overly profound, just something that drooled out of my mouth, but suddenly everyone else at the table is silent. Said in a different tone, I might have sounded like a spoiled brat or an egomaniac but instead, I sound like a woman completely and utterly defeated, which I am.

I feel Julia moving her chair closer to me, as if the mere heat of her body can somehow bring me back to life, like some form of mouth-to-mouth resuscitation where one person gives existence back to another. Claudia reaches out again to touch the one hand I've left on the table.

"I'll bet you haven't," Claudia says. "A woman can't get as far in this world as you have by quitting or losing all of the time. But this is why we're here for one another. The biggest successes as well as the biggest screw-ups in the world can find themselves in this position. Do you know why you're here? You're here because you love your husband."

I pull my hand away with a start. Here I am, a mixture of every bad feeling I've ever had in my life, one of which is that I've somehow been unfaithful to Kyle by going behind his back to this group I've joined, and then Claudia just sums it all up in one short little sentence. *I'm here because I love my husband.*

"I shouldn't have taken partial information from Gabriella and run with it," I say groggily, my head still hanging over the back of my chair. "I fucked up. I never do that at work, never. I check and double-check everything before I rush into things."

"I know you do," says Claudia. "How else would you have gotten to where you are? And that's why we understand. Someone from the outside looking in might not understand people like us. It's a bad cliché: 'My mother-in-law is so awful.' 'How awful is she?' Usually it's men doing the complaining. But that's usually superficial stuff—how they felt they were nagged by their mothers, then got married and were nagged by their wives, but lo and behold, now they have another woman to nag them as well — another mother.

"But with us, it's different. There's this weird sort of Oedipal aspect. Some mothers of men get downright territorial and possessive. They view us as the competition and so they fight back. But we're not fighting! We fell in love with a man and we simply want to go along that whole path — living, loving, maybe having children, whatever. Marriage is a life decision and we went for it. It's not always a bed of roses, but we can deal with that, one way or another. But dealing with this other woman, that's the part we didn't bargain for. Not only that, but deep down we really don't want to 'win.' I know you said you've never lost before, but I know you realize this really isn't about winning and losing. Check that — it *is* about losing. It's about losing our marriage and our family and that's crucial for us. But what we really want, what makes us crazed, is we want all parties involved to win. We *like* mothers. Some of us *are* mothers. Part of what we looked forward to when we got married was having another mother. Some of us have wonderful relationships with our mothers and so the word 'mother' has a positive ring to it. One was good; two could only be better. For others who, perhaps, did not have mothers, or did not have wonderful relationships with their mothers, it was the chance to start over again, to have something very important we had been seeking for a very long time. Oh look at me; I'm pontificating."

She may have felt she was rambling, but Claudia's words feel like a warm shower massaging my tired body. I glance over at Julia and she looks so soulful, as if she's just heard the words, 'I love you' for the first time. Julia shared with me about her damaged relationship with her own mother, so I know Claudia's message touched her.

"So what's next?" asks Gabriella, not in a rude way, but perfectly appropriate for a businesswoman with places to be and important people to see.

"Gabriella, please forgive me."

Gabriella's lips ripple into a small smile. "Honey, if you think this is an irreconcilable fuck-up, you have no idea what my life is like. At least once a week I have to bail one of my clients out of jail, sneak them out the backdoor of the police station, check them into Betty Ford — again, through the back door—then keep a straight face when I say to the media my client is suffering from 'exhaustion.' Everyone fucks up. Most of my clients simply *are* fuck-ups, period. But they make the big bucks and by working with them, *I* bring in the big bucks, so it all goes around. You and I are cool. Just… well, try to learn from it as best as you can. I'm with Claudia on this one — we're all, all of us, in the same boat together. You didn't mention my name to anyone, did you?"

"No, no, hell no. I keep corporate secrets all day long."

"Good, then we're truly cool on this. Moving on…"

Claudia and Gabriella exchange looks. Julia and I do the same, pensively, like two kids in the principal's office waiting to see if we're going to be given detention. Finally, Gabriella grimaces a smile and Claudia sighs. "Level Three?"

"Yeah, I think so. I don't see any harm," adds Gabriella.

I sit more upright in my chair. "Level Three? There's a Level Three? Ladies, with all due respect, this is getting weirder and weirder. Do we keep going up a ladder until we reach Level Sixteen, and does that one involve aliens inside a volcano?"

Gabriella chuckles. "No, Level Three is as high as we go. Past that we just move on to hitmen or divorce attorneys."

"I've been wondering about those two options," I respond, half seriously.

"Why don't you lay out all the levels right from the start? We should know what we're getting into and what's available to us," adds Julia, with a far more pleasant tone than her words belie.

Claudia leans toward her in a motherly manner. "Julia, I don't believe in killing fruit flies with a bazooka. It isn't necessary. The techniques we use in Level One — cataloguing incidents, speaking to issues as they occur rather than letting them fester; all the other things we do — that's the foundation; that's what every woman should know about this sort of conflict resolution. If someone were to skip all that and go right for the private detectives, that's all we'd have — a bunch of women hiring snoops so they can blackmail their MILs. We'd be making the world a worse place. People talk about our 'carbon footprint.' I believe in minding our emotional and karmic imprint. Most of our Sisters succeed quite well with just the tools we give them on Level One. That other girl who joined with you, Kat — Debbie. The one who broke down and cried when I welcomed you all to the group? She's been doing wonderfully. You see her every Thursday. She still comes to meetings, but she's progressing steadily. I think she's going to be one of our success stories."

"So we're…" I begin.

"You're about to say, 'fuck-ups,' but I'm not going to let you," says Claudia. "Furthermore, you two aren't the only ones who've not been roaring successes using the techniques of Level One. I simply invited you today because only the four of us know about this AA debacle and I knew you'd want to talk about it in private.

"They say you can only kill a werewolf with a silver bullet. On Level One, we give out good ol' regular bullets. The fact the other Sisters succeed because they are only shooting quail has no bearing on the fact you're stuck having to hunt werewolf."

I manage a laugh. I feel downright hungover, what with my depression as well as my cold turkey abstinence from caffeine. I'm tired, cranky, headachy, and pretty much sore all over.

"Okay, Level Three — the Silver Bullet. What the hell is it?" I ask.

Gabriella and Claudia look at one another and the more they do that, the more I think this is somehow going to involve animal sacrifice and creepy children with glowing eyes.

"We'll tell you," says Gabriella, "but you've got to be open-minded."

Chapter Eleven

Day spas are what heaven must be if God is a woman. Today, Claudia has invited Julia, Ashley, and I — the DILS version of the slow kids on the short bus — to a wondrous spa just outside of the megalopolis. Gabriella is here as well, which makes me wonder — are we three so pathetic that Claudia needs a classroom aide? Ashley wasn't invited to our last get-together when we lunched, but needless to say, she's here now, so I'm figuring Level Two didn't work for her, either. Strange, since it seemed a perfect match for her — the forensic accounting and espionage and all.

The only trouble with spas is the other women in them, especially in this town. Back in North Carolina, I was considered pretty hot. Granted, that was in my teens and most girls can only dream of being as tight and toned as they were at mile-marker eighteen. But here in Southern California, home of the model-actress and those forced to compete with them, every barista in every coffee shop has had a boob job and big, collagen BJ lips, even if they had to go without eating for two months in order to afford it.

Check that — most every woman in Southern California *does* go two months without eating solid food — quite frequently. They call it cleansing. I call it starving.

So here I am on the island of naked and half-naked ladies, lolling around, being pampered in the second most sensuous way, and I have to avert my eyes from the competition for fear of losing my high due to poor body image. Julia is a perfect pixie, not an ounce of fat on her, but I can handle that because we're such totally different physical types. How can one aspire to lose about eight inches in height, and why would they want to if they could? Claudia is how I want to look in about ten or twelve years, for basically, despite being around that much my elder, she looks the same age as me, which is maddening in its own way. What's the point of being around older women if they can't look at you and get jealous?

Gabriella is the problem. Gabriella has a bosom men have gone to war over. And my white-girl hips and ass are fine, thank you, but lately guys seem to have developed this fetish for Gabriella's type of junk in the trunk and hips that don't lie. I doubt any doctors, even in this land of plastic, can grow me trunk space like that. I find myself looking everywhere but at her as we get our wraps, massages, and all sorts of things laid upon us and splooged over us. She's either going to think I hate her or that I'm attracted to her and trying to conceal it, but there's not much else I can do about it. People like her should get their own section of spa.

And then there's Ashley. Ashley is hot, I must admit, but in a slutty, cheap sort of way. Her boobs are definitely not natural, but furthermore, she went at least two cup sizes too large. Add to that the tan that is way too dark and the blond hair that is bleached too much and you've got a cheap imitation of Pam Anderson, which may work for you if you're a stripper, but it's a little too overt for most people around here. She looks like the girl guys sleep with but don't marry, which is the only reason I don't feel completely inferior around her.

I still don't have my best take on Ashley yet. The slutty look and the shitty attitude have definitely rubbed me wrong, but she does come to every meeting and she seems to really feel it when she tells her tales of woe. I knew a lot of girls like Ashley back in Carolina. They came from rough homes and developed tough exteriors, but some of them were like the preverbal "hooker with the heart of gold." It was an act, a shell, but deep down they wished they had a do-over in life, a chance to start fresh without all the baggage. Although I know little about her home life growing up — it simply hasn't come up — I'm imagining there must be some bad scenes she's tried to bury. I can't quite explain how I know this; I just do. And I suppose, in her own way, she's been attempting to right her ship, marrying a dentist with a trust fund and all, and trying to create a better relationship with her MIL.

Julia has shared her childhood stories with me and it makes me all the more impressed she came out the other end of it as well as she did. All told, she's the one who should be looking like a truck stop trollop and acting like one, too. But she retreated into her creative dream world and that's what got her through. She hasn't talked about it, but I imagine she must have been picked on and called "nerd" a lot growing up — "bookworm." I caught some of that flack myself, being the bookish math and science girl, but I had the two most wonderful parents ever and that's what held me together.

There's a maddening thing I've come to expect from a get-together with Claudia—she seems never in a rush to get to the point. We're all here, but I'm still not sure if this is purely social or another special meeting of some sort. It's been a week and a half since I first heard the phrase "Level Three" and now I'm here, waiting for something, anything. Meanwhile, I'd be quite pleased if Level Three was merely, "Ladies, we've arranged for you to stay in this spa forever. If you need anything, just ask. *This* is Level Three — complete avoidance of mothers-in-law altogether."

Gabriella sashays over to where Julia, Ashley, and I are clumped together and faces us, with Claudia following her, a step behind. Even with her make-up off, her hair up, and just a towel around her, Gabriella's looks still intimidate me. At any moment, I expect the towel to give way as those breasts of hers break free, reaching for freedom, looking for the opportunity to mock those belonging to us mere mortals.

"I have a confession to make to you all. Like you, I am not a Level One success story, but you probably imagine, since I'm so intimately involved in it, that Level Two did the trick. Unfortunately, Level Two didn't do it for me, either. This does not mean those two methods have not been effective for others, but even when I put my best P.I.s on my own MIL's case, I came up with nothing I could effectively use in order to change the dynamic of our relationship. Not to say she didn't have some issues she'd rather I not know about, but the purpose of Level Two is not just to get something on them — it's about whether or not it's something that can be used effectively, and in that area, the exercise was a failure for me. And like you, maybe even more so than you three as I've come to know you, I really hate to lose. It's a lawyer thing — so hate me."

"You used this 'Level Three' thing yourself?" interjects Julia.

"Yes."

"Are you going to tell us about it?" she follows up.

"Yes. Just as Level Two was about meeting me, Level Three is about meeting another one of our Sisters, which you'll be doing shortly. But meeting me and learning about Level Two was fairly straightforward and conventional, relatively speaking. Level Three is a little…"

I've never heard Gabriella pause to parse her words so much before, which causes me concern. She finally continues, "… It's a little controversial."

"More controversial than private detectives? I thought espionage was already on the cutting edge of legality," I quip.

"Controversial insofar as asking you to take a bit of a leap of faith from traditional thinking. Challenging what you know and what you think you know about the human mind. And yes, it does travel into the realm of the quasi-legal."

Okay, she's got me hooked. Even if this is the most repulsive idea since "man purses," I cannot go another minute without knowing what it is. I look over at Julia and I can see the wheels turning in her head: *If this involves alien mind control, maybe I can use it in one of my books.*

Finally, Gabriella lets out the single word she seems to have been dreading. "Hypnosis."

"Oh dear God," says Ashley, the way most people would say, "Bullshit!"

"I told you," Gabriella shrugs.

"That stuff doesn't work. What are you going to do, make my MIL squawk like a chicken? They do that bullshit at cheesy family resorts. It's all crap," Ashley adds in her impeccably diplomatic fashion.

Gabriella delicately winces through a closed mouth smile. "Your reaction doesn't surprise me. I knew one or all of you would think that way. *I* thought that way when it was first presented to me. But the person in our group who does it is one of the best in the world. It's an art, it truly is, and she's a doctor, not some cruise ship magician."

Julia, Ashley, and I exchange looks, each of us at one point or another snickering like a schoolgirl.

"I know, I know," says Gabriella, rolling her eyes along with us. "God, this is such a re-enactment of when it was first presented to me. That's why I can't take your reaction personally. But let me tell you my own version of how it helped me.

"My thing was that my MIL was a racist. Or at least she acted like one. But she had people of color and people from other countries and other religions and cultures in her life all of her life. She didn't hate them all. Some of them she loved dearly. The problem was, she had a picture in her mind of what her daughter-in-law would be like and look like and I didn't fit that fantasy, so she freaked. But even she didn't quite know how to express her feelings on the matter, so it ended up coming out in the most vulgar offensive manner — racism."

"You sound like you're making excuses for her," said Julia.

"Maybe I am. That's a lot of what I do for a living and perhaps it's a part of my personality and how I'm wired. I own that and I can live with it. The thing is, deep down, there was a part of my MIL that was open to loving me. That's the key to it all. I *am* a good person. And like most people, my MIL has some racial issues, but she is not some cross-burning Klansperson. It was just that her discomfort with something new did not have a place to go. I know that sounds like psychobabble, but everything DILS does has a psychological component. We may do mani-pedis, spa days, movie nights, and lunches, but we're merely reveling in the physical while we're working on the mental and the emotional. Level One is all about that. We've taught you how to outthink your MIL, how to listen to her and perhaps outsmart her — to get to what it is that's wrong with her and with your relationship with her and mend it. Often times it works. With Level Two, we bring in some bigger guns so you can look her down and realize you're dealing with a flawed human being and by knowing those flaws, perhaps you can re-approach her and try those Level One techniques anew, albeit with some occasional modification."

"And now we're going to hypnotize them," says Ashley. 'No, I am; if you want me to.'

The words came from a new figure, a somewhat older woman of around forty with short, strawberry blond curly hair and freckles, who had surreptitiously joined us. "Hi, I'm Stella, Stella Diomare."

Unlike Gabriella, Stella is certainly not a current or former model-actress, unless she made a living modeling sensible shoes. She's what people graciously describe as "handsome." If that sounds like an oxymoron because men are called "handsome" and women are called "beautiful," it's because, at best, Stella would be considered the most beautiful man in the room, but as a woman, she's rather plain. Her body is neither fat nor thin, although in this town, thin is no longer a criticism. Her face shows her age, which is not so old as to require convalescence in a retirement community, but it is also not botox-filled, lip-plumped, and plastic-surgery-altered beyond recognition. In LA, she would be considered an endangered species.

Stella sits down and makes herself at home. Her attitude is professional, yet modest. I get the impression she feels as I do about the ravishing beauties strutting around this spa— a bit jealous and uncomfortable, determinedly drawing upon her other natural strengths — her internal ones—to the best of her ability.

"I'm sure all of you have an impression of hypnotism, most of it bad. I admit, its been treated as a cartoon-like subject by the entertainment business for years," she pauses for a second, then adds, "sorry if I offended anyone with that remark."

"My Ryan hasn't made any screwball comedies involving hypnosis in years, thank you very much," says Claudia with a grin, piping up for the first time in a bit, happy to let others take the floor.

"I studied psychology at the University of York," Stella begins.

"NYU?" asks Ashley.

"No, England. York, England. I was an army brat. I attended more than fifteen schools from kindergarten through high school all over the US as well as in Europe. My father was an officer and my mother was a stay-at-home wife. I developed an appreciation for different cultures and people. I guess I escaped into that — the exploring, the analysis."

I watch Julia on the edge of her seat, as if she were

listening to a soul mate, a fellow oddball finding a way to get by in a tough situation. Julia did it through her writing. Me, I may have had a better go of it growing up, but my science fair/Star Trek "nerd power" escapades still isolated me at times. In Chicago, I found I no longer had to apologize for getting A's, and once I moved to LA and met and married Kyle, I should have been complete. But then came Momma Lana...

"During my studies, I took a course on hypnotherapy and that was it—I'd found my niche within a niche. I took extended journeys to India, China, Germany and the US to study with leading hypnotherapists. I eventually ended up here in Southern California, laid down roots, and set up a practice. So here I am, years later, a doctor of psychology with a specialty in hypnotherapy."

"What is your connection with DILS?" asks Ashley, probingly.

Stella exchanges a quick look at both Claudia and Gabriella. "All is not perfect in the world—not for me, not for anybody, for that matter. I met and married a wonderful, wonderful man — my soul mate. His name is Aaron. He's in real estate and hotels..."

"Diomare. Hotels. You don't mean those really nice hotels in all the major cities — the Diomare Paris? The Diomare London? The Diomare Tokyo?" asks Julia.

"Yes," Stella says, blushing appropriately.

"Those were the nicest places I've ever stayed! My first book, my publisher put me in rat holes when I was touring. But once that one made money and the second one came out, they put me up in all of your hotels wherever I went. That's the moment I truly knew I'd made it," Julia gushes. "So you're the heiress to the Diomare empire."

Stella chuckles. "No, that would be my husband. According to my MIL, he was the heir, I was the error."

We all have a nice laugh over that one.

"See, Aaron was one of those 'World's Most Eligible Bachelors.' God, I sound like I'm bragging, but trust me, I'm not. If you were to meet him you'd wonder, 'What does he see in her?' I mean, not only is he wealthy, he's drop dead gorgeous. Before we met, he was dating all these Playboy bunnies. How can a girl like me compete with that?"

"So you hypnotized him?" asks Ashley, oblivious as always to how insulting and hurtful it is to say out loud — even if we were all thinking it.

"No," Stella shakes her head, again blushing while looking at her feet. "There are some lines I would never cross. Especially back then. I have to admit, my ethics have been tested more and more in recent years but… I'm getting ahead of myself here. Anyway, when we met, it was just one of those things — instant soul mates. The problem was, he was already engaged to one of those 'bunny girls.' And his mother couldn't be happier.

"Truth be told, as centerfolds go, his fiancée wasn't too bad a person. Megan was her name. I shouldn't even put it that way. I'm sure there are all sorts of centerfolds like there are all sorts of dental assistants and television journalists. It just so happened that Megan was not like any sort of cliché that would make her easy to hate. Oh, I could hate her for being far more attractive than I, but that's about the worst of it.

"Anyway, Aaron and I got to know one another and there was that special something. Pretty soon, he dumps Megan and he and I start up together in earnest.

"His mother was not at all happy. A lot of it was simply over the cancellation of the engagement. Aaron's mother — Ilene — was already planning the Wedding of the Century. It was going to put Charles and Diana's nuptials to shame. Now she had to make the big disappointing announcement and go back to square one.

"I guess it might have been easier for her had Aaron gone back to wooing starlet after starlet. Then she could say he simply wasn't ready for marriage. Instead he brings me home only a few months later and says he's asked *me* to marry him…" Stella looks embarrassed again, her insecurities as obvious as the silicon in Ashley's double D's.

"Ilene's face betrayed everything she felt. 'He goes from Miss September to Miss Frump! How am I ever going to stage a royal wedding around *this* ugly duckling?'"

"You are *not* ugly. Don't say that!" I blurt out. I've known this woman for all of ten minutes and already I'm defending her. I can't help myself. It's my own special cross to bear in life. I hate it when nice people get shit on.

"You're too kind," Stella replies, then takes a deep breath in order to continue. "Anyway, we get married. It isn't quite a 10,000-person guest list, but it's big and it's nice and I'm in love, so what more can I ask? Before you try to answer that, I'll spare you the trouble. Ilene's heart was broken. Aaron got over Megan — totally forgot her — but for Ilene, Megan was 'the one that got away.' Crazy, right? And she *should* have gotten over it. I wasn't sharing a bed with Ilene; I was sharing one with Aaron. What was in it for her? But that's not the way she saw it. Ilene had an image in her head and I didn't meet it. Great woman, but not a trophy wife; if you catch my drift. And I may have been brighter and wittier than Megan, but Megan, as

I said, wasn't too bad. When you're Miss September, they lower the bar a little when it comes to intellect and charm."

"So where does hypnosis come in?" asks Ashley, bored and irritated as usual.

"I was one of Claudia's first Sisters," Stella says, looking over at a glowing Claudia. "I was at one of her first meetings. We've come a long way, haven't we, girl?"

"You betcha!" says Claudia.

"I was there when all we did was vent, vent, vent. We hadn't a clue of what to do about our MIL issues. We were just happy we had a place to go to talk about these things, a place where we were with others who felt the same way. Some had it worse and that made us feel better. Some weren't doing so badly and we felt a little worse, but we still felt we weren't alone."

"Actually," says Claudia, "it was Stella who, being a psychologist, began moving us all towards finding solutions. We worked together, she and I, and developed many of the steps the rest of you have been using all this time. Level One was as much Stella as it was me, and I love her for that."

"Did you charge?" I didn't have to wonder where that came from. It was "Miss Inappropriate" herself — Ashley, as usual.

"Stella and I have an arrangement. Believe me, had she charged each of us what she should have had we been private patients, she would be opening her *own* line of boutique hotels by now!" Claudia quickly adds, coming to her friend's rescue.

"I have to admit, a lot of what we tried on Level One worked. I'd also be lying if I were to say Ilene was the world's worst mother-in-law, even then. Most of what we now call the 'Level One Techniques' helped a lot with her, too. But it wasn't perfect. When she'd throw big soirees, Ilene would actually invite Megan. Invite her! This was years after Aaron and I had married. We had two little boys — beautiful kids. Ilene would say, 'I've always hoped for a 'Little Megan' around the house.'"

"No!" says Julia.

"Yes. In Ilene's eyes, Megan was the ideal, even as she envisioned grandchildren. We had two boys. Ilene wanted a boy and a girl, and for the girl to look like Megan — God forbid she look as average as me! Aaron confronted her once and she said she felt he would eventually get bored with me and start running around, looking for some other centerfold girl. Ilene may be a lot of things, but she doesn't condone scandal. She just felt that had Aaron married a Megan-type, he wouldn't be as tempted. I guess, in some perverse and misdirected way, Ilene's heart was in the right place. She just didn't acknowledge what Aaron and I had together and it hurt me constantly. Every time I saw her I held my breath, waiting for the next shoe to drop, the next inadvertent insult.

"I met up with Claudia, we did DILS, blah, blah, blah. Gabriella came aboard and we went to Level Two. There was quite a lot of dirt we dug up on Mother Ilene, believe you me, but we just couldn't seem to finesse it. Ilene was cowed into keeping her mouth shut more often, though a lot of it could have simply been the passage of time, but she still didn't love me. I mean, she didn't hate me, but I wanted to be loved by her. It didn't seem too much to ask and that's what I was asking for.

"And so—and this is the part you've been waiting for — I hypnotized her. No more Megan. No more digs about my looks. No more feeling like she's shopping for my replacement. We get along famously."

I turn to Julia and her eyes are bugging out of her head. She's looking at me and I feel the muscles in my face and I realize my eyes are bugging out as well. I lean forward a hair and there's Ashley and she's looking over at us and her eyes are doing likewise. All three of us look like we've just seen Marilyn Monroe crunking with James Dean risen from the dead and none of us has a digital camera. For the first time ever, Ashley's eyes are larger than her fake breasts.

Chapter Twelve

There is silence. Someone has come into our lives to say, "Here is a magic lamp. I know you've heard about these in storybooks and Disney movies, but this one is real. You rub it and a real genie comes out. He will indeed grant you a wish. Yes, I know, you were expecting three, but c'mon, let's get real. There's a recession on and so the best we can do is one. And you don't have a choice as to which wish because, well, we got this genie because there was a volume discount down at the magic lamp store. He only does one trick and that's to grant you the wish of making you and your MIL bosom buddies which, in your case, Ashley, means *really* big bosom buddies."

I am the one to break the dead air. "Treat me like the skeptic I am and explain to me — how does it work? Not necessarily 'what is the clinical definition of hypnosis,' but how do you get someone to like you who doesn't like you?"

"Good question," says Stella. "First, let's lay down some basics. As you've probably heard, hypnosis cannot make you do something that's completely and utterly against your moral and ethical code. That still leaves a lot of room with which to operate. Take killing for example…"

"There's a summer blockbuster movie thriller in this, I'm betting. You're going to have one of us kill the President," quips Julia.

"Been done before. It was called *The Manchurian Candidate*," responds Claudia, our resident movie expert, "as well as at least a hundred poor imitations of the 1962 original."

Stella smiles knowingly. "Killing is a frightening possibility because, for as much as we deny it, most of us do have the capacity to kill."

"She's scaring me," I say, and Julia giggles. Ashley, on the other hand, seems to be counting her newfound money.

"The point I'm making is, as abhorrent as murder is to most of us, it's actually less abhorrent to most than, say, eating a live rat," Stella says as we all wince at the mental picture. "The issue is more about 'murder who?' If someone has truly wronged us, or if it were a stranger we were led to believe meant us or someone we loved harm, there's that little 1% of our psyche that could possible kill that person."

"I don't understand the point you're trying to make," says Ashley, stone-faced, having just come down off the orgasmic high of mentally killing off her MIL and spending all her money.

"Love and death. Love and hate. Love and murder. Our strongest human impulses. Look around this room," says Stella. "See that woman over there? It's possible to hypnotize you, brainwash you into thinking she meant you harm and you had to kill her to protect yourself. Just as easily, perhaps even more so, you could be made to envision her as your best friend, someone you wanted to go up to, introduce yourself to, and make a wonderful connection with. So let's drop death and murder for a second — and the only reason I brought it up in the first place is because Hollywood has, in fact, done so much with that plot device coupled with hypnosis and mind control, and instead focus on something more positive — that woman over there who is a complete stranger but could become our new best friend."

Ashley is showing her usual exasperation. "I still don't get your point. What can you do and how do you do it?"

"She's trying to tell you we have the capacity to love or hate, kiss or kill. If I told you that woman across the room fucked your husband, you'd stomp right over and punch her out, right?" I say, finally getting as agitated at Ashley as she does with everyone else.

"Probably."

"So, I've just given you a suggestion. I planted a seed in your head. I played with your mind. I happen to know that woman did not fuck your husband."

"Are you sure?"

"Ugh!"

By now Claudia and Gabriella are holding their stomachs in laughter. Stella, the mental health professional, merely smiles. "Kat has it right on the money. What she just demonstrated through example is merely the power of suggestion. Hypnosis takes suggestion a step further. Let me ask you all, do your MILs hate you?"

"Yes," Ashley, Julia, and I mutter in unison.

"No, they don't. I know you think they do, but unless one or all of you did something totally unforgivable, they still have the capacity to love you."

"I beg to differ," I say.

"Kat," says Gabriella, "She's not completely oblivious to the fact you two have not been getting along, right?"

I think for a moment. "No, I guess not. I complain to Kyle, he says he tells her some things — in fact I know he does because often times she throws my complaints back in my face the next time I see her, so yeah, she knows I'm unhappy with her."

"And she's somewhat unhappy with you."

"Ha!" I can't help myself. "Yeah, once I pointed at her and accused her of being a mean, rip-roaring drunk, if she wasn't 'unhappy' with me before, she sure as hell was then!"

"Kat," says Gabriella, "things like that happen. I know you're mortified by it now, but the truth is, especially within families, things happen. Some day you'll laugh about it."

I inhale to begin my protest, but Gabriella cuts me off and says, "I am not minimizing the pain you're feeling right now. I am merely pointing out you did not gun down her entire family."

"Good example," says Stella. "None of you has gunned down your MIL's family."

I actually lean forward a bit to get a good look at Ashley's face to see if she's showing any poker player "tells." I don't see any, but I'm watching her; I'm watching her.

"Next question. Assuming you feel your MIL does not love or like you very much at this moment, answer me this — does she love or like anybody? Anybody at all? Does she have any friends? One friend? A relative she loves or likes? A pet she cherishes?"

By now even Ashley is smiling, against her more evil wishes. "I'll accept your silence as acquiescence. Each of your mothers-in-law currently loves or likes somebody.

Just not you — or so you feel."

"Right," I answer.

"Capacity to love, just not loving you — maybe."

"Why do you keep saying it that way?" asks Julia.

Stella looks at her in a motherly manner. "I'm not going to hypnotize any of you, but I am going to plant within you the seed of possibility that your MIL does not hate you. She may not even really dislike you. I know, I know, I haven't been to your meetings lately so I don't know all your personal stories. But one thing I want you all to hold onto is the possibility that, perhaps, your MIL actually does not hate or dislike you. Call it one last gasp of optimism, if you will."

"Okay," Julia says, willing enough to go along for no strong reason.

"I am telling you there is a part of them that likes you, loves you, or has the *capacity* to like or love you. Because of that…"

"You can hypnotize them into tapping into that love!" says Julia.

Stella shrugs impishly in an "ah-shucks" manner. "Yep."

"So how do you do it?" It's Ashley in her role as "Little Miss Downer" again.

"Hypnotism? It's done in relatively idiosyncratic ways depending upon the practitioner, but by and large, you've probably seen it depicted fairly accurately in TV, movies,… cruise ships," Stella jokes at her own expense.

"How do we get our MILs to you? How do you pull it off without them asking, 'What the hell am I doing here?'" Ashley follows up.

"That's a little tricky sometimes. We've come up with a few effective ruses, haven't we, girls?" Claudia turns to

Gabriella and Stella and they share a knowing chuckle.

"One of our favorites is the weight loss scam," says Gabriella. "That's the one we used on my MIL. I started wearing really baggy clothing around her for about a month and complained about gaining weight. Then I started showing up wearing next to nothing at all and she couldn't help but compliment my figure. I told her I was going to a hypnotherapist and I'd lost twelve pounds. Her ears perked up like a Great Dane. I asked if she wanted me to introduce her. She bit. I took her to Stella and the rest is history."

I'm lost in thought for a moment or two. It seems so easy, and yet it also seems too good to be true. "Does it last?" I say, finally.

"Kat," says Gabriella, "You remember what I told you about my MIL? How she didn't like that her son married a Latina? Remember I also added she was not a complete and total racist? People are like blended fabrics. If she were 100% racist, it wouldn't have worked. If you had gunned down your MIL's entire family, she would 100% hate you. So long as there is a percentage for Stella to work with, she can pull this off for you. You've got to believe some part of your MIL is open to liking and loving you. If so, Stella will find it and get her focused on it, to the absence of her opposite feelings. My MIL sees me now and she doesn't see a 'spic.' She sees a very successful lawyer who loves her son and is a good mother to her grandchildren. None of that is an illusion — it's all true. There were always things about me worth loving, and once Stella helped her block out the racist, hateful things, she was able to focus on the good. Now we get along fine. I still do things I learned in Level One. I accept that I have to do certain things in order to be a good daughter-in-law and I work on that. And yes, my MIL is still a human and capable of doing things that get on my nerves, but I handle those to the best of my ability — again, using what we talk about in our meetings. It's a comprehensive program; it's just I no longer feel I'm trying to run through a brick wall, making no progress. Our relationship is the way a MIL and a DIL should be. That's all I ever wanted."

"How specific can this be?" asks Ashley. "Can you make them do things?"

Geez, this broad is a piece of work. I can just see Ashley walking around with her MIL, saying, "When I tap your shoulder, you will sign checks, big checks, and they will all have my name on them." As for me, I want my MIL to love me. I don't want to enslave her. But the thought does tempt me…

"Well," and I can see Stella wiggling uncomfortably, "I don't like to get into that whole 'cluck like a chicken thing.' It's stagy and the sound hurts my ears. I also struggle with the 'playing God' part. See…" and what I can see is more wiggling and embarrassment from Stella, "I'm rather good at this. I don't mean to sound like I'm bragging, but it's true. I'm not an entertainer. I study this stuff clinically. I study the human mind. I've had offers to work with the CIA."

"Jesus," I say, uncontrollably.

"I told you I married a man who was used to beautiful women. It made me feel good being with him, but there were times when I really wondered if he would stray, if he would look around a room and wonder why he'd settled for something less than the girl on the cover of *Vogue*. I toyed with the idea of hypnotizing him into believing I was that beautiful, that if he saw any other woman he would find her revolting. You can't believe how tempted I was. "God," Julia says. "With great power comes great responsibility," she muses, quoting Spiderman. I don't know if I would have so much control. "Truth be told," Julia continues, I used to work with a guy who I felt was the most handsome creature on this earth. His name was Jason and he was breathtaking with a body like a Roman god and a face to match. He and I got along so well that I would hear wedding bells every time he walked past my desk. Unfortunately, he put me in the Friend Zone. As he put it, he thought I was beautiful and amazing and was the only woman in his life that he could be himself around. He didn't want to ruin that. Personally, I believe a higher power plopped me in the no-bone zone because I was not his genetic equal. Whatever the reason, he ended up marrying a nine. Feature-wise she was a six but she knew how to put herself together so well that she could have stepped right out of a magazine ad. Even if a tornado whipped through her house, every strand of hair on her head would fall perfectly back into place. Yes. She was one of "those" type girls. I was heart-broken but never let him see it. Instead, I remained the friend that made him smile and laugh. The Seven with a friendship ring instead of the real bling. Jason was also the reason I wanted to leave Colorado. A few years later, I met Mark. I guess my insecure scars left from Jason not wanting me gave me more reason to rush our nuptials. Jason was The One. Just the one who didn't want me." Stella cleared her throat, bringing us out of lost love land and back to planet earth. "Sorry about that, Stella. Things with Mark just are not what I hoped for and Jason still holds a very soft spot in my heart. Perhaps I can book a private session with you at some point to work through my inability to know when and how to let go." Julia gives the group a weak smile and sinks down in her seat, obviously still pained by the rejection.

We all turn our attention back to our magic genie, Stella, who continues with her story. "In the end, I couldn't do it. If he left me for another woman, the hell with him. The mother-in-law, that was different. I was doing that for him. I was doing it because I love my husband."

There's that line again. Every time I hear it, it focuses me. Maybe that's exactly what Stella and Claudia had in mind when they developed this entire program. Half of all marriages end in divorce, but divorcing or living a life of misery seems ridiculous if the only issue at hand is not getting along with your MIL. *I'm doing this because I love my husband.* If I were an old-fashioned gal I'd embroider it onto a pillow, but I'm a digital chick so I think I'll make it into a screen saver for my flat-screen monitor.

Chapter Thirteen

I do a bad job imitating a fat person. Don't go hating on me, but it's true. I'm frenetic to a fault, always in motion, burning up calories without even thinking about it, and when I've eaten all I can my throat simply shuts, period. Add to that my natural frame. I was the girl who didn't think she'd grow boobs until she saw her first grey hair. Tall, thin—yes, I know one shouldn't complain — but I looked liked a stick-figured boy until I was nearly sixteen. In addition to being teased as "Flatsy," what hurt even worse was the moniker, "Horseface." With budding breasts and adult hips (finally!), the "Flatsy" talk faded, but God still left me with a long, narrow face, or at least *I* think so.

I haven't thought about any of this for years, but now I find myself looking in the bathroom mirror puffing out my cheeks. It's no use. Thank you, God, for the high cheekbones and hollow cheeks. I love them, I really do. My face doesn't look bloated even when I'm retaining half the Pacific Ocean.

"What are you doing?" I hear, and I see Kyle's head

behind mine in the mirror, his brow furrowed as it often is when he sees me. I'm a flake; I know I am. Kyle grounds me. Thankfully, he does it unconsciously and innocently, not like some demented male rodeo clown trying to break me so I vacuum his house while wearing pearls.

"I'm gaining a little weight."

"No you're not."

Men are taught to say this from birth, right after, "I'll call you," and "Wanna beer?" My case, though, is further undermined because I am standing in my bra and panties and even a blind man can see there's no fat anywhere on my person. A woman, well, she might notice, as I do, the little pouch of skin above my pubic bone and the slight dimpling on the backs of my thighs, but men note this about as much as women follow professional wrestling. But I must persist, and not because I'm fishing for compliments. "The scale doesn't lie."

"You look great," he says, and nuzzles my neck. Then, he comes back to his senses, if only for a moment. "Why were you posing in front of the mirror bulging out your cheeks?"

"Trying to see how I'd look if I kept putting on the pounds."

"Honey, I'll bet you're one of those women who even looks svelte when she's eight months pregnant."

Suddenly, we both recoil a little. Kyle, in his innocent attempt at inoculating my neurosis, has hit the third rail of our marriage and he knows it. This time, though, I can *see* he knows it and I actually feel sorry for him.

"Someday," I say, letting him off the hook. It's a far gentler reaction than I've tended to show him, but I'm making peace with him despite my questioning the future of our relationship. Since the last time his mother came over for dinner, I've been The Bi-polar Wife, diligently going to DILS meetings the way gym rats go to the health club, all in order to save our marriage, while at the same time distancing myself from him because I have my doubts we can truly overcome his nightmare of a mother. I wonder how much of this he truly understands. He doesn't know I belong to this cult of frustrated women and yet he knows I'm distraught. I've shared with him my concerns about his mother literally from the first time she and I met. But six years into this marriage, here we are. If time heals all wounds, Momma Lana Ding Dong is the festering sore even penicillin can't kill.

I turn around and kiss him sensuously and he reacts in kind. We don't make love as often as we used to, but this seems like one of those great, classic "good-bye romps," or at least it is for me, and we gently slither and stumble into bed together. It's good and I lose myself in it, but it's erotic as well as melancholy. Melancholy because I still fear we're on a pathway to an ending; erotic that because of this I'm able to forget this is my husband, my lifemate whose underwear I toss in the wash and whose breakfast I make, and instead think he's just a hard and ready man with a hot body. In the end, it's probably somewhat dissatisfying to my soul, but my body rocks.

In the afterglow, I turn to him and ask, "When's the next time your mother's coming over?" My tone is blasé which, when it involves his mother, is never the case. Again, Kyle furrows his brow and if he keeps that up he's going to look sixty before his 35th birthday. Since our last dinner debacle, combined with the AA atrocity, I've not seen hide nor scare of my monster-in-law. From my end, I've always tried every excuse known to womankind to stave off having to entertain her. I've been doing that for years now but usually it doesn't work, yet lately it has. What's different is Momma Lana no longer seems to want to see me — or Kyle. "I invited Mom over but she says she's playing bridge;" "I asked Mom to dinner but she says her stomach's been acting up lately." It's clear she's so damn angry with me she's putting off the Big Confrontation until she has her words and moves choreographed so well I'll never be able to thwart or rebut her in front of Kyle. The woman scares me. I can't fight anymore. I'm mentally battered from losing. And yet there's still this hypnosis thing, this new harebrained twist from my mentors at DILS.

"Do you want me to invite her over?" Kyle asks excitedly. Oh, dear boy. I fell for your body, your face, your mind, your sense of style, your kind soul, your love for me, your wit and your sense of humor. But when it comes to this aspect of our marriage, I swear, you are clueless.

"It just occurred to me she hasn't been over in a while," I reply, stating the obvious and nothing more, certainly not inflected in a way that could make any rational person think I was pining away for her. But people hear what they want to, and that means Kyle suddenly thinks I've had a roadside conversion and for no practical reason think his mother is the new cool kid in school who I'm dying to hang out with so we can braid each other's hair while discussing fashion and music.

He scrambles to get out of bed, pulling up his boxers so fast I'm afraid he might rip them in his haste, and then runs downstairs to make a phone call. I lie back in bed, feeling as if I've done nothing more than set the date and time for my own suicide—which is as suicides should be, if you ask me. The last time she was here, my mantra was, "Be the Gandhi; serve the Julia." Now it's, "Be the chubbette." Ha!

Two days later, my doorbell rings and, of course, it's Lana, right on time. Though Kyle never mentioned it, she must have been totally thrown when he extended our dinner invitation, particularly since I'm sure he made a major point of mentioning it was my idea.

Lana's face, a personal nightmare of mine akin to how vegans must feel about looking into slaughterhouses, is a blend of her typical "I smell a fart" puss, blended with a haughty, "I'll get you my pretty, and your little dog, too!" Me, I could care less. I really could. If she wants to spill the whole AA episode on Kyle right here, right now, so be it. If a coward dies a thousand deaths, I'm already onto my thousandth demise and frankly, I've just about had it. Bring on your worst, Evil Woman, for I have given up my will to live.

Through a pair of lips that combine a sneer with a baby about to imitate a motorboat, she says, "Hello," possibly the most evil and insincere "hello" ever uttered.

I look her right in the eye through squinted slits Clint Eastwood would be proud of. "Hello," I respond, just as icily. This throws her a bit, as she expected to find me quaking in my boots, pulling her aside to plead with her not to tattle on me. Yeah, like that'll happen. Maybe a week or two ago, but now I'm far past it.

"I've been looking for you every time I leave the house," she says. "Have you given up stalking me or have you left that for the professionals?" Ooh, snap. The lady is good. Cold, utterly cold.

"No, no stalking. Too busy making a living." She looks inside her head for a comeback, but what I said was too broad, too general. She plops herself down on the sofa and I completely ignore her. I've actually never tried this before and I hadn't planned on doing it tonight, but here it is and frankly, it's more pleasant than I'd ever imagined. Once in a while I catch a look at her from the corner of my eye as I finish the preparations on the meal and no, she does not look happy — she never looks happy to me — but she also does not quite look like the ominous queen of the damned she usually sets herself up to be. I am almost liking this. She must have come here expecting to put me on the defensive and make me sweat, but I've driven past the point of caring. If Kyle finds out about what happened, I may just come completely clean and tell him, "Your mother and I have issues. You know it, you've known it, and I've been at my wit's end trying to formulate an accommodation. If that caused me to do some crazy things, so be it."

Kyle is upstairs fiddling as he always does, but eventually he joins us. He's got this dipshit look on his face that indicates a renewed sense of optimism about the relationship between the two women in his life. I love that about him. Like me, he's the patron saint of lost causes. Stalwart. I know he loves me and he'll never leave me, which is part of why I love him so much. I don't want to leave him, either. I just want this one gushing wound between us to stop bleeding.

His head swerves from side to side, first to me and then to his mother, nervously looking for some fight to referee, but there is none. Lana has been sitting rather quietly on the sofa, not bothering to project her voice far enough for me to hear her usual ranker about something, anything, having to do with me or my home. I expect she's been muttering, but what the hell do I care?

The first thing that catches Kyle's eye is how I am dressed. I have a lot of very cute workout outfits — my Stella McCartney tennis wear is to die for — but I am schlumping around the kitchen in the world's most unflattering gray sweat suit. And when I mean unflattering, I am being far too kind. There is not, nor has there ever been anything this gauche in my closet at any point in my life. The top set me back $4.99, as did the bottoms. I made sure they were not some hideous thing that were actually haute couture disguised to be so ugly as to actually be cool, but no, the designer label read, "Dave's". Yes, there is some Third World designer named "Dave" and he has a line of clothing you can only buy at your local neighborhood poverty store. It made me wonder if there really was a person named "Dave," and did he actually sit around staring at a large design pad saying to himself, "Sweatwear. What would be really utilitarian and classic? Something that says, 'I don't give a shit. I'm going to sweat in this, dammit, and then I'm going to throw it in the wash and maybe it will come out in one piece and maybe it won't, but either way, I don't give a damn because I'm a 'Dave's' kind of customer — cheap and practical.' Oh, and I'll make it out of belly button lint. That's my idea of an environmental statement."

Kyle creeps over towards me. "What are you wearing?" he asks, his voice a semi-loud stage whisper, unaware how much he sounds like he's initiating phone sex.

"Sweats. What does it look like I'm wearing?"

Confused, he rephrases. "Why?"

"I like to be comfortable. Do *you* want to cook?"

If Kyle's brow furrows any more I will begin giving names to the valleys of flesh on his forehead. "But wouldn't it be more appropriate to wear something less… frumpy?"

"Look, you can make this meal or you can go shopping for me and pick out all of my clothes. It's up to you." I go back to my stirring, flipping, and seasoning, all the while realizing he's the one making all the sense while I'm acting like an insane person, albeit a rather subdued one.

When everything is ready, I get Kyle and his mother to the table and I flop down as if nothing were awry.

"Lovely outfit," says Lana, in a sarcastic tone.

"Glad you like it. It's a 'Dave's.' I imagine it would look good on you."

She doesn't quite know how to take this and neither does Kyle, as my delivery is unusually blasé and devoid of inflection. Then I decide to change course for a moment. "I'm wearing it 'cause nothing I own fits me anymore."

Again, no one really reacts. Looking at them both, I know I'm confusing the hell out of them and frankly, I kinda like it. Without trying at all, I am the center of attention, and so I decide to expound with a somewhat renewed vigor. "I'm getting fat. And no, before you start asking—no, I am not pregnant. My cycle comes like clockwork. "

"Are you sure you're not just temporarily bloated?" asks Lana, in a tone far more concerned than I'm used to.

"Nope, just fat. Fat, fat, fat, fat, fat."

"Honey, you're not fat," says Kyle, mouthing the perpetual male point of view.

"Yeah, you said that two days ago. You should see what I look like today."

"She must be getting that 'anorexia' all the young girls

are getting. They say they starve themselves just to get attention," sniffs Lana, trying to get back into her normal cycle of abuse, talking about me as if I weren't there.

"If I wanted attention, this is not how I'd dress," I reply, and then take an unusually large forkful of food into my mouth. "Actually, I've been repressing my true self for years now and I really can't keep it up. I think I've reached my breaking point." For emphasis, I belch. "'Scuse me."

Now Lana's brow is furrowed, too, and I begin to see resemblances between her and Kyle I've never seen before. Frightening.

"Kyle, you remember when I took you to North Carolina to visit where I grew up? You remember all those restaurants we went past, all selling that 'funny food,' as you kept calling it?"

"Yeah," he says hesitantly, "I can't remember the name of the cuisine. What was it again?"

"Calabash. And the reason we never stopped to eat at one is because it's the most fattening thing on earth. All calabash really means is fried and batter dipped. Down where I'm from, we'll batter and fry just about anything. Go to a calabash buffet and all you'll see is a sea of golden brown. Everything looks the same except for the shape. Imagine trying to pick out your food, trying to decide what it is by nothing but the shape. You could be getting steak, you could be getting catfish; hell, you could be getting a piece of pecan pie. We might just batter and fry that, too. And did you recall the size of the people coming out of those restaurants? They all had 'Wide Load' stamped across their behinds. Yep, those are my peeps," and I can't help but notice as I'm unloading this soliloquy I am suddenly drifting into my Southern drawl, something

I never, ever do, but somehow, as I spin this yarn, it just seems to fit. Without planning it, I am creating some kind of character for myself, some redneck yahoo woman. Kyle and his mother can't keep their eyes off of me. Neither of them has chewed a bite of food since I sat down.

"What's the point of this story," Lana finally asks?

"The point is this is who I am. Calabash. Big eater. Big eater of bad food. I've tried to suppress it, but recently I've fallen off the wagon. Momma Lana, you know what I mean by that."

Her jaw hits the table. If she had no idea where I was going with all this southern-fried hoo-haw before, now she thinks I've gone completely mad. Me, I kind of like it. It's something a mentor of mine once passed along as we sat in on a meeting where we were trying to sell an idea to a client and were failing miserably. Not only was the client not buying what we were selling, he downright hated us for whatever reason. So Jerry, my mentor, just went off. He didn't yell or scream or anything. He simply pulled out all his guns and went out blazing. He ripped the shorts off all of our competitors as tactlessly as humanly possible. He told the client his own company had its collective head up its ass and would be shuttered down in less than two years — and, in a final irony, he was right about that. He remained calm and professional, after a fashion, but he said exactly what he thought — the sorts of things you think but never say. The client tossed us out of the office and, of course, we did not make the sale, but then, as Jerry recounted to me later, we weren't going to make it anyway. "Kat," he said, "when you know you have no chance of winning, give them something to remember you by. Burn down the room. Not literally, but set it on fire. When you've got nothing to lose, speak your truth and let the explosion blow back your hair. It'll be cathartic for you, but also, you'll be remembered. You may even be the person they come out respecting the most, even if you don't feel that respect for four or five years."

As they continue to sit in astonishment, I press on with the act by shoveling everything off my plate and into my waiting gullet. "Ah! Anybody else want seconds?"

As much as I'm loving this absurdist comedy, my throat definitely is closing up on me and if they were to call my bluff and challenge me to an eating contest, I would barf up right then and there, but both of them merely pick at their salads; Lana, for once, not complaining about anything I've served for fear I might start ravenously gnawing on one of her mighty meaty legs, but only after breading it and having it deep fried.

Kyle breaks the silence with, "Honey, where did this come from? I've known you for years and you've never been a big eater. I've hardly ever heard you talk about food. To you, it's just been something you had to do, not something you craved. And you are not fat. Absolutely not. This is all in your head."

"Not to worry, honey. I plan on doing something about it. I conquered this food obsession for years and I will conquer it again. I've got a friend — she's a novelist — and she told me about a hypnotherapist she went to."

"I never knew you knew a novelist. What does she write?" asks Kyle meekly, hoping desperately to change the subject and bring me back to what he used to know as Earth.

"Fantasy!" I say, almost demonically, while staring wide-eyed at Lana. "Really wicked weird stuff. Unicorns and witches and goblins in some never-never land somewhere. She told me she used to get high on Twinkies in order to visualize it all. She went to this hypnotherapist to try and kick the stuff. Sugar's a drug, you know."

I haven't had so much damn fun in years. Kyle, poor Kyle, has never seen me like this and the bewildered look on his face is so precious I just want to push him down on the table and jump his bones right in front of his own mother. This is the first moment I've felt truly in control in my own house in what seems like forever. Even when Lana is nowhere to be found, she's haunted my dreams. So many days and nights I prayed she would retire to Nova Scotia or somewhere far, far away like that, but old folks don't tend to retire to frozen fishing villages so here she is, only a few miles away from us in Southern California. It's cast a pall over our marriage, especially during her frequent visits to our home. But tonight, with no real plan in mind, I've regained my life-fire through pure, bug-eyed insanity.

"I'm going to go to her hypnotherapist. I have to. Look at me." They both look. "I know, with this baggy thing on I don't look all that different…"

"Your face looks the same. When people gain weight, it usually shows in their face," Lana interjects timidly. Timidness from Lana? I really *have* done it, haven't I?

"Yeah, but it's here, in my butt…" I run over to her, turn around, and drop trou, as close to her face as one can without having the other person stick their foot up your ass. I'm having a terrible time containing my own laughter. I am officially insane. Oh my God; wait 'til I tell Julia and the girls this one!

"Oh, I'm sorry," I say as I turn around to catch Lana's look of abject horror. Kyle, for his part, has lost the entire lower part of his face, his jaw lying useless on the ground. "The food, the food. It has me manic. I've been starving myself for years now. I exercise, I run from place to place, but I also eat all the right things and have these teeny tiny little portions and it's *so* against my nature. I just want to calabash everything, from ice cream to pizza, and shove it down my throat until I feel full, *really* full. All this denial and now finally, satisfaction. It's throwing off my body chemistry, and you know what comes next after body chemistry, right? *Brain* chemistry."

"I can see that," says Lana, gulping for breath as she nearly hyperventilates.

"That's why I need hypnotherapy. It's the only way. My friend, the sugar junky, she did it. A couple sessions and boom! She no longer craves gummy bears and licorice whips."

"Fad fixes never last," says Lana, bracing herself against the back of her chair for fear I might shove some other naked body part in her face.

"I knew you would know that. I mean, look at you. I bet you've tried everything. What are you, a size sixteen? Eighteen?"

Combine offended with scared for her life and Lana is now totally mute. I know she wants to let me have her worst, but I've just gotten away with calling her a fat, fat, fatty right to her face and she's got no comeback. This is so juvenile of me and not at all who I am, but I'm venting all the pain I've felt over the past six years through the obfuscation of temporary insanity.

Kyle is still only in possession of half a face and I think his tongue may have gone down with his lower jaw, for he seems incapable of even making guttural noises let alone words. I turn back toward Lana. "Momma Lana, I can't do this alone. You know what it's like. Having to go to the Big Lady's department all the time when you go shopping. Wearing stretch pants and sweat suits. Oh, but you've got really nice sweat suits; not like this old thing. Where do you get yours? I'll bet it's by some fancy designer. This 'Dave,' I've never heard of him before. I've got a feeling he's not very fashionable. What do you think?" I don't wait for an answer. "You've got to go with me. We can go together. We can both get hypnotized. It works, it really does. My friend is living proof. If you met her, you'd never know she ate Snickers bars by the case-full. She used to, but now she has her food addiction under control. That's all I'm asking. I want to get myself back under control. Wouldn't you like that? Me, under control?"

In the horror movies, there's that look on the face of the victim right before she's about to have a dagger shoved right up her nose. That's what Lana looks like right now as my jittery, crazy eyes and rapid-fire delivery have her pinned up against the back of her chair, wishing she could slide away, running out our door, screaming, "Help me! Help me! My daughter-in-law is on crack!" But I have to seal the deal. Like Jerry taught me; I've blown up this room, so there's no turning back. Only this time, I'm not leaving — or letting anyone else leave — until I close the sale, dammit.

"I need you, Mom. I *need* you. This food fixation, it's making me crazy. I need a friend — a sponsor, if you will — to go through this with me. I believe in this hypnotherapy and that's half the battle, right? Finding a system you can put your faith in. C'mon, I'll bet you've tried lots of things to lose weight, but look at you — you're fat. There, I said it.

I'm not saying it to hurt your feelings. I am trying to keep this real for both of us. I know you don't want to be fat. If I don't kick this again, you'll be ashamed to introduce me as your daughter-in-law. I've tried conventional ways, but they only make me miserable. Look how I get when I fall off the wagon. I can't go around like this. C'mon, let's try this together. We've never done anything together before. We can… bond. Yeah, we can be like mother and daughter. All I need is for you to go with me. What's the worst that can happen? It doesn't work! Then all we'd be is right back where we started; am I right? You in your size sixteens and me in my Dave's, craving deep-fried Oreos. So what do you say; will you do it? Will you go with me? Will you do it for me? Will you do it for yourself?" And then I throw in the kicker. "Will you do it for Kyle?"

The silence is deafening as I stop my infernal, hyped-up blathering for the first time in ten minutes or so. Lana is shaking as if she wants to wet her pants as I stand over her with my manic expression. Finally, I hear Kyle behind me, having reattached his lower face.

"Uh, Mom, that, that sounds nice, don't you think? You and Kat doing something together? Getting some help for her… together? You, the two of you… together? Doing something?" His face may be working again but he still hasn't mastered the art of cogent sentences.

"O-o-okay," Lana stammers, willing to agree to anything in order to get the hell out of my house and away from the crazy lady in the grey sweats.

"All right!" I shout like a cheerleader. "I'll call you. I *love you*, Mom. I *really love you*."

129

Chapter Fourteen

I have never cruised the throughways of LA with my MIL sitting next to me in my 'Benz Roadster. As expected, all she has done is complain and yet, unlike when she comes over to my house for dinner, I actually relish her discomfort. Maybe it's the newness of it all; the fact I know that, with her hair helmet, she will exit my convertible looking like Marge Simpson after a windstorm. I also drive fast — make that quickly — and every time someone swerves from lane to lane, or another car stops short, she smacks her hands against the inside of the car door as if to express her shock, much like a heart patient grabbing for her chest. When that's not happening, she clutches the car door handle as if she's ready to open it and roll out while I'm going sixty-five miles per hour; a sight I would pay to see.

"You know, if we really do have an accident, your arm is going to snap off right above the wrist," I say. "The best way to survive an accident is to just relax your body and go with it. This car has the best safety equipment money can buy. You've got airbags and crumple zones galore. Besides, we've got lots of fat to cushion us, right Mom?" I laugh hysterically, only partially faking it. I am *so* happy.

Lana doesn't say much in reply, but continues her frantic physical reacting. Despite her complaints on this trip, I seem to have muted her significantly ever since I stuck my bare ass in her face. She appears to seriously question my sanity, and who would have thought this would give me an upper hand in our on-going war?

We're off to see Stella, who roared with laughter when I gave her the blow-by-blow of how I managed to convince — or shall I say coerce — Momma Lana to come see her. I must admit, for as much fun as I had acting like a hyped-up loon, I actually feel a little guilty for the overt potshots I took at her weight. That was evil and I deserve some sort of karmic punishment, although the way I look at it, perhaps my life with her thus far has already been the punishment and now I have simply added in the crime.

I screech up to Stella's office address — a very nice glass and steel post-modern rising high above the pavement below. As I had hoped, Lana's hair is in laughable disarray. I really shouldn't take such pleasure in another person's pain — and I absolutely never do — but this woman has buggered me ever since I started getting serious with her son and now it's payback time.

"I don't know why I'm doing this. I don't know why *you're* doing this," she says. "You're skinny and I am what I am, period."

"Oh, but don't you want me to be the best that I can be? Don't *you* want to be the best that *you* can be?"

Lana winces and slowly moves along with me towards the revolving front door. I know her gears are grinding and she wants to simply confront me; I just know it, but something is stopping her and I think it's the way I've gone from being the world's most predictable person to being this total wildcard. We had this set routine where she was always three steps ahead of me and now I've changed the game, and not in the way she expected.

In the elevator, Lana's hair looks so bad I almost feel sorry for her. I thought about wearing my "Dave's" gray sweat suit, but I couldn't push my luck, taking the chance of seeing someone who knows me, so instead I am wearing a loose-fitting, blousy tunic dress — cute and fun, but not very form-fitting, so I can still whine about my burgeoning buttocks.

"If this doctor tries to me make me cluck like a chicken, I'm walking right out," she says, finally.

"Why is it that everyone uses that same example? When I first heard about hypnotherapy, I thought the same thing. Has everyone who's ever been hypnotized had that experience? Do you think they make you cluck like a chicken just to keep the urban legend going?"

She looks at me like I'm a freak again, and once more, I like it. Who would have thought such a thing would be so empowering? All my life, all I've done is try to be taken seriously. High school, college, grad school, work. The longer time has gone on, the more studious and staid I've let my public persona become, so much so that I'm probably not half as much fun as I used to be. It's the whole "glass ceiling" thing — being a woman in business. I show up at a big meeting to make a presentation and I can almost hear the males whisper, "Eye candy," and so I feel I have to work rings around them in order to get the respect I deserve. Sure, the ogling attention is flattering, especially when you didn't grow breasts until the tenth grade. I'd been in a training bra for over four years, until finally I said to my mother, tearfully, "Maybe I need a *personal* trainer." I can still recall the look of shock on her face, and then the cascade of good-natured laughter. I'd heard the phrase, "personal trainer;" I just didn't quite know what one did — or what exactly they trained. Nor, for that matter, did I understand the concept of a training bra, especially since mine wasn't earning its keep. Thereafter, when my mother and I were alone, usually when I was changing or trying on clothes, she would stare at my chest and mock-shout, "Drop and give me twenty! Grow, darn it; grow you two!" It was all in good fun as we laughed together. What a fabulous relationship I always had with my mom. I'd hoped for the same with Momma Lana, but alas, I'm here trying to have her hypnotized into simply tolerating me.

Stella's office is beautiful, full of antiques and objects d'art. Lana appears at once relieved, yet pensive. Because of the surroundings, she certainly has no reason to think she's in some roadside palm reader's shanty, but instead, she looks as if she's worried she might accidently break something. "She must get a lot of suckers in here to be able to afford all this," she says to me, a little too loudly for my personal taste. I want to quickly defend Stella, but I shouldn't make it appear she and I already have a personal relationship, and so I ignore it.

After a very short wait, Stella appears in a doorway. "Hello. You must be Lana and Katherine."

"Yes," I reply, excitedly.

"So, who wants to go first?"

"After you," I smilingly say to Lana.

"Why? This was your idea. Why am I the guinea pig?"

"Please don't say 'pig' around me right now. I'm feeling very vulnerable," I reply.

Lana huffs and rolls her eyes. "If this does anything at all, I hope it just knocks the crazy out of you. You need to lose weight the way I need another migraine."

All the while, Stella just stands there, smiling, watching us interact. She must have seen it all, having been with Claudia and the DILS all this time. Mothers and their daughters-in-law. What is it exactly? I know someday I'll want children and eventually he, she, or it will grow up and most likely find a mate, or at least I hope so. Will I be this way? Will I bust chops and give my child's lover such a hard time? My parents love Kyle, they really do. They love him because he loves me, and that's all they really care about. Why is Lana so damn complicated? She must have enough baggage to fill a train.

"Please. I'm nervous. That's why I need you here for support. Help me," I say. Lana looks at me as if she finally suspects something is awry. I've never talked this way to her and her antennae are up.

"Me," she repeats.

"Yes."

"Why not your husband? Why not one of your girlfriends? Or why couldn't you do it alone? You've never been the shy flower before."

I'm feeling trapped and caught and the fear must be evident in my eyes, my eyes that no longer have the ability to feign craziness. My body language says, "I'm begging you. I've got you this far; now get your fat ass in that office so I can finally be free of the pain you bring me." It's like pushing a recalcitrant cow onto a cattle car, bound for the stockyards.

"Maybe she's expressing feelings she hasn't been comfortable sharing before," says a new voice — Stella's —

quietly, yet firmly.

It takes Lana by surprise. Stella's a doctor, after all, a mental health professional, and she's acting like one, which sort of brings both Lana and I back to what is before us. Silently, albeit reluctantly, Lana gets up and slowly heads towards Stella. "Fine, I'll go first," she says, and nothing more. Right before they both disappear behind the closing door, Lana turns and looks at me. It's a look I've never quite seen from her before—a resigned, plaintive look that says "You owe me one," which I really don't know how to react to.

I settle back in my chair and wonder how long this will take. After a few minutes, I lean forward and rustle through the magazines on the coffee table, unable to find anything that holds my attention. I lean back again and ponder. *What the hell am I doing here? Can this really work? And if it does work, will it all be a sham? Will I have to go smacking her three times on her shoulder in order for her to treat me with civility? And if so, how do I get her to not accuse me of assault after the first two smacks?*

I don't know exactly how much time has passed, but when I hear a hand on the knob on the other side of Stella's interior office door, I think my heart will break out of my chest with excitement. Out walks Momma Lana. She looks… different. I mean, she looks like Momma Lana; she's wearing the same outfit, she's got the same build and all. But the look on her face is, dare I say it, pleasant.

"Your turn," Lana says with a smile. "Not that it will do any good."

I lean forward in my seat, as if straining to hear. I did hear; I heard quite well, but Lana has never smiled at me in such a way, unless it was a mocking smile as I tripped over an ottoman or something. No, this is a kindly-old lady-being-sweet smile. I know; I've seen them before, but only on kindly sweet old ladies, not on Miss Misery.

Slowly, I rise and as I do, Lana gently touches my hands as if to help me to my feet while also steadying herself as well as reassuring me. Again, she smiles warmly. "It'll be okay. It didn't hurt a bit. Nothing to be scared of."

As she sits, I can't take my eyes off of her. I must indeed look scared because, actually, I am. I turn and look towards Stella, who is also smiling, leaning against the door frame. I make a beeline to her as fast as I can so I can shut the door behind us.

"What the hell did you just do?" I ask.

Stella continues to proudly smile. "What you asked me to do," she says quietly, her voice softer than mine, indirectly encouraging me to lower my tone as well. She turns past me and leads me to another room, further from the waiting area and Lana's ears.

Inside, the lights are dim and there is definitely some sort of aromatherapy going on here, though I can't tell if its incense or a candle or what, but it smells and feels good. Against my own wishes, it relaxes me.

"Did it work?" I ask.

Again, Stella smiles, almost embarrassed, looking down into her lap. "She was quite easy. Some people just are."

"Lana? Easy? I never thought I'd hear those two words spoken in the same sentence. Is she done? Is it over? Will she have to come in every day for a year until it takes for good?"

Stella chuckles demurely. "No, it doesn't work like that. What's done is done. She's been hypnotized. I believe you'll find a change in behavior. I hope it's what you've been looking for."

I sit in silence a moment or more. "Are you hypnotizing me right now?"

"What?" Stella asks, politely giggling again.

"It just seems too easy. Like, I trust you and all; we're part of the same secret society, but I don't know. It seems too good to be true. I imagine if you're really good at this what you could also do is hypnotize *me* into thinking you've hypnotized *her* so I would think she's changed, but she really hasn't. Sort of like when dentists give people laughing gas. They're still in pain; they just don't give a damn."

Stella's smile remains as she shakes her head back and forth. "No, Kat; I'm working for you. I'm not trying to anesthetize your emotional pain. I am not putting you under a trance. I am sitting here talking to you, being a friend, being a sister, making myself available for your questions. Tell me, what else do you feel you need to know?"

"I want to know whether this will work."

"I don't know."

"What?"

"I said, 'I don't know.' That's the same answer any good doctor would give you about just about anything if that doctor were being totally honest. If I did surgery on you and you asked whether I had completely cured you of all that ails you, if I were being honest I would say, 'maybe, maybe not. But what I have done is what you asked me to do; what we both agreed was the proper course of action, and I am pleased at this point with the results.' That's where we're at. Your mother-in-law is under hypnotic suggestion as we speak. You don't have to do anything to her to trigger the action or to untrigger it. There is no aftercare. Just go out there and use all the basics you were taught at DILS. Be a good daughter-in-law, be good to your husband, treat your MIL as you would have her treat you, and be good to yourself. I believe you will find positive changes in her attitude towards you. Beyond that, every individual is unique. I can't tell you in advance exactly *which* Lana will present herself to you because you seem to have only seen one, and it's not been a positive or constructive one. But there are many sides to her, as there are many sides to all of us. I can't make her into something she's not, but I believe you are likely to see parts of her you've rarely seen before and I believe those parts will be kinder and sweeter — more respectful and loving towards you. I'll look forward to hearing from you so you can tell me about it."

I feel strange. I feel like they say lottery winners feel. There's the initial rush of exhilaration, but it's combined with an odd, ominous dread, as if they're worried about all the negative ramifications such as taxes and leeching relatives. I stand up and I'm a little unsteady on my feet. Stella notices and comes closer to me, helping me rise and embracing me — quite unlike a normal doctor would.

"I know; I know," she says. "I can tell you've been in a lot of pain. That's the reason I do this. You seem like a good person, Kat. All the other girls tell me so. I hope this helps you."

I start to get a little weepy and sniff back a few tears.

"Let me know," she repeats, and I make my way out of her office.

Chapter Fifteen

Returning to the waiting room, there she is again, this person who looks like Momma Lana, is dressed like Momma Lana, and yet is not Momma Lana, or at least Momma Lana as I have come to know her. She is demurely smiling at me, which again, she never does, and looking up from her magazine.

"My, that didn't take long at all," she says. "How long was I in there? Was I only in there a few minutes, too?"

I stare at her and feel perplexed. It's not like she's a zombie; she just seems to have lost that time she spent with Stella. Okay...

"I don't quite know how long I was in there, either. Only a few minutes, you say? Oh my. Well, I guess we should get going then," I say, recklessly ambling towards the outer door. As I exit, I turn back and Lana is right there behind me, still smiling that dopey smile I don't know how to react to or what to do with. I continue this clumsy walk of mine all the way to the elevator and out the front door of the building, all the while turning every few seconds to look at Momma Lana and each time finding her with that same, beatific smile on her puss. She looks like she's having an all-day orgasm. Put in that context, I'm actually jealous.

I can't quite bring myself to say much to her. I don't know what to talk about. Of course, that part is not new to me. In the beginning of our relationship, I would talk to her as I would most anyone else. I would ask her about her life and her day and although she would rarely ever ask me about me and mine, I would give her an obligatory breakdown of it. In each case, the reaction was always the same — I would regret having entered into a conversation with her the moment I'd started. If I had good news from work, she would shit all over it. If I reported that someone I cared about had gotten ill or had an accident, she would surmise that they would only get worse until they finally and blissfully succumbed to death. In short, the woman is a downer. This was, of course, when the issue wasn't simply complaining, particularly if it was something I could take personally. Even when I didn't have her over for dinner, if she, Kyle, and I went out for a meal, she would castigate the food and the service, asking, "Did you pick this dump, Katherine?" Even when Kyle would step in and admit it was his choice, she would counter by saying, "Probably to please your wife."

The old Lana and I were sort of used to not talking to one another. But this new and improved Lana smiles like a simpleton and can't seem to take her eyes off of me. Whenever our eyes meet, I actually get creeped out, like I'll turn into a pillar of salt or something. Yet that blissful smile of hers makes me feel as if… *as if she's happy to be with me*! Naw, couldn't be.

"So, what do you wanna do now?" she asks. Her tone is optimistic.

Do now? With her? I've daydreamed of throwing her in front of a bus many times, but if I admitted that out loud, I'd lose the element of surprise. But she's never asked me such a question in such a way. It infers she wants to spend more time with me. She *never* wants to spend time with me.

"Well… I was going to drop you off back at your house and then grab a bite to eat." After saying it, I realize how unintentionally cruel that sounds. Yet it's a subtle kind of cruel. There's never been any subtlety in the way she has talked to me. I've been told my outfits were "trampy," as opposed to "not quite my personal taste." I'd even settle for, "I wish I had the body to wear something like that." In fact, that's exactly what I'd love to hear, but I've given up dreaming of such a thing.

I look at Lana and she looks up at me, hopeful, like a puppy waiting to be adopted. "I haven't eaten yet, either. Do you think maybe we could eat out together? My treat."

The last time Momma Lana picked up a check, gasoline was ten cents a gallon. The last time she wanted to go out to lunch with me, just the two of us, was… never.

I can feel my eyes bulging out as I try to collect myself. She's hypnotized. Stella told her to like me. People who like each other go to lunch together. Okay, so far so good. But Lana is still Lana and Lana doesn't like anything. Even if she likes *me*, which I still cannot fathom, being out in public with Lana is like walking down the street with a grizzly bear. At some point in time you know she's going to metaphorically shit somewhere other than the woods, since we don't have many forests in downtown LA. That, or maul a park ranger. She knows I do not like or make public scenes; I'm too staid and polite. On the other hand,

I've seen Lana bring seasoned urban warriors like valets and busboys to the brink of tears. I've wondered forever whether this was simply how she was, period, or whether she did it most of the time because she could see and sense how badly it made me feel. After a night out anywhere with Momma Lana, I would go home and want to change my phone number, then browse through magazines for a picture of a new face to bring to the plastic surgeon so I could successfully go into the witness protection program. Embarrassment barely describes the feeling.

"O… kay," I reply, thinking on my feet as to where we could go where there's no chance of being seen by anyone I've ever met. Would the Grand Canyon be too far a drive?

I suggest a place a few blocks from where we are. It's small, as I figure the lower the number of tables, the lower the number of diners, thus the least mathematical chance I'll run into anyone. Who says a background in math isn't helpful in this world? It also has no tables outside, which cuts down on pedestrian traffic. I feel like I'm looking for a no-tell motel for a hot tryst with some hunky guy I'm keeping on the side. Then I look again at Momma Lana and cringe at the thought. No, sorry babe, you're just not my type. *Way* not my type.

She says nothing during the short car ride — nothing unusual about that — but she still has that blessed-out look on her face and I make a mental note to say something to Stella about that. *Dear Stella, the constant smiling makes her look mental. Can you substitute a blank expression? Thanks.*

I hand my keys to the valet and still, she says nothing. Usually this is when she'll make one of her patented remarks like, "You know, they race around town in your car once you give them those keys, don't you? And they run down to the locksmith and make copies so they can steal your car whenever they want. Before we leave, walk all around the car looking for damage. They always damage your car when they take it. They don't care about it at all. They don't hire good drivers; it would cost too much. They only hire illegal aliens—even the ones that *look* white. They don't have roads in their country. That's why they're used to flying over potholes, as if they're dodging roosters and chickens. That's how they live."

But Lana says nothing.

We are seated and again, my sense memory reminds me no seat in any restaurant is ever to her liking. "This one is too close to the door. This one is too close to the bathrooms. This one is too close to the kitchen. This one is too squished in next to the party at the next table." But again, this time, not a peep.

Next come the menus and here I know I will catch hell. First off, the entrees are rather pricey; something I should have thought of when I picked the place, even more so since Lana volunteered for once to pick up the tab. Yet once more, I hear nothing negative.

All of this defensive thinking has me reflecting upon myself and what I have become in these years with Momma Lana. It's the perpetual feeling of dread, of feeling at any moment — at *every* moment — she will do or say something that will ruin my mood. It's like being on the bomb squad in a war zone. It's less a question of "where are the bombs?" than "where *aren't* the bombs?"

I look across the table and see half of her face through our tall menus. The happy look is still there, undaunted by the food prices or the menu selection. I begin to think Stella has installed some sort of high tech vibrator inside of her and she's simply enjoying the unending moment. Finally, she lays the menu down and asks with a smile, "What are you having? And for goodness sake, don't worry about calories!"

"Uh… the salmon?" I answer, as if unsure, hoping I might get the answer right and win a million dollars.

"That's what I'll have, too!"

She looks positively pleased with herself, as if she's having tea and crumpets with the Queen. *What the fuck did Stella do to this woman?*

The waiter comes over and Lana says, "My daughter-in-law will order for the both of us. We're having the same thing. I want to lose weight and I know if I do whatever she does, I may stand a chance. Look at her; just look at her! Isn't she beautiful?"

The waiter smiles while drool drips off the lower lip of my gaping, open, wordless mouth. "Salmon," I say, but I'm sure it came out more like "Za-ma" because my tongue is dragging along the tablecloth and lint is getting in my mouth. *Did she just call me beautiful?*

"I am so glad you agreed to bring me along with you. I know how busy you are and how hard you work. I can't believe Kyle snagged a girl like you. You're the total package! You're smart, you're beautiful, you're young, you're refined, you know everything about everything, you dress like a model, you *look* like a model, and you make enough money on your own that you could have a harem of men at your beck and call. I am so envious of you!"

Who the fuck is this woman and where did she hide my mother-in-law? I put my tongue back in my mouth because it is getting dry—so dry, in fact, that I flag down another waiter and ask for, nay, I *demand*, a glass of wine, stat!

Chugging it down, I stare at this pod person across from me and wonder when she's going to say, "Ha! Gotcha! Thought you were going to have me hypnotized, didn't you? Well it won't work 'cause I've got mirrors for retinas and black tar for a heart and if you thought I was a pain in the ass before, you ain't seen nothin' yet, sister!" But she doesn't. It's a stare down contest, except I'm staring and she's gushing. She's looking at me like I'm a teen idol and she's a 10-year-old girl with braces on her teeth *and* her legs and she just won a dream date with me — unchaparoned.

"So… weight loss. Well, salmon is good for you," I say. I'm at a loss to discuss anything of greater depth.

"And red wine! Just like *you're* drinking. I hear that's great for your heart. I have to watch mine. I'm getting older, you know. Oh, but you ordered fish…"

Here it comes. I knew it. I knew no matter how good Stella was, she could not turn Momma Lana Ding Dong into an agreeable sort; someone who isn't always looking for a way of making me feel like I'm in the wrong about something, anything, all of the time.

"… But of course!" she counters herself. "I read somewhere that those old 'white wine with fish and fowl; red wine with meat' rules were passé. Of course you'd know that! You're on the cutting edge of everything. Besides, I don't remember ever reading where white wine was as good for you as red. Maybe you have. Have you?"

Is this a question? All I know about wine is it's too damn early to order scotch in a public place and not get looked at like I was an alcoholic or something. Ah… alcoholic…

"You don't have a problem with my drinking in front of you?" I ask.

"Why heavens, no! Why would I? Why should I? It's your right. Wine was meant to be drunk with a good meal. People have been doing it since biblical times."

"But I thought you were anti-alcohol. AA and all?"

"Pissh! Look, my Lenny was a drunk. There's nothing else to say about it. That doesn't make drink the culprit. Personal responsibility, that's what I say. But you, I've never seen you drink to excess. And even if you did, I'm sure you would be careful. I don't judge."

"Ha!" I bark so loudly that people in office towers seven blocks away are turning their heads and saying, "Huh?" Embarrassed, I slap my hand over my mouth and duck, waiting for the wrath of Lana to come slamming down upon my head. I wait. And I wait. Nothing. After a few moments of awkward silence, the restaurant begins to buzz again and the rest of the diners go back to their own lives, leaving mine alone for the moment. But that does not make Lana disappear. I'd afraid to look up, but eventually, I know I have to. Raising my head, my hand still over my mouth in fright, she's still there. I expect the worst turd-mouth sneer of all time, but no, what I see is a look of concern.

"Are you okay? Did you choke on something? Your face is all red. Did that wine go down your windpipe? Can you breathe? Please tell me you can breathe!" With that, she bolts out of her chair faster than I've ever seen her move. Her little ham hock legs are churning and I'm afraid the friction will cause a fire of some sort. In a blink she's behind me, grabbing me. "Can you breathe? Can you breathe? Does anybody here know the Heimlich Maneuver?"

She's grabbing me and clutching me so hard that, whereas I was fine before, now I *am* choking; choking because she has a death grip around my lungs and she's squeezing tighter, tighter, tighter...

My eyes open. The chair suddenly has a headrest that it didn't have before. It's also quite firm — good for the posture. Then I realize I'm lying on the floor. I know this because Lana's face is looming over mine. Looming as she comes closer, closer, closer... her lips about to meet mine.

"Agh!"

"Are you okay?" she asks.

"Yes, and I don't go that way!" I sit up and the room is spinning ever so slightly. "How'd I end up on the floor?"

"You passed out. You seemed to be choking." The voice is not Lana's, but our waiter's. As I sit completely upright and assess the situation, I have once more brought the entire restaurant to a screeching halt, only this time they continue to stare, their forks in mid-air arc, their cell phone conversations temporarily on hold.

"I'm fine. I wasn't choking on anything."

"Then how did you end up on the floor, passed out?" he rebuts, daring me to argue with his waiterly omniscience.

I want to say, "Because miniature Hulk Hogan over here wrapped her chubby little arms around me and squeezed me like I was the last life preserver on the Titanic until I lost consciousness, I suppose," but for once, she looks to me like the saddest, most pathetic and apologetic creature on earth. Instead, I climb back into my seat, but not before Lana brushes off the back of me with her hand, like a personal dresser on amphetamines. "Don't touch my ass!" I hiss, as I straighten my dress and sit, regretting it no sooner than I said it as she scurries back to her own chair like a genuflecting English butler. In the last few minutes she has molested me more than Kyle has in weeks.

"Are you sure you're okay? Can I get you anything? Will you be all right?" she asks. She isn't faking it. I mean, if she is, she deserves an Academy Award, and this place probably has enough industry types for her to get great representation.

My head still whirring, I turn to the waiter, "More wine, please. In fact, bring the bottle…"

Chapter Sixteen

"**N**o, I am not making this up. She wasn't just nice to me; she acted like she was the president of my freakin' fan club! If she got any weirder about it, she would have been cutting off locks of my hair and pressing them into her Memory Book."

"Oh my God, you are not serious," says Julia, over-enunciating each syllable like it was an entire page full of important words.

"Swear! I mean, am I happy? I don't know. I sincerely don't know. It's like dating a porn star. It's something you think about, but once it happens, you ask yourself, 'what am I gonna do with that big damn thing?'"

Julia laughs so hard that, unlike me in the restaurant with Momma Lana, she actually does sound like she needs resuscitation. "Glad I could make you cheery, deary, but I'm telling you, it's like an out-of-body, out-of-mind experience. She's no longer Momma Lana Ding Dong. She's... she's not even my dream idea of the perfect mother-in-law. She's just plain possessed."

Julia's convulsing laughter ebbs only slightly, just

enough so I can make out her words, "Kat, are you *ever* happy?"

"Yes, I'm happy. Just not… for the past few years, that's all."

Julia's siren-howling guffawing finally winds down, although I get the feeling that if we were in person and not on the phone, she would crack up again the moment she tried to look me in the eye and act seriously. "All right. In spite of your tale of woe, I have *my* appointment with *my* MIL and Stella tomorrow. And as much as you've given me pause, I'm not canceling it."

"I'm not telling you to cancel, sweetie; I'm just letting you know I may be experiencing buyer's remorse. It seems I've traded in one loon for a loon of a different color."

Before Julia can say another word, another line rings. "Jules, I've got another call. Call me after your appointment tomorrow."

I grab the other call. "Katherine?" I hear.

Certain words spoken by certain people have the effect of a hangman saying, "Next!" as you stand in line, realizing there's no one else in front of you.

"Momma Lana, how are you today?" I literally sing. I don't want to know how she's doing today. Every other time I asked her how her day was she actually told me. Where was she on the day everyone in the world was informed that no one actually wants to know how your day has been, particularly if you have a reputation as a chronic malcontent?

"I'm fine, dear," she replies, as sing-songy as I, only more so. But then she stops, which is disconcerting, forcing me to be the one to keep this conversation going.

"Sooo… to what do I owe the pleasure?"

"I'm down in the lobby."

I notice she called me on my super secret private avoid-my-professional-call screener line, but she did it from some number with which I am not familiar. Her home phone I know by heart, as does my assistant. That's the number that gets sent to voice mail quicker than a phony African prince looking for a short-term loan.

"What lobby?"

"Your lobby. Where you work. I'm on my cell phone. I never use this thing, but Kyle made me get one. Can you hear me all right?" she screams into the phone, blowing my ear off and, I'm sure, scaring the righteous shit out of every person entering our building.

"I hear you fine, Momma Lana," I say, picking myself off the floor and slipping back into my chair. "So, as I was saying… what's up?"

"Is it okay that I called?"

"It would be too late now if it wasn't, wouldn't you say?" It's quippy and snippy and I regret it the moment I emit it. Maybe I've taken to waving red flags in front of this red-haired baby bull. Maybe our relationship has gotten so caustic and I have gotten so defensive that I raise my sword and shield at the mere mention of her name. I don't like this about myself. I never dreamed my husband's mother would entice me into losing my civility.

"Can I come up?"

Even Fortune 500 CEO's wouldn't think to just "drop in" on me without an appointment. Lana has never even been here before. What the hell is she doing here now?

"Is there a problem?"

"I'm disturbing you, aren't I?"

She says it so weakly, so softly, that I am sympathetic

and apologetic by instinct. "No, no, you're fine. I'm just trying to ascertain what it is that brought you here today. I was wondering if you needed a kidney or something."

"No," she answers, ignoring my sense of the ridiculous. "I just never saw where you worked before. I probably should have called first and made an appointment. You're such a busy and important girl. Please forgive me for being so forward. I'll go…"

Any other day, any other time, these same words would have been laced with such venom, such sarcasm, that a person who knew not a single word of English would have gotten the gist that Lana was pissed. But today I don't detect a single ill-mannered, ill-tempered feeling from her. "No, don't go," I say, immediately questioning my own sanity. "I'm on the 23rd floor. Ask for me and they'll direct you to Robin, my secretary, who will bring you in."

I hang up the phone, shaking my head and pulling back my hair. What in living hell is going on here? This is the worst practical joke I have ever suffered. She wants to see where I work? Does she think I'm doing volunteer work at a soup kitchen and can come and go as I please because they don't pay me?

A few horrible minutes go by as I attempt to get my mind off Lana and back onto my tasks at hand, when Robin leads Lana in to see me. Robin's been with me for a while now and despite our different levels of power within the corporate structure, I've been personable enough around her that she knows how I feel about my MIL, as I've regaled her with numerous Lana episodes of the not-so-distant past. The look on Robin's face is precious. She stands behind Lana and makes a face that mimics my own confusion, as if to say, "Is this the three-headed monster? If so, why is she here and why is she acting so human today?"

"My, this place is so impressive! This whole office is yours?" Lana asks.

Working here as long as I have, I've stopped being impressed with this place and take it for granted. For me, it's just another place to slave away for the almighty dollar, but for a first-time visitor, particularly one who is not from the corporate world, she's right — the damn place is huge and it definitely rocks. "Thanks."

Lana wanders around looking at every little thing as if she were from an impoverished Third World nation, a look of shock and awe on her face. She touches and admires everything in sight and it gets so uncomfortable that I'm tempted to offer her a souvenir pen or something.

"So, what do you think?" I ask.

"This is the nicest office I have ever been in. Not that I've been in that many corporate offices. I'm just a stay-at-home wife and mother. But Katherine, my God! How did you get to be in a place like this? I asked for you and people around here act like I'm coming to see the president."

"His office is further down the hall," I say.

"Mr. Obama?!"

"No, no; oh geez, never mind. Misunderstanding." She's here in my realm, my lair, but wherever I have ever been with her, especially in my own house, I have felt like her servant, her slave, and in doing so have become a blithering, dithering idiot, afraid I might trip up and give her more ammunition to use against me. Now she's practically bowing to me and I don't know how to act. "Uh, so glad you like it. That means a lot to me."

"It does? Oh thank you, Katherine. Thank you," and she pumps my hand like a politician desperate for a vote.

"So…?"

She continues to diddle with every little thing. I expect any moment now she'll start flipping the light switches off and on as if she's been living in a cave all her life. But she never quite addresses why she is here.

"Was there any particular reason you came to see me today? Is everything all right?"

She looks up from a burled wood dictation desk adjacent to my own much larger desk and smiles that loopy new smile of hers. "I'm fine. Am I disturbing you? I hope I'm not."

I can't turn away her overtly desperate look. "No, no, I'm fine. I was just wondering if there was something you needed or if you came here to get something off your chest. As we both said, you've never been here before so I was fearful something was the matter."

"Oh, don't be concerned for me. I'm fine. Thank you for asking. You've always been so thoughtful; really, you have." As she says this she strides over towards me and takes my hand and forearm in a show of earnestness. I fight the impulse to recoil. Polar bears look cute on TV commercials, but they're said to be huge and unfriendly killers and I feel like my arm is engulfed in the grip of just such a creature.

"Uh, thanks. Thanks." I know if this were anyone else I would reciprocate the compliment, even if it was total BS, but with Lana, it would be like saying to Satan, "Love your work. Let's do lunch sometime."

She continues working my arm until emotion overcomes her and she takes a step closer, pulling me in for a hug. I catch the scent of the polar bear's breathe and it smells like an Altoid. Right at that moment Robin pokes her head in, her eyes bug out, and she quickly runs out so as not to be seen by Lana, perhaps surreptitiously on her way to grab security, maybe even an entire SWAT team. I've warned her to expect anything and to agree to take a bullet for me from this woman.

"So, what are your plans for the rest of the day?" I ask uncomfortably.

"Could I watch you?"

"Watch me what?"

"I promise, I won't get in the way."

"In the way of what?"

"Whatever it is you have to do. Lady in a big office like this, you must have a million important things to do. I've never seen anything like it. This life you lead, it's so foreign to me. I'm fascinated by it. You know, I watch a lot of TV. All they seem to have are lawyer shows, cop shows, and doctor shows. They never have a show about people like you, and yet look at all this around you. I'll bet people would pay to watch what your day was like."

I raise my eyebrows cynically. "It's not quite as exciting as finding a dead body and solving a crime."

"Oh, but I'd love to watch anyway. I tell all my friends about you as it is, but when they ask me questions, there's so much I don't know. I guess I just don't understand very much, but I'm willing to learn!"

"So you just want to hang out here today?"

"If it's all right with you."

"You just want to shadow me."

"I promise; I won't get in the way."

I'm flummoxed. Part of me thinks this is all just an act, another part wants to treat her like any other stalker and say, "Thanks, but no thanks," while my remaining instinct is to take this moment and use it. I mean, this is what I asked for. She's being nice to me. She hasn't criticized a single thing about me and she's been here almost three whole minutes. That means she's already beaten her personal best by two minutes and thirty seconds.

"Well, I'm flattered, really I am, it's just that, well, I really wasn't expecting you and I do have a full schedule..." She picks up her purse, the universal non-verbal indicator that she's about to leave, when I say, "No, wait! Uhhhh... sure; why not? If you don't mind me just going about my normal business, what the heck? Just let me apologize in advance if I can't stop and answer a ton of questions, okay?"

"Oh, Katherine, you do whatever it is you have to do. I promise, I won't get in the way, honestly. This is so exciting! Watching you, I feel like I'm looking at the 'road not taken.' You know that poem, don't you? Me, I took the well-worn path," she sighs. "I married Kyle's father and I did whatever was necessary to support his life decisions. That's how I was taught. Around that time, women were starting to break free of those kinds of 1950's roles, but I couldn't seem to pull it off. My mother... she was just so... *old fashioned*. And my mother-in-law... don't get me started!"

"Kat, call on line three," I hear Robin say over the intercom.

"Put it on hold a minute. What did you say?"

"I think she said you have a call on line three."

"No, not that, Momma Lana; I mean the thing that *you* said. Your mother-in-law?"

"Oh," and she sits down, fiddling with her purse. "The woman was a total monster! Made my life a living hell. Nothing I ever did was right. The mere sight of her gave me nervous diarrhea. And when I had the children, it only got worse. Why do you think Lenny and I moved out here from Philadelphia? The first opportunity that came his way, I begged him, begged him on my hands and knees, to take it, just so long as it meant being as far away from that woman as possible. Ugh, I get those same old feelings in my intestines just thinking about it."

My face unconsciously curls into a grin. "Wow. I can only imagine what that must be like. You poor thing."

"Oh Katherine, you don't know the half of it. Let me tell you something, if I ever get like that, I want you to tell me. No, I want you to *shoot* me."

I press the intercom. "Robin, could you come in here and take some dictation? I want something put in writing."

Chapter Seventeen

Momma Lana has become my lap dog. Sure, there's no way I could ever support her full weight while sitting in my chair without falling to the floor and breaking my tailbone, but as requested, I have allowed her to tail me as I work and frankly, were she a prospective intern or new hire, I would sign her up on the spot. She keeps so close to me I can smell her perfume. She asks questions. The problem is, she's Momma Lana and not an ambitious young college grad. As such, she's slowing me down, and yet I haven't the heart to toss her out.

"I have a meeting now in the conference room."

"Ooh. That sounds exciting," she replies. Everything I say sounds exciting to her today. She spent at least five minutes ogling the hand sanitizer on my desk, asking me how it works and why I use it. Each word from my mouth is like a parable from Moses. "Go forth and sanitize!" And ye, verily, it was good.

"Actually, you may find it kind of boring," I say, hoping she will beg off. But if I told her I planned on getting on my hands and knees to count carpet fibers she would probably buy us matching knee pads and want to take pictures for her scrapbook. It's all so over the top that I keep wondering when she's going to admit to me it's all a game and who the hell do I think I am, thinking I could have her hypnotized into treating me in a civil manner.

"Ooo, this is nice," she says as we enter the conference room, just as she has as we've entered each and every room. Even the hallway held her attention like it was a new feature at Disney's Magic Kingdom.

"It's a small conference room. We have some that are much bigger."

"You have multiple conference rooms? Wow. This most certainly must be an important place. And you're the boss here?"

"*A* boss, not *the* boss. I'm in charge of Sales and Marketing." I look at her and I can tell she's wondering if my job somehow involves grocery shopping. Still, she seems to be going through the logical steps of this misnomer in her head, perhaps concluding that even if it did involve choosing which melons were the sweetest, to have such an office in such an office building I must be pretty darn good at it.

She's actually not a stupid woman. She asks a lot of questions, but seems to avoid asking too, too many, and appears to be stifling herself from asking the most terribly dumb ones out loud. She seems to be in a trance all right, but not suffering from complete mental disconnection — or at least no worse than before she met up with Stella.

We sit — me at the head of the table, while Lana, who again seems to be of this world, knows enough to seat herself further down away from me.

"It's not a big meeting; just a few guys I work with

every day and know well. You might find it a bit dry and boring."

"I find this all so interesting. But if I do get bored, I have my knitting," she says as she pulls out some yarn and a pair of needles. Oh great. If she didn't look like a clichéd old lady before, she sure as hell does now. The thing with tech industries is that hardly anyone is over thirty-five. Most of the guys, when you can get them to dress up at all, which is almost never, appear to be wearing their bar mitzvah suits — which still fit.

Eric, Joel, and Bruce all troop into the room, each feeling totally at home until they see the old lady with the knitting down at the far end of the table, to whom each says a tentative, "Hello," which Momma Lana graciously and smilingly reciprocates. "That's my mother-in-law; she's visiting." It's a simple explanation, but still, I see each face searching the far recesses of their brain, looking to see if there was something on the calendar about "Bring Your In-Laws to Work Day." I await some sharp-witted quips, but no one's brain can spew one out quickly enough. We get down to work.

"Ad revenue is down, but that's industry-wide, not just limited to us," says Eric, the reliable source of data, most of it bad.

"The problem is, less people are clicking on sponsored links. The consumer is getting smarter. They're beginning to understand the difference between paid listings and organic rankings. And the advertiser is being more careful as to how and where they spend their dollar. Plus, we're no longer the only kid on the block. Ad networks are popping up left and right, and social applications are helping merchants push their product with good results," adds Bruce.

I have nothing immediately to add because they've told me nothing I don't already know. My simple charge to them is, "Well, fix it anyway," which is, of course, Management 101. My job is not necessarily to fix problems myself; it is to acknowledge problems and assign some other schmuck to repair them or else start sending out their resume during lunchtime. It's good to be queen.

There's more jibber-jabber around the table, most of it in tech jargon. Me, I'm used to it; it's my second language. Lana? I look down the table at her from time to time and I can see she's trying valiantly to look cool and clued in, all the while knitting away so as not to seem too desperate to be included. Just so long as she keeps her yap shut; that's all I pray for. *Be quiet, be quiet and knit yourself a cloak of invisibility, but more than anything, just be quiet.*

"Push downs, hulks, trolls, big brothers, stealths—no sooner do we create them, they figure out a way to block them. And even when they don't, most consumers are developing banner blindness."

"Bruce, is it your contention they're being actively blocked, passively blocked, or people are deaf, dumb, and blind to them? Make up your mind. Which one is it? At least if we knew what we were fighting against, we could fight the good fight," I say.

Eric, the one who most desperately wants my job, suddenly tries to hijack the conversation, his favorite ploy. "Let's ask her." All eyes slither down the oak table to the pudgy little lady with the purple wool and the two orange needles. Oy…

"What?" Lana asks, a tentative smile on her face that attempts to mask a nervous quivering in her voice.

"Guys, focus. This is my mother-in-law. No offense, Lana, but she has no idea what we're talking about."

"That's the point," says Eric, who I want to strangle so badly that my French tips are taking on a life of their own, quivering with the anticipation of freshly minted MBA blood. "She's the perfect focus group. We know that first adaptors are way ahead of us, but the problem is that second and third-wavers are, too. I say, let's stop trying to do battle with the first adaptors and instead fight this battle from the back lines forward." He looks so God-awful pleased with himself I want his face to melt so it glues his lips shut. The others look tentative, trying to decide who to side with — Lancelot or King Arthur. Every one of these kids would cut the brakes in my car if it meant getting my office and my parking space, yet on the surface they love and fear me.

"Eric, how does one woman constitute a focus *group*? Do you plan on cloning her?" As I say this I cringe at the nightmarish thought.

"I understand," he says condescendingly, "But she's here now; we're here now; let's use her. Ma'am… when you are searching for something online, do you click on the links to the right or the ones in the middle of the page?"

Lana looks both happy and scared, like some wanna-be contestant on "The Price is Right" who also happens to suffer from stage fright.

"She has no idea. Sorry, Lana; I didn't say that to hurt your feelings. I set up her computer. I taught her how to properly use a search engine to find relevant results. Ironic, isn't it, all things considered?" As I wait for a response I reflect back on the day I spent at Momma Lana's condo, setting up said computer. If I'd been hired to do that job I would have stomped out after about twenty minutes of her interminable insults, but no, I am the daughter-in-law from Silicon Valley so I had to take it all right in the face. I shiver as I remember it as one of the single worst days of my life. It also led to me being used as her personal 24-hour tech support, although even the nameless, faceless support desk people in India never had to take as much abuse as I signed up for. "What's an attachment? Why can't I open anything my friends send me? You gave me a piece of junk computer. I'm going to have to go to a professional."

"Mrs.… can I call you Lana?" he asks.

"Why yes," she says, looking so flattered she might adopt him.

"You use your computer. You use the Internet, right?"

"Yes, sometimes."

"Do you ever see ads like this?" Eric, carrying his laptop, has moved over to the seat next to Lana. "I know, even if your daughter-in-law set you up and told you how and where to find the information you're looking for, I'm sure you click on these links. Am I right?"

"Uh, um," Lana says, searching for an answer. "I think so. I'm not sure. I can't remember."

"Let me ask this in a different way about a different product of ours. Have you ever seen an ad on your computer and really used it? I mean, did you stop and read it or did you click on it?" Eric sounds like he's cross-examining a witness at a trial. I'd pull him off since I think this is all pointless, but the vengeful side of me is almost enjoying seeing Lana get grilled, although she is still acting more like someone Al Roker decided to chat up on "The Today Show". I suppose no one asks her opinion very often… thank God!

"No, that I am sure of. I can't remember ever stopping

to read one, and I know I never clicked on one. I'm afraid to click around on things. When I do, bad things happen. I really don't know what I'm doing on those computers." She looks helpless yet hopeful, and again I feel a pang of guilt for what I've just put her through and how I still harbor such anger towards her.

Eric smiles and continues to speak to her in a calm, soothing voice. Sure, *he* can be patient with her. He never had to take her on vacation with him.

"How does your husband feel about you parading around the hotel pool like that?"

"I'm not parading; I'm swimming and sunbathing."

"Humph! I've seen prostitutes showing less skin."

"It's a bikini. Look around; lots of women are wearing them. Some are far more revealing than the one I'm wearing."

"Well, they're probably single. And unlike you, they have the bodies for it."

Lana — old, pre-trance Lana—has not just rented space in my head; she's built a freaking 108-story office tower there with a 99-year lease.

Eric moves as close to Lana as a young gigolo at a senior citizen's resort. "What would it take for you to notice an ad on the Internet? What would the ad have to say? How would it have to be presented so that it didn't annoy you, but instead, drew you in?"

Lana pauses for a second, looks around the room at the others, looks at me nervously as if seeking approval, and then finally speaks. One word. One stinking word. "Coupons."

My head actually thumps off the conference room table, making a loud noise and causing me to see stars. I rub my forehead to make the pain go away and Bruce, Eric, and Joel are all looking at me like I've just had a seizure and they don't know whether to call 911 or apply for my job.

"Coupons," Eric repeats calmly.

"Jesus Christ!" I finally blurt out, and everyone looks at me and wonders if indeed I am still in the middle of some sort of neurological episode. "Everything is coupons! If I ever hear the word 'coupons' again…" My voice trails off as I see the faces of my minions looking at me as if I've finally lost it for good. Lana. Lana did this. This must be her plan. Ruin my career by making everyone think I'm the crazy one.

"Tell us about coupons," Eric says to Lana, calmly as ever, as if to offset the rantings of his crazy boss at the head of the table, the one with the big red welt puffing up on her forehead.

"Well, when I see an ad, all I think is, 'So what am I getting? Why should I act now? Why should I buy here? Most ads never give you a reason to buy.'"

Eric does a three-sixty and faces me with a demonic look on his face like he's about to say, "It's ALIVE!" He turns back to Lana. "Give you a reason to buy. A reason to buy. Yes!"

"Eric, this is Marketing 101. Of course an ad must give the consumer a reason to buy. Geez, you'd think she invented advertising!" I say.

"Actually, my Uncle Lewis, may he rest in peace, had the first off-price men's clothing store in Philadelphia. And he built that business on *coupons*."

"Argh! Must I hear the Philadelphia men's clothing store story again?!" I say, loudly at first, then draining to a whisper by the time I finish. Again, everyone looks at me like I'm a few lobes short of a brain. Lana seems perfectly normal — the classic little old lady acting like a fish out of water in the big, high-techy boardroom. Me, I rage at every single thing that comes out of her mouth, none of which, for once, is a slur directed at me. How sinister!

"Coupons," Eric says softly, like a mantra, steepleing his hands in prayer-like fashion.

"Eric, you're acting like she just invented a new word; a totally new concept. Coupons have been around forever."

"What if we ran a column down the right or left margin…" says Bruce.

"Right is better," adds Joel.

"… And instead of just placing an ad — which might be blocked — we just run a list of product categories. Food, computer supplies, automobiles…"

"It could be part of our standard page setting, so it wouldn't register as a pop-up or an ad of any sort," Joel chimes in. "It actually wouldn't *be* an ad. It would be an offering for… coupons!"

"Yes! I do a search on whatever, I get my hits, but I always know that in the right page margin there's a listing of product categories that all have coupons available. All I have to do is think, 'Hey, I wonder what electronic accessories are featuring coupons this week. I'll click on and see!'" Eric says as he continues pacing.

"Guys, this is not a new idea; why do you think it is? People get coupons from every on-line retailer they've ever done business with via e-mail. Don't you people ever use the Internet?" I practically scream.

"No, this is different. Sure, I know if I go to Store X, I will get e-mailed coupon offers…"

"You will?" says Lana, truly amazed and excited. She's never bought a thing on-line in her life. She thinks typing in your credit card number sends it immediately to the Russian mob, which in turn uses it to buy cars, planes, and women of loose virtue. Meanwhile, she trusts every restaurant and gas station in America with the same information.

"Yes," says Eric, "But this is better, better for our clients. They don't need us to retain the customers they already have. They need us for new customers. Like…what's your name again sweetie?"

"Lana," she says, blushing, probably thinking of how to change her will to put this little putz Jon in it and leave me out.

"Like Lana says, this is how our clients can create a reason to buy. Businesses that people haven't done business with before. If I know that in the right page margin there will always be coupon offers, listed by category, I can always go there and see what's available for me. One click and I'm taken to a colorful page that only features coupons in the product category I'm interested in. I see a good deal, I click the coupon and I'm redirected to the company's site, AND I get to print out the coupon for terrestrial buying or simply use it right then and there for cyber purchasing."

"It's brilliant," says Joel, who never gets excited about anything.

Joel and Bruce's heads nod like bobble-head dolls. Eric struts around the room like he's just invented electricity. I want to scream. I want to crawl down the length of the table on my hands and knees in order to choke my mother-in-law to death. I look at her with steam pouring out of my ears. All she does is wear a dim-witted smile, amazed by it all — a female Forrest Gump in Sears ready-to-wear.

I am defeated. Now that Lana is so sweet, I have also

become one confused mean bitch. I barely can stand being around myself. What the hell is happening to me?

Chapter Eighteen

"I always love our 'Darla and Julia' lunches," Darla Klein said as she sat behind her brimming bowl of greens at a small café. She smiled, as she always did when they were together, and her daughter-in-law, author Julia Rader, who kept her maiden name because her fame had begun prior to her marriage to Darla's son Mark, looked at her with her typical anxiety, awash in the confusion of whether Darla had a sincere bone in her body.

Julia always admired one thing about Darla, no matter how she felt about the woman personally: the lady had class. Her blond hair was perfectly coiffed, kept long enough to still be sexy and stunning while not making her appear as if she were attempting to hold on so tightly to waning youth that she appeared desperate and ridiculous. She dressed in couture, yet never seemed to look down her nose at Julia's occasionally anti-fashion fashion statements. And that, of course, was the crux of the problem: How do you confront a person who is completely non-confrontational? How do you accuse someone of something you've never seen nor heard in your presence? Even the worst backstabbers in the world eventually crack and let their bile spew all over the place, but Darla Klein seemed in a class of her own. At times like these, Julia couldn't help but feel a loving bond with her. And therein lay the problem. They would have these times together — *every* time they were together they would have these sorts of times together — and then Julia would return home to her husband, Darla's son, only to get kicked in the proverbial gut by his replay of what really went on from Darla's point of view, courtesy of the phone calls she and her son incessantly shared. It was the height of betrayal, something she had trouble relating to but which she now seemed to face constantly. It even merged into her writing. In her first novel, all the major conflicts were transparent: there were bad guys and good guys and each knew who the other was and stated their reason for existence accordingly. By book three, Julia's perception of Darla had begun to creep in. Now no one was to be trusted.

"So, how did you like Dr. Diomare?" asked Julia.

"Fine. Great. She had some wonderful ideas about how to relax before bedtime. I *so* need my beauty rest," she gaily chuckled.

Julia had known the "fat" ruse would not work. For one thing, she herself didn't weigh 95 lbs. dripping wet and her MIL had six-pack abs a twenty-five-year-old would envy. But who doesn't wish they could sleep better?

"What about the hypnosis?" Julia asked tentatively.

"Wonderful. I don't recall a thing. Just the most relaxing rest I've had in years. God, if she could come to my house every night and do that, I'd be in heaven!"

Julia smiled, feeling a cornucopia of emotions: pleasure, guilt, nervousness, and hurt. "So, the movie opens next week." She let it lay there without adding anything like, "And I'm so excited," or "I hope it does well." Both would sound like she was fishing for compliments and positive reinforcement and she wanted above all else not to appear as if she were fishing for anything positive from Darla. Just honesty. True feelings from the heart.

She'd struggled the night before this day. So ironic, using the trick of claiming they were going to see a sleep specialist — Julia hadn't slept a wink. *Is this ethical? Is this right? She already says nothing but nice things to my face. How will I know whether or not it's working?* Those thoughts and others had run through her mind over like a broken record.

"Oh yes, darling, I won't be a needy nag by asking for tickets to the premier, but for the second showing, I'd like to buy a block of tickets for all my friends. And don't just give them to me; I want to pay. You're far too nice. I know how those movie studios operate. If you don't do well the opening weekend, they cut your legs out from under you and it's straight to DVD. But I know that won't happen to 'Children of the Forest.' Your fan base is deeper than the Pacific. You'll set records; I know you will."

"How many?" Julia asked.

"*Everybody* wants to see your movie. I've been hyping it to my friends ever since you got optioned. I'd say… put me down for one hundred and twenty."

"One hundred twenty tickets? To a movie?"

"Yes. I'll get them all to arrive early so they can see the aftermath of the red carpet. I promise, I won't embarrass you. I'll just wave to you from the crowd and point you out to my friends. They'll be so thrilled!"

Julia picked at her salad without making much

headway. "You've already discussed this with them? Your friends I mean."

"Why certainly. It's all I ever talk about."

Julia fidgeted. "You have one hundred twenty friends and you've already been saying good things about my book — my movie?"

Darla looked a little perplexed. "The book, yes; I've read the book. I've read it and re-read it. The movie, I'm just excited that it's happening. Obviously, I haven't seen it; it hasn't come out yet. But I've told all my friends about it and they're dying to see it and witness your big success."

"You have one hundred twenty friends?"

Darla Klein sat back in her chair with the oddest, most confused look on her face. "I don't know what you're getting at. I know at least one hundred twenty people. I'm sure you do, too. Maybe I'm being a little presumptuous to call them all 'friends,' but I know them. A lot of them are close personal friends, but some of them, I admit, are just acquaintances. Why do you keep asking about this as if it's so strange?"

Julia continued to rearrange her veggies with her fork, not motivated to stick any in her mouth. "Dunno. Just asking."

A pregnant pause lay between them. "Is everything okay, dear? You don't seem yourself," Darla asked.

Julia bit the inside of her lower lip. "It's just that… one hundred twenty people is a lot. I'm trying to figure out what would motivate someone to invite that many people to see a movie. I know it's not 'high art.' It's a popcorn movie; I know that. It's just… it's what I do, that's all. It's my passion and I'm proud of it." Her words took on a defensive tone. This was how she expressed herself to

Mark when he came carrying tales to her about the precise nature of Darla's criticisms of her work.

"You're my daughter-in-law. I love you. I'd bring everyone I know if you made a movie about the mating habits of flying squirrels!"

"So that's it. It's just about the celebrity. It's a movie and people who get movies made are suddenly glamorous. What does it matter whether it's good or not? People like me get published and get on the Best Sellers lists even when they can't string together cogent sentences, right?"

Darla, who had straightened up in her chair before, became even more rigid, as if her body was nothing more than a stake in the ground holding earthbound the helium balloon that was her head. "Did I say something to offend you?"

"I don't know; did you?" Julia countered, irritable from her lack of sleep.

"Like what? When? What's going on here? I thought we were having a nice lunch and now it sounds like you're attacking me. What did I do to deserve that?"

Julia held onto her fork as if she were planning to use it as a weapon. "Just tell me how you really feel about my writing. That's all. Just tell me the honest truth about what you think of my work and my talent or lack thereof."

For once, Darla Kline's face appeared stern. "I've talked to you about your writing a thousand times before. You know what I think. I'm your biggest fan. Why do you suddenly sound like I've been lying to you?"

"Well, have you been?" Julia snapped back.

Darla's jaw slackened as she slowly arose, gently placing her napkin on the table. "I'm going to give you the benefit of the doubt and write this off to you being stressed about the premier. But I am no longer enjoying this time we're spending together. It's getting ugly and I'm feeling hurt. I've never seen this from you and I hope it's just something you'll work through over the next few days. Until then, I'll stay my distance. Good day," she said as she left the table, her heels clacking against the floor, her head never turning to look back.

Chapter Nineteen

Many boutiques on Rodeo Drive keep their doors locked, even during peak business hours, requiring one to be buzzed in by the staff. *Joel Wayne*, named after it eponymous designer-owner, is so exclusive it often goes beyond the buzzer, its exclusive client list making appointments simply to browse in private. Me, I've never been here before, not because I can't afford it, but because I rarely make the time for such indulgences. Joel Wayne's clientele are predominantly the idle rich and I have not yet evolved to the level of being so idle. But Claudia Steadman is another story entirely — as always.

It's another day with just the Short Bus Level Three crowd — me, Julia, and Ashley—along with our mentors Gabriella, Stella, and the omnipresent Claudia. I wonder how Claudia manages to come up with new and exciting meeting spots and themes for these soirées. DILS is worth joining just for the amenities — kind of like some sort of tricked-out time-share club. Models put on a private show for us as we sip champagne, and we're encouraged to try on anything we like — strutting the mini-catwalk to mutual tittering laughter. It's a great time. Were it only that we were here with no real purpose whatsoever. *That* would be the dream.

I look around and it's impossible not to notice that Gabriella, Claudia, and Stella are happy as vacationers, while Julia appears on the verge of a nervous breakdown, Ashley looks pissed, and me, well, I don't need a mirror to see I look anxious and frustrated. Still, it seems like a giant game of chicken. The Three Misfit Toys all look like they want to vent and get down to business, while the others are happy sipping bubbly and running up their Centurion cards.

Julia cracks first. "My MIL was actually better *before* you hypnotized her. What's up with that?"

"Results may vary. Warrantees are limited. Read the fine print for details," sniffs Gabriella good-naturedly, as she takes another sip of Cristal.

"Is it safe to talk here? I've wondered about the legal implications of this ever since it was suggested," I add.

"Ladies, the staff here is used to controversy. Over the years they've heard so much dish they could each write bestselling tell-alls," says Claudia languidly.

"And this place would shut down forever and ever, amen. Don't worry; they know better. Carry on," says Gabriella, the lawyer among us.

"I just want to know when it's my turn. When did we draw straws with me ending up with the short one?" pouts Ashley, unhappy as always.

The only one not entirely effusive in some manner is Stella Diomare, the hypnotist extraordinaire. Seeing her sitting rather demurely, almost apologetically, I feel sorry for her, even if I'm not the world's happiest client right now.

If there's one vibe I get from her, despite not knowing her very well, it's that she is, if anything, sincere and dedicated to her craft. Perhaps she doesn't feel like appearing too defensive, feeling more comfortable with Gabriella and Claudia doing her fighting for her, but still, I can see that our words and attitudes sting.

"Well, if we're going to do this, let's get down to it. Kat, what has your experience been like?" Stella finally asks.

"My MIL has gone from Satanic to being a potential lesbian lover, although the thought of that sickens me. Sorry if that offends anyone. I have several friends who are lesbians but none who would want a piece of Lana either."

"Oh honey, if you ever want to go that way, I know much hotter women," cackles Claudia.

"It's just… it's too much. Can't there be a middle ground? She doesn't just like me; she loves me. Check that; she doesn't just love me; she's obsessed with me. I wouldn't appreciate this sort of smothering dedication from a man, any man, let alone my MIL. I'm on the verge of taking out a restraining order."

"Does she stand outside your bedroom window at night, her face pressed up against the glass?" laughs Gabriella. "Does she toss pebbles at it and recite sonnets to you? Has she tried tying you to her bed and breaking your ankles while telling you she's your biggest fan?" Either Gabriella has had too much to drink or else she's simply having way too much fun at my expense.

"Okay, okay; let's leave little sister alone. Kat, just remember that, compared to how things were, this is something I'm sure you'll laugh about some day," says Claudia.

"Kat, hypnosis deals with what is real within the brain.

The shy person who starts belting out a Broadway tune is, deep down, a repressed woman who has not been able to express her true self. The thing is, there are many parts to us all. We're at the same time shy and extroverted, repressed and wild, sweet and bitchy. All the contradictions in the world, we possess them all. What I've tried to do here is get your MIL to tap into the positive feelings she has toward you. What neither of us knew was how many there were."

"You mean to tell me she's always felt this way towards me?"

"Exactly."

I ponder this a minute. "Poppycock," I say; a word I've never spoken out loud in my life. Maybe *I've* had too much champagne.

"I've seen this before, Kat, but never as dramatically as you've described. Your MIL has done one hell of a job repressing her true feelings toward you."

"But… but why would she have repressed them by being so horrible to me before?" On this cue everyone leans back a little into their seats and focuses their attention on the next outfit being modeled, a beautiful jacket and skirt set that would be perfect for a cool evening out.

"I've never done this myself, but have any of you ever heard of girls, little school girls, who kick boys in the shins to show them they like them? Anyone?" asks Stella.

Ashley raises her hand slowly. "I guess. It was quite a while ago."

"How about playing hard to get? That's a bit more accessible," asks Stella. We all mutter our agreement. "Well it's sort of like that, only in Kat's case, picture it on steroids. Kat, it appears to me your MIL had such strong, positive feelings toward you that she did everything in her power to tamp them down. From what you've told me, it seems she saw in you an ideal. You were everything she ever wanted for her son. In fact, you represent everything she ever wanted for *herself*, everything she ever wished she could be but never was. You're young, you're beautiful, you're smart, you're successful, you're nice, and you're interesting."

"Keep going; it feels good," I reply.

"That's it. None of the rest of us ever had a reaction quite like this."

"Here, here," Gabriella and Claudia say in unison, raising their glasses in a toast. "Kat dear, my MIL is civil towards me," says Claudia. "She likes a lot of things about me. We have a pleasant relationship today. Pleasant. Civil. What's in the past is in the past. Sort of like Poland and Germany."

"Let's say I buy into this theory. She loves me so much she wants me to think she hates me. What on earth is the point behind it? The 'playing hard to get' analogy doesn't link up, in my mind. You do that to attract someone; to not let them think you're too easy or too desperate. Why would a MIL do that to a DIL?"

Again, everyone decides this is the perfect cue to ignore me and instead focus back on the mini-runway, where a model is wearing the most dynamic black lace mid-calf skirt.

"I'm too short for any of this. When are they going to have models who are five foot one? That last one had to have been six-two if she were an inch," pouts Julia, not usually this much of a grouch.

"Jealousy," says Gabriella, as all the other voices chime in in unison. I grimace.

"No, really," says Claudia. "It's as simple as that. We're

making this far too complicated. Put yourself in her place. You want the best for your child, right? So what would be the ideal DIL? Smart, pretty, successful, etcetera, etcetera. Your husband shows up with you on his arm. Mission accomplished, right? Except you're actually *too* good. You're so good, part of her wishes you weren't. She wants her son to be happy, but she doesn't want herself to become irrelevant."

"Soooo…" adds Gabriella, "she makes every attempt to knock you down a few pegs. That way she can have her cake and eat it, too. She still has the great DIL her son brought home, but she gets to keep her in her place so she doesn't feel totally inferior. It's a sad commentary, but we've seen it before."

"But we aren't dealing with the new issues! My MIL was perfectly swell to my face before and now she's not. Kat's used to treat her terribly and now she stalks her. The hypnosis was a bad idea. I regret it. I'm sorry; I don't mean to be mean, but that's the way I feel," says Julia, her arms flopped across her chest like a child in a huff.

"I don't know about either of you two, but I still haven't had my turn and I'm willing to take the gamble," says Ashley, piling on.

Stella, not one to dominate a room, pensively looks down at the Persian rug beneath her feet, saying not a word. Finally, "Okay, let's take this one at a time. Kat, do you want a redo? A reversal? It's easy. I can do it any time you'd like. Just bring Lana in and I'll take her out of her trance. Is that what you want?"

I stop and ponder the offer. Die by the gun or die by the knife. Either way you're dead. "Isn't there a middle ground?"

"No. She's either in a trance or she's not. How she specifically reacts to hypnotic suggestion is unique to her and how she truly feels. What you have to do is ask yourself, 'Am I happier with her now, or would I prefer her the way she was?'"

Now it's my turn to look down at the expensive floor covering. "Can I get back to you on that?"

"Sure. You know where to find me. I'm not going anywhere. Now, Jules…"

"You can have my answer right now. Yes, I want you to put my MIL back the way you found her. The sooner the better."

"No."

"What do you mean, 'No,'?"

"Jules, I'm not just a hypnotist; I'm a therapist. I want you and your MIL to come back to my office. I want to do some sessions with the two of you."

"Why? With Kat you just gave her an either/or. I don't get it."

"Ladies, Level Three is more than a service, and DILS is more than vendor," injects Claudia.

"What are you saying?" asks Ashley.

Claudia composes herself politely, yet regally. "When you three first came to us, you described your situations in quite a lot of detail. In return, we provided support and suggestion. With Levels Two and Three, we offered even more. What DILS does is attempt to assist women achieve happiness and fulfillment in their relationships with their husbands and their MILs. Occasionally, though, the patient makes a lousy doctor, if you catch my drift."

No matter how beautiful the clothing still being displayed, I am far too rooted in this conversation now, yet

I have no way of verbalizing how I wish to respond. Old Lana or New and Improved Lana. The Monster-in-Law or the Smother-in-Law. I have no answer. But Julia has a few.

"I resent that. I don't like being spoken down to. I'm just as smart as anyone here." I've never seen Julia so enraged.

"Julia, no one is talking down to you," says Claudia. "I understand you're stressed about the movie…"

"Screw the movie. I wish I'd never agreed to it. I wish I'd never been published. I wish I was still in Colorado, sitting under a tree, writing for my own pleasure. And single!" No, not single! I wish I wasn't a *Seven* because if I was a *Nine* or at least a phony *Nine* I would be living the life I was meant to live with Jason, a man that would be proud of my success. Lift me up rather than try to find all my faults. Laugh at my jokes because I am pretty damn funny, not annoying and loud like Mark says. My damn best friend! But no, Jason saw a better match with Ms. Fake Nine!" With that, she storms out, or attempts to storm out before she realizes she's locked in, the glass door refusing to give way. We all shout after her but she doesn't care to hear us, instead just bellowing over us, "Let me out of here! You don't even sell petites!"

The store manager moves faster than the rest of us, protecting the sanctity of her door from being reduced to shards of glass from the incensed little dynamo.

"Julia, wait!" But it's too late; she's gone. The rest of us are left to metaphorically rearrange our blown back hair, until finally Ashley breaks the shocked silence.

"So when is it my turn?"

Chapter Twenty

"Honey?"

"Yes, Kyle."

"Honey, did you do something to my mother?"

Reflexively, I pull the bedcovers over my head and try to hide, a silly strategy since Kyle knows I'm here; he can probably feel my body heat and hear my breathing, although, to my credit, I don't create much of a lump.

"Like what?" I answer with a question. *Please don't catch me; please don't catch me,* I pray to whatever deity might be listening.

"Kat, I can hardly hear you under the covers. Can you come out?"

"I'm cold."

"I could warm you up," he sing-songs sensuously.

"That's okay," I say quickly. "Pass."

"Honey, I know you've complained almost every day since we got married that my mother has had trouble accepting you," he continues in this strange lyrical tone that seems to infer he knows what I've done even though I have no idea how he could have found out.

"Yes," I say in my same clipped tone, the sound still muffled under silk sheets and a cozy comforter.

"But now she seems... different." He stops there and that's enough to capture my interest.

"Do you have a problem with that?" I ask as I pop my head up from its hiding place.

"No, no, it's just... very sudden. And intense. Severe, really. I mean, I've seen people mellow over time, but usually there's a transitional period. Not in this case."

"So, again I ask — do you have a problem with it? Or did you like it better when she hated me?"

"What?!"

"'What' is right. What's the matter with how she's been treating me lately? Hmmm?" The best defense is a good offense.

"Nothing. I couldn't be happier," Kyle replies, suddenly looking like he wished he hadn't started this topic. "I just think it's strange. Not strange that she — or anyone — would like you, but strange she would swing so violently from one extreme to another."

"Oh!" Now I'm sitting straight up in bed and Kyle actually flinches from my quick movement. "After all this time, the hundreds of nights we spent in this very bed with me crying on your shoulder about how your mother treated me and you, you making excuses for her or attempting to make me think it was all in my head. Now *you* are sitting here finally admitting that she really did treat me like shit?!"

He's speechless. I'm livid.

"She's... my mother," he whimpers.

"And I'm your wife!" I am now standing on the bed. "Kyle, this... this..." I am so pissed right now I want to hit him with something. "I have been confiding in you since the time I met her and you always defended her."

"Did not!"

"Did, too! You always took her side."

"Did not!"

"Did, too!"

I stand here realizing I am resorting to the most infantile debate technique in the English language. In a fit of anger, I pull my negligee over my head, nearly ripping it in the process, and throw it in his face. "Me or your mother!" I scream, buck naked and bouncing on the bed before him, my teeth clinched, my eyes ablaze.

He stares at me a moment, then says, sheepishly, "Looking like that, do you think there's any choice?" and tackles me around the waist. I love make up sex.

Chapter Twenty-One

I buzz the call box at the end of the long driveway. "Yes?" a tiny female voice crackles through the speaker.

"It's Kat. I'm alone. And unarmed. Can I come up?"

There's a pause, or maybe it's just my imagination, then finally, "Fine."

After I drive up and park, I approach the massive castle doors. For a poor girl from rural Colorado, she's done quite well for herself. When I first met her, I had no idea who she was or what she'd done, but since then I've made a point of reading her books, which is a chore for me since I'm no longer much of a recreational reader. They're okay. I'm not really her demographic. She aims for the teen girl crowd and they're buying her up. But through it all, I can see she knows how to string together a sentence or two. Still, I can understand where the slings and arrows of critics might take aim. It's very commercial; not fine art. And even in her fantasy genre, she's not a deep study. She's a good commercial writer, and in this case, one who has caught fire and made the kind of money 99.9% of authors could only dream of.

"Hello," she says with little enthusiasm, her arms wrapped around her chest in a self hug. "Come on in."

The feeling of being in a modern day castle continues as I gawk around like a tourist. Julia looks back and sees me craning my neck this way and that and without waiting for the expected compliments says, "Claudia helped me decorate it. Nice, huh?" From someone else, this might sound haughty, but from Julia, it sounds like she's giving a tour through someone else's house, as if she's completely divorced from it. I've heard this same sort of attitude from a few women in my day, but in those cases it was because it was all from their husband's money and they didn't even have much say in the decorating or anything else for that matter. I guess compared to the opposite end of the spectrum—the ones who act as if it represented the blood, sweat, and tears of their own labor when there was none, this was preferable, but with Jules, it's almost like part of her is ashamed of it, this ostentatious thing, far too large for only she and her husband.

"Mark's not here; he's at the driving range," she says, still very reserved, moving around like the walking wounded. She sits and, without offering me a chair, I can figure that much out for myself and join her.

"Good. I mean, not good that I don't ever want to meet him, but good we can be alone. I mean... oh, I don't know what I mean. Jules, I'm so sorry you're blue. Is it... is it the opening? Does that have you stressed? I'm not asking that in a way to minimize how you feel about your MIL, but..."

"Yes," she sighs, "the opening is definitely contributing to it. It's bringing everything to a head. If you were to sit here and tell me, 'Jules, I read your books and I'm sorry to say, they're not my cup of tea,' I could live with that; I really could. I'm not an egomaniac. I take criticism well, I think. I don't require blind fandom from my friends. What I can't handle any more is the dishonesty."

"Where is it all coming from — your MIL?"

"I don't know. That's the tough part. That's what none of what we've been doing in DILS has been addressing. Before she was hypnotized, she said she loved me and my work, but said the opposite to Mark behind my back. *After* she's been hypnotized she does the same thing. So what have I accomplished?"

I ponder a moment. "Has it always been centered on your writing? Again, I say this not to minimize your pain, but if my MIL had only hated one thing about me, I probably could have lived with that."

Julia stews for a minute. "You may be saying that, but I sincerely wonder if it's true. No offense, but my writing is who I am."

"No, it's not. You're a lot of things…"

"No, listen. Let's say I was a model. If you called me 'ugly,' that pretty much tears down the center of whom and what I am. A model's job is to look a certain way. You can say I'm not to your taste — maybe you like full-figured women, or super tall ladies, which I'm not, obviously. But there's a big difference between that and 'ugly.' Ugly, in this case, means I suck at what I do and you can't believe I get paid for it — I don't *deserve* to be paid for it. It may even be an attack on what it is I do, period.

"I'm not saying there weren't other things Mark reported she said about me. She didn't like that I was this way or that. But at the center of it all was my writing. And I repeat — it wasn't just a matter of taste. The way it was expressed to me was it was so bad that it was an affront to her sensibilities. When someone breaks it down like that, what they're saying is they completely disrespect you. From that point forward, there's nowhere positive to go. Everything else follows suit. It's like if I was a street corner, STD-carrying hooker. Did your MIL ever look at you like that?"

"Well…" and I look for a good zinger but my sense of humor is muted by Julia's sincere tone of pain and vulnerability.

"Look, I'm getting kind of uncomfortable being the center of attention here. That's not who I am. Do you know what writers enjoy most? Being alone. That's how we're wired. That's why we don't become actresses or stand-up comedians. We don't want the spotlight. Hell, we don't even want to be in a normal workplace. Put a whole bunch of other people around me and I can't write; I can't do my job. Have you ever seen those putzes who bring their laptops to Starbucks to write? What's with those people? They're poseurs. They're not really writing. No one can write anything of quality in a busy coffee shop. They just do it so people can look at them and whisper, 'Ooo, look. It's a writer. Maybe he's writing about us. Maybe we'll be in his next bestseller.' Meanwhile, the guy is probably adding up columns of numbers or watching YouTube videos of guys being punched in the family jewels."

She finally chuckles and so do I. It's the first I've seen her break character from Pensive Girl in days. "So enough about me. What's new with you?" she asks.

"Well…" a 'well' that hangs in the air for a seeming eternity. "I'm thinking of not returning my gift."

"What?"

"My new and improved Momma Lana. Lana 2.0. I think I'll keep her. She comes over for dinner every single night now and she eats everything I cook — everything — without complaint. I've even learned to stifle the urge to spit in her food. She helps bus the tables when she's done. She's even shown up for breakfast a few times. I finally taught her to keep that habit for the weekends because Kyle and I are too frantic at that hour during the week and sometimes only have time for a granola bar while driving on the freeway. And that's sort of the breakthrough, believe it or not. She's now open to suggestion. When she gets too stalker-ish, I give her a good, practical reason why it's a bad time to drool down the back of my neck and she accepts it without throwing a pity party for herself."

"So you don't have a problem with the fact that it's all fake?"

"That's the point. It's not fake. I had that paranoia at first, but living through it these past few days, I've come to understand it all much better. The part of her that couldn't get past the jealousy of me has been buried. That was real, too. But the part of her that thought highly of me…"

"Worshipped the ground you trod upon."

"Yeah, that part; was always there. Like Stella said, if she didn't feel that way at all — if she thought of me the way vegans think of roast beef — she couldn't bring herself to be this nice to me — even under hypnosis."

Julia is no longer holding her arms around herself as if she were trying to prevent an alien worm from bursting out of her chest. Still, she dawdles her hands around any little trinket on her furniture — looking bored, tentative, depressed, and undecided. "So you're accepting the obsessive 'I love you so much I wish I could jump inside your skin and be you' part?"

"From what you've told me, that's an extreme version of what you've had all along with *your* MIL. You just never believed it to be true."

"But it's not. Mark says it isn't. He's always said it isn't," Julia replies. "Except now. Now she tells me when I'm being distrustful and ungrateful. Is that a step up?"

I'm beginning to discover the answer, but she's so pissed at the world right now, and strung so tightly about her movie opening, that I'm afraid to say it. I saw what she nearly did to that glass door on Rodeo the other day. She may be small, but she can pack a punch. "Here's what I think. Stella suggested you and your MIL come visit her for a therapy session — pure therapy. The way I see it, your opening on Friday should be the best day of your life, or at least one of them. Why have this cloud hanging over your head? Even if you don't like the answers you discover, I have a theory about that. The truth is always better than what terrible things we imagine it to be. It doesn't mean everything will always be great, but it means that we tend to imagine utter catastrophe when we should only be dealing with minor irritation."

"You're saying my MIL may have more in common with painful rectal itch rather than inoperable cancer?"

"Perfectly put. That's why you're the author and I'm just a lowly chiphead."

"Thanks, Kat. You're a real friend. You're one of the only people I've met since I left home who likes me for me, and not because I'm 'Julia Rader, famous author.'"

She goes in for one of those twig-armed hugs I've learned to enjoy so much. Julia and I could have been friends anytime or anywhere—rich, poor, Colorado, Carolina,

Chicago or California. There's nothing I wouldn't do for her and I feel she'd always be there for me. DILS really is a sisterhood, for those who wants sisters, and a sister is what we both need right now.

Chapter Twenty-Two

L ike the old song says, "The waiting is the hardest part." Julia Rader tucked her tail between her legs and begged her MIL to accompany her back to Stella Diomare's office. "I'm having trouble sleeping and I believe part of it has to do with the tiff you and I had the other day — for which I take full responsibility. As I see it, perhaps the best way for me to move past it is to bring you along so we can reconcile whatever exactly it was that went down between us that day." It worked. Darla Klein was never one to hold a grudge, and had never had a cross moment with her DIL prior to that moment, so burying the hatchet was no biggy to her. Now, though, as they sat waiting their turn, the quiet between them was deafening. Darla wanted to talk about Julia's pending movie opening, while Julia looked like she was wound so tightly a mild breeze would make her vibrate like a bowed cello.

Finally, Stella invited them into her inner sanctum. Once seated, both looking rather uncomfortable despite the plush furniture, she began. "Usually, my job is to sit here and say as little as possible — just get you two to communicate with one another. I do that for a few months, send you bills, buy more artwork, and smile a lot. In this case, I'm going to admit that I have a personal relationship with one of you — Julia — and since that alone puts me on shaky ethical ground, it also means I know she has some issues she wants to resolve sooner rather than later. Is this okay with you so far, Darla?"

Darla Klein pursed her lips but seemed relieved by the honesty. "Fine. I've haven't been sleeping well lately, either. Sort of ironic since that's why I first came here. But sure, yes, if you want to do things a little differently — more expediently — then by all means, do your thing."

"Fine. Here goes. Darla, your daughter-in-law values your opinion greatly. What appears to concern her most is your honesty and frankness. She's willing to accept your opinions even if they are negative, so long as they are sincere. Are you with me so far?"

"Yes, of course. I feel I've always been sincere with you, Julia."

"Good. So, how long have you known your son, Mark, has been jealous of Julia's success?"

Darla Klein glanced down at her lap a moment, while Julia Rader's mouth opened wide enough to let flies in. "What?!"

"Darla?" asked Stella again.

"Well… Mark has had some issues in that area for quite a while. And I don't just mean with Julia; I mean ever since he was a little boy. He's very talented, very smart. Always has been. He just doesn't deal well with disappointment. It's not uncommon with a talented person. They work hard and they expect results."

"That's understandable. Can you relate to that, Julia?"

"Uh, sure. People expect results. Got it," she said, still looking quite stunned at the line of discussion.

"Julia, Mark is a writer, too; am I correct?"

"Yes he is," answered Julia.

"And, in your opinion, how good a writer is he? And please, don't let your mother-in-law being here color your opinion. The reason we're all here is about honesty, and if we all make a pact to be honest in our opinions, we can all move forward," said Stella.

"He's very good. Better than me. He's been better schooled. His vocabulary alone is almost twice what mine is."

"And how do you think it makes him feel, then; you with all of your success and him with… well, with what exactly?"

Julia did not expect to be in the hot seat, but here she was, her tiny buttocks getting warmer by the instant. "He… he… always seemed very supportive of me. I tried to help his career. He asked me to do things and I did them. I gave his work to my agent. When she said it wasn't the sort of thing she represented, I asked her if she knew anyone else and I sent it along to that person. I told Mark I would do whatever I could to help his career."

"But still, nothing came of it, right?"

"Is there something more I should be doing?" Julia asked.

"No, not for the moment. Now Darla …"

"Yes?"

"Darla, does your son confide in you as to how this all makes him feel?"

"Why yes. He's been very bitter about the whole thing. I told him not to be, but that's been a part of his personality ever since I can remember. I love him; he's my son, but he doesn't take disappointment well. His father was much the same way. He could get very vengeful, very unfocused. They both have a tendency to place blame on others and get very, very bitter at times. It's Mark's worst trait. I had hoped when he got together with Julia things would start to go his way. I told him, 'Maybe you should befriend more writers. Join a writer's group. Get out there and network. Perhaps someone will agree to mentor you.' He didn't like me mentioning the mentoring part, though. He really is quite good, you know. But the kind of writing he does doesn't always pay very well. I think he should teach writing; that's what I think."

"The business about networking with other writers — did that have anything to do with his meeting Julia?" asked Stella.

"Sure. I mean, I didn't tell him to mix networking and dating, but lo and behold, one day he walks in the door with Julia. The next thing you know, they're engaged. Me, I couldn't be happier. I mean, not because of his career or anything. I just immediately thought the world of Julia. I could care less what she did for a living. She's such a genuine person. Sweet and kind. That's why I was so upset when we had that spat the other day. They were the first cross words to ever come between us."

Julia edged to the end of her seat and looked at Darla. "Do you mean to tell me that Mark married me because I'm a successful writer?"

"Well, I don't know about all that. I do know that right from the start he talked about you helping him with his career. He was walking on air from the time he met you until — oh, I don't know; about year ago or so."

Julia sat stunned for a moment, clueless that Mark was in any way unhappy with her or their relationship. "What does he think of my writing?"

Now it was Darla's turn to look down into her lap in silence.

"Does he think I'm talented? Does he like my books?" Julia stared intensely at her mother-in-law.

Finally, Darla huffed and said, "Honey, I like your books. I'm not as smart as Mark. I'm just your average, run-of-the-mill reader. Give me Ashley Cornwell, Nicholas Sparks, Danielle Steele, James Patterson. I like your books because I enjoyed those Harry Potter books so much. I thought at first they were just for kids, but I like them, too."

"So *you* like my books."

"Yes, I sincerely do. And that thing the other day — about the one hundred twenty friends coming to your opening night — that was as sincere as I've ever been in my life. I've recommended you to all my friends and all my friends read you. They're fans."

"But what about Mark? Has he ever discussed what he thinks of my writing? Darla, tell me; I have to know. Did you know that ever since the wedding all he's told me is how much you hate my writing? That you think I'm a talentless hack?"

"Me?! Me?! That's him!" There was a stunned silence as Darla clenched her hand over her own mouth. "Oh God, I'm sorry. I never meant to say that. Please forgive me. I told Mark I'd never say that. He made me promise."

"Too late now," said Stella in a monotone.

"Listen, I couldn't make my way through the sort of books Mark likes for all the money in the world. He gives me these books and I'm lucky if I can get through the first ten pages — and that's with a dictionary in my lap. How can someone enjoy themselves if they have to look up the meaning of every other word? And that's just the half of it. The references, the… the I-don't know. The things he likes are like homework assignments. The same goes for his own writing. As my son, I respect it; I respect him. But I'm not his audience and I'd like to think I'm not a complete dummy. I graduated from college, but that kind of stuff… forget about it. I enjoy your books, Julia. I really do."

Tears welled up in Julia's eyes and Stella handed her a tissue she had readily available. "Darla," asked Stella, "were you aware that Mark has been telling Julia for quite a while now it was you—not him, but you — who disliked her writing? And not just her writing, but just about everything about her *and* her writing?"

"All he's done is criticize me, everything about me. But he says it's not his opinion; it's yours. That he's just the messenger and these are the things you feel about me — that I can't write, I can't cook, I'm not smart, all my friends and advisors manipulate me and give me bad advice because I don't know the difference…" By this time it became hard to hear her as her weeping garbled her speech, but the sentiment came through.

Darla sat stunned. "He blamed this all on me?!"

"He says he talks to you on the phone almost every day and that's what you have to say about me," Julia continued to shudder.

Darla reached over and gave her daughter-in-law a loving rub on the shoulder, "Honey, Mark hardly ever calls me. I call him maybe once every two weeks, and that's just to nag him that he hasn't called *me*. I'd like to think we're close, but not as close as I'd like. I wish we did talk every day or so. And now that I hear what he's been telling you, I have a heck of a lot I'd like to say to him." Darla shook her head in frustration. "Just like his father," she hissed. "I hate saying things like that; I really do. I believe we all have our unique path in life and we make choices. He saw how arrogant and jealous his father was and I always tried to tell him not to ever be that way. It was hard, though. You don't want your child to grow up thinking one of their parents is bad. I always told him, 'It's not the person who's bad; it's the act.' I don't know. I wish I knew where I went wrong. I always gave him praise. He was such a bright and talented boy."

Julia continued to cry, as Stella rubbed one bony shoulder and Darla the other. "Darla, could I ask you to step out for a moment? I want to go over a few things with Julia alone. Is that all right with you?"

"Of course," and then to Julia, "I'm sorry, dear. You're such a sweet girl and I never meant to be a party to your feeling hurt in any way." She gave her a semi-side hug and exited to the waiting room, leaving Julia alone with Stella. Stella waited until Julia was finally ready to speak.

"Is she telling the truth, or is this part of the trance?" she asked.

"There never was a trance," replied Stella.

"What?"

"It didn't take me long to figure this whole thing out when I got her in here alone. I have a pretty good sense of when a person is being honest with me. It's part of the job. There was no trance because there was no need for one. Your MIL loves you and respects you and your work. A trance would have accomplished nothing."

"But…"

"But what you never did was ever hear a single negative thing from the horse's mouth. You believed Mark. You believed every single thing he ever told you about her — about her, about himself, and about how he felt about you. Did you ever question anything he said; anything about him at all?"

This only brought on a new geyser of salty tears, which again Stella waited to subside. "Putting my Jason issue aside, Mark was my prince. All my life, he's exactly what I dreamed of. Those days I spent sitting in the woods—writing, drawing, dreaming. He was in all of those thoughts. When he finally appeared in my life, it was as if all my dreams had come true," she said, her voice still trembling.

"Even more so than all your fame and fortune?" asked Stella.

"Yes," she cried.

Stella allowed Julia's head to lean in upon her shoulder. "I know. I know," she said as she patted her head. "And that may be the difference between you and Mark. You were waiting for your knight in shining armor, while he was the one who dreamed of bestsellers and movie openings. You got each other's dream. Life is like that sometimes."

"So now what?" Julia whimpered.

"I think you have to have a very long talk with your husband. Listen, DILS isn't really set up for couples counseling, but I am, although, truth be told, I would strongly suggest you go to a more neutral mediator." On another note," Stella continues, since meeting you, I've read your books, Julia, and from the little you've said about your past relationships, including friendships, I can't help but think that your friend/co-worker Jason was your true Prince, the man of your dreams. Mark is the one you settled for when you felt dismissed by the true love of your life. It's not my professional opinion, just an observation from a friend."

Julia huffed and puffed a few times, trying to collect herself. "This was supposed to be the best week of my life. Red carpets, flashing cameras, interviews, beautiful gowns, fans calling my name. And now… now I don't know if I even have a husband," she said as the tears flowed anew.

Stella sat with her stoically. "Julia, sometimes truth is relieving in and of itself. I know right now you're probably thinking you'd rather still be under the illusion that your husband loved and respected you and your accomplishments, and maybe, perhaps, if someone in your world had to think ill of you it would be your MIL instead of him. But that doesn't appear to be the reality of the situation. Your MIL has nothing to gain by telling you she loves you, but your husband might."

"Why didn't you tell me you didn't hypnotize her?"

"I needed to let you have this all unravel itself in its own time. I knew you'd eventually confront her — or him — and at some point the truth would come tumbling out. If I just sat here and told you what I thought, you'd never believe me. You'd say I didn't know either of them well enough to know what I was talking about.

"Jules, even if you lose your husband over this — ask yourself what exactly you've lost. At his worst, he may be an opportunist who deceived you to help his own career and then became embittered when his plan went awry. But at best, you now know what's it's like to have a MIL — a mother — who loves you and respects you. I'm pretty good at reading people — it's what I do — and I honestly believe Darla is sincere. I think she really does love you and your work. Try giving her back that love and see if I'm right. The next few days are going to be very stressful and precarious. I'll be here for you; so are your other Sisters. If you don't reach out for us, we'll be checking in on you. And we're still going to be with you for your premier."

"Ugh! The premier. I wish I could just skip town and never come back."

Stella patted Julia's hand. "I know part of you feels that way. Some of that is the writer in you, which loves to be alone. The other part is even more obvious — you have to figure out where you're going next with your relationship with your husband. You know, though — and I can say this from having done some couples counseling — your MIL will always side first with her son, but it's not inconceivable she may still be open to having a continuing relationship with you. When we find good people as we pass through life, it's important to hold onto them. Speaking of which, when is the last time you spoke to that friend of yours?"

The first resemblance of a smile crosses Julia's face. "We have kept in touch throughout the years, usually a joke here on email or text. I make him laugh, he makes me laugh, and then I remember we are both married." Julia's face is becoming more flushed by the second and she blurts out, "I invited Jason and his wife to my premier. I need to see him even if I have to see her." Before any of us can respond, Julia is out the door.

More than anyone, Stella understood how it felt to love a man far more beautiful than she. The differences between her and Julia were that the man that should have been unattainable to Stella fell madly in love with her, and secondly, unlike the average looking Stella, Julia was pretty and there should have been no reason for Jason not to snatch her up. Stella's thoughts begin to head in a moral no-go zone. Stop thinking what you're thinking, girl. It's a line you can't cross.

Chapter Twenty-Three

Hair up or down? That is the question. I have never been to a Hollywood premier before, thus I have no idea what would be most chic. Down. I'm going to emphasize my youth and wear it down.

"Honey, the limo is here," Kyle shouts to me from a floor away, his voice echoing off the walls. "Hurry."

Tonight I want to look perfect. Not only am I going to a premier; I'm strolling the red carpet. Wowza! Who would have thought the DILS was going to be like this?

For the life of me, I cannot make up my mind what to wear around my neck. The problem with this whole thing is I dress up all the time for fancy, work-related functions. I go to weddings and bar mitzvahs. But do all the same fashion rules apply for movie premiers? Shouldn't I be… flashier? I mean, I bought a new dress for the occasion — I had to. To wear something I already owned, even if no one I knew was going to see it — would be the faux pas to end all faux pases. And so I sprung for this Joel Wayne original, a blue gown with one bare shoulder and one lacey arm with a floor-sweeping fishtail, spending about quadruple what my freaking wedding dress cost. But it's for a good cause — friendship.

I decide to do what women have been doing for ages — ask the opinion of their man, which is a study in futility unless one happens to have absentmindedly married a gay dude. Such is not the case in my house. If I ask Kyle to suggest accessories, he would give me a new set of speakers.

"What do you think — the gold or the silver necklace?" Kyle smiles a nervous smile, which is nothing more than a cover-up masking his complete inability to give a shit. Not that I'd put much stock in what he'd prefer anyway, which further makes me wonder why I'm asking him.

"They're both nice," he says. Well, duh! They both also cost about as much as his last car. I smirk while I hold each necklace against my cleavage. Why is it I know he's no longer looking at the necklaces and instead looking at my breasts? Straight men — gotta love 'em.

"Gold. But what do I know? Ask my mother."

I stroll down the rest of the stairs and there she is. I smile. There stands Momma Lana Ding Dong, all decked out as a shorter, older, version of me. She insisted on coming with me to Joel Wayne's to pick out my dress, then put on puppy dog eyes as she wistfully mused about how swell it must be to be invited to a major Hollywood premier. "The closest thing to it was when I went to a taping of *American Bandstand* when I was just a teenager, but I didn't get to dance. Frank Rizzo was chief of police in Philadelphia and later became mayor. He always came to my Uncle Lewis's store for his suits. Always brought a coupon! So Chief Rizzo arranged for tickets from Dick Clark. Dick Clark! He was so handsome! Ah, when Bandstand left Philadelphia, it was as if youth itself had died."

It was about then I thought about how much Kyle had been whining about having to escort me. Like most men, he dislikes tuxedos, which has always struck me as odd since they all look so good in them. "Can't you go without me?"

"What kind of loser do you want me to look like? I am not going alone. I'm even renting a limo. We're doing this in style. When's the next time I'll get a chance to do something like this?"

"Whenever I see people on the red carpet, if it's a couple and only one of them is famous, you only see the famous one. Famous people must go to premiers alone. Without me as your date, people will assume you're a somebody," he replied.

"No, no one goes alone. If one person is famous and their escort isn't, the unfamous one is pushed to the side while they shoot pictures, then the couple regroups once they're inside the lobby. It's ok that you don't know anything about red carpet protocol. You can't be perfect."

"It's kind of like when guys have to carry a woman's purse in the mall. That sucks, too. Who started that trend? Have you ever tried to look straight and macho while having a little purse slung over your shoulder? And besides, isn't your friend's book part of a series? There'll be two or three more events like this one. Couldn't I skip this one and catch the next? I promise, with more time, I'll be able to psyche myself up more for the boredom. And drink more heavily in advance."

It was about then I stepped back and looked at my situation: One Embers standing in a pool of imaginary tears, wishing she could go with me, and another wading in a pool of depression, wishing he could have a "get out of jail free" card. "Momma Lana, would you like to be my date?"

"And go with you to the premier?" Her look of excitement was so genuine you'd have thought I asked her to move in with us.

"Yes. Would you like that?"

"Oh… oh, oh, oh, oh, oh…"

"I'll take that as a 'yes'"

"But what'll I wear?" Which is how we ended up here. Once the sales clerk overheard a mother and daughter-in-law discussing attending a premier together, she couldn't jump in quickly enough to suggest matching outfits. Me, I thought the whole idea was beyond gauche, but Lana nearly peed on the rug so here we are — me looking as beautiful and elegant as I've ever looked in my life, standing beside what I will probably look like when I'm about to retire — a living, breathing "before" and "after" shot. How poignant.

"You two look marvelous," says Kyle. "Mom, I'm so glad you're pinch hitting for me. You'll get a lot more enjoyment out of this than me."

Lana beams, while I reply, "Let me guess. Your plans for the evening are football, beer, blue jeans, and pizza, followed by some strippers."

"The strippers are coming early, before the football and pizza. That way there won't be any uncomfortable overlaps if you come home early."

"Ha! When I look this good, no stripper can compete."

"Kyle, you don't look at other women, do you?" says my new biggest fan and protector, Lana.

"No, Mom. I know how good I've got it. No messing around."

"All right. Our chariot awaits," I say as we trundle into

the limo — Lana first, and then me.

A little while later, we pull up to Julia's McMansion—a home that puts mine to shame. Lana's mouth is open so widely she's drooling. I take a moment to think about how pleasant this trip has been. Even a short car ride with the Old Lana would have necessitated my breaking into the wet bar and downing all the single malt scotch they carried. But no, this was pleasant, and Lana's fawning over me seems to have hit its stride — water finding its own level, so to speak. She still repeats herself — what older person doesn't? — and much of that repetition is her endless compliments of me — I look so good, I'm so smart, what an exciting job I have, what an exciting life I lead, what marvelous taste I've developed. But after a while, what the hell? It's all good; it's good stuff. It's nice to hear, even if it's lost its originality. Maybe that's why the rich and famous have posses full of fawners. Now that the shock of it has begun to wear off, I think I could grow to like this, in its own weird way. And Kyle? Things between us have never been better. His mother was the skeleton in his closet; the thing about him I most had to accept with reluctance. No matter what the purists may say, when you marry someone, you really do marry their entire family. His brothers and their wives I can tolerate, and his aunts, uncles, and cousins are so geographically distant I haven't seen most of them since our wedding. But Momma Lana Ding Dong came along with Kyle as a package deal and up until Stella's trance, she was excess baggage with a bad attitude. Now she's becoming "my California mom;" a stand-in for all those months that go by when I don't have my real Carolina mom around, which is most of the time. It's good. It actually feels quite nice. And so with this new bliss, how could I not love Kyle all the more? Heck, I'm so pleased with him, I may just call up and send him over beer and pizza myself, my treat for his evening in. But no strippers. I'm not that open-minded yet.

"God, have you ever seen a place this big?"

Well, actually, Claudia's manse matches it quite nicely, but why be argumentative? If you're standing next to someone who's looking at the Grand Canyon for the first time, you don't break their awe by saying, "Oh, you think this is great; you should see…" Why play "can you top this?"

We walk up to the front door and it's open; no one coming to answer it to let us in, so we stroll in independently, the chauffer having used the call box at the front gate. "Jules? It's Kat. We're here." Both Claudia and I volunteered to go with Julia to the premier for the purpose of moral support, but Julia felt Claudia would already have her hands full, being the wife of the producer and all. Me, I'm just a techie. The only thing I'm in charge of this evening is having a good time and helping Julia hold it together.

Like in a princess movie, Julia Rader appears at the top of her long, wide, winding staircase, a vision of loveliness in a strapless ivory column dress featuring a folded-over panel at the bust that extends down the front of the skirt.

"Oh my," I hear Lana say, "She's radiant." I'm thinking the same thing, but a trained eye can see she's a very sad wealthy girl, with issues and blues only a few of us know about.

"How do I look?" she asks.

"You're kidding, right? You were born to wear that dress. You look lovely." As she descends the staircase and reaches the polished marble floor, we embrace. "How are you?" I whisper in her ear. "Really."

"Fine, I guess," she whispers back. "I'll be fine." She sniffs a little, as if she's been sniffling back tears for a while now. "Oh, and when I heard who you were bringing for a date, I decided to follow suit. Meet Ms. Darla Klein." As if on cue, a taller, older, yet equally stunning woman appears at the top of the stairs — wearing a similar dress, just like me and Lana.

"Oh my, are you Julia's mother?" says Lana.

"Mother-in-law," answers Darla as she strides towards us, offering a manicured hand.

"I'll have someone to talk to then. This is my daughter-in-law, Katherine."

We exchange the requisite small talk and introductions. Somehow I manage to pull Julia into the next room on the premise of allowing Darla to give Lana a mini tour of the house. "So, what's going on? The husband is nowhere in sight, but the MIL is still on the scene?"

"Mark is… on vacation. My treat. Anywhere he wants for as long as he likes."

"He's not coming back?"

"It's not up to him. It was my decision. It's my house. Well, that's not completely true, either. California is a joint property state and we never had a pre-nup."

"You should have met Gabriella earlier," I opine.

Julia grimaces a small smile. "Yeah. But it doesn't matter to me. The money… oh hell, half of all this is still more than I could spend in a lifetime. I'm not about the money; I never was. Maybe Mark is; I don't know. He can have half of it; I don't care. Maybe it'll bring him some sort of happiness."

"You're very generous. Gabriella could still probably bust him up in court for fraud and deception."

"Aah," Julia says with a wave of her hand. "Like I said, who cares? I can still write, and what I write still sells. I'm not even thirty-years old. There's a lot of life ahead for me."

"You sound pretty well-adjusted for a girl who just broke up with her man."

"No, I'm just a good bullshitter," she says and we laugh weakly. "If you don't laugh, you cry, so I'm choosing not to cause a scene by crying tonight — at least not while any strangers are looking OR in front of Jason and his wife."

"Wow. Jason is coming?" I ask. "Do you think that's a good idea? I mean, having him with his wife there and all. I've never been a fan of opening old wounds. I wouldn't want you to start feeling bad about yourself, because you have to know that you are an amazing, beautiful, funny, smart woman and he missed out, Jules! And more importantly, I don't feel like getting into a fist fight should I catch her giving you a dirty look. Don't think I won't drop the bitch with a left and then a right for my sister!"

"Kat, I need to see Jason. I don't care if he is with his wife. I respect that. The fact remains that I loved him as my friend and still do. Plus, I can't lie and not say that I will get some satisfaction having both of them see me in all my glory. Neither of them made me feel like a seven. I branded myself with that number. The only thing she really had over me was about six inches in height," Julia says as she walks around on her tip-toes. Seeing Julia get her glow back over the idea of seeing Jason is giving me the nervous jitters.

"So, the MIL — what's that all about?" I ask.

"She's genuine. I mean, it's not like she's really choosing

sides. She still loves Mark; he's her son. But for now he's in… Tahiti, Bimini, Hawaii… I have no fucking idea, nor do I care. It wasn't like he was going to bring his mommy along. He needs to soothe his fractured artistic soul and look for a new muse. Or a new excuse."

"Fucking phony," I say.

"Hey, I gave him everything he wanted from me — contacts, meetings with agents, what-have you. And still, it went nowhere for him. I said it before: It's not like he has no talent. He just has no audience. Maybe if he sticks to it and keeps writing for the pure joy of it, once he's dead someone will discover his stuff and he'll be known as the Shakespeare of our time. Or not," she giggles. "He's actually more talented than me. I told him that all the time and I'd still say it to anyone who asked today. But that doesn't make up for the deception and the lying. And Darla! To implicate *her* in all this? She's furious! I think that's part of why we're hanging out together. We're the only people in the world who really understand how the other feels — present company excluded."

I can't help but wrap my arm around her. "You'll come out of this all right; I can tell."

"Who would have guessed — our MILs, strolling around my house together? Dressed the same as we are."

"And they're our dates for your premier. Who would have predicted *that* when we first met?"

"Yeah," says Julia, "Who would have dreamed you and I would be so damn pathetic?" We both laugh. "I gotta find me a MAN!" We howl.

Chapter Twenty-Four

As we're whisked away to the theater, Claudia, who is lucky enough to have a man as her date this evening, is on the phone to Julia, giving her all the tips and protocols for being one of the red carpet stars of a Hollywood premier. Me and Lana, we're just part of the great unwashed, much like the nameless, faceless, mid-level executives who will also be there, the ones who make the movie industry function yet only see their names in flyspeck print as the closing credits roll by.

I still find myself worrying about Julia and so I do, in fact, open up the wet bar and start poking around. Out of the corner of my eye I see Lana about to say something, something negative, but then she suppresses it. Therein lies the change, the difference between Old Lana and the New. New Lana thinks before she speaks. Since she no longer has an agenda to put me down in order to not feel so personally threatened, she can stifle herself and accept that, like most people, I like to knock back a drink or two once in a while.

"Here, you can thank me later," I say as I hand a glass

to Julia.

"I may need one as well," says Darla, and I smile and pour some more. Julia finishes on the phone, taps it shut, and sits back with a resigned look on her face. It could be worse. I'm sure part of her wants to jump out of the limo — while it's still moving — and begin walking back to the woods of Colorado on foot, never again to face all this tumult, never again to let a man ruin her life. But she's erudite enough to see what she's got and realize most of the civilized world would give their left breast to be sitting in her **Louis Vuittons. Still, I have no trouble imagining this i**s all bitter sweet.

As we round the corner, I see the crowd and the adrenaline starts to flow. "Oh my God," says Darla. "Will you look at that!"

Suddenly I start to imagine how The New Kids on the Block must have felt in their prime. I almost expect mobs to begin climbing on the hood of the car trying to beat through the glass. Julia's fans are — well, fans, as in fanatics. I have never seen so many teenage girls in my life, some reluctantly toting along their mothers, others grouped together like the entire scene is a gigantic rave.

Security, outfitted like Secret Service agents, all in black suits with earphones and cuff mics, hastens us out of the limo. There, I catch my first glimpse of the red carpet. At the end of the day all it is is… a red freakin' carpet. It's not even nice carpet. Purely utilitarian stuff you could pick up at the local Home Depot. But in this context, it's the yellow brick road and everyone who is allowed to walk on it is Dorothy going to see the wizard.

"We're not actually walking on that thing, are we?" asks Momma Lana.

I think I know the answer, but then again, I'm not totally sure myself. I figure the men in black will push and pull me wherever they want, and judging by their size and demeanor, I shall do whatever they request. Silent men dressed like that always bring out the docile sheep in me.

"Julia, darling; there you are!" The voice is unmistakably Claudia's. She's knocking my eyes out in a yellow Carolina Herrera gown with a massive statement necklace. She looks damn near perfect. Next to her is what I can only assume is her husband, a silver fox with a week spent in Lake Como type of tan and teeth whiter than Antarctica, the kind of sexy grandpa even a girl my age would consider allowing into bed. Next to them is Gabriella Eastbrooks, aka "The Body," in a black, strapless, basic-but-beautiful Elie Saab that accentuates her every bountiful curve, held in place by her gravity-defying bourgeoning bust. I also get to see what her race driver hubby looks like and I am not disappointed — a small, wiry man, which is usually not my type but I suppose that in order to slide into those Formula One cars one must be the male equivalent of compact, not-an-ounce-of-fat-on-her Julia, although for him I could make an exception. Handsome, très handsome. I shouldn't be doing this; staring at all these married men and drooling, while my comfy Kyle sits at home with his pizza and beer, wishing for strippers who shall never come. But hey, this is what he gets for refusing to join me. If he'd have come I'd have made him look his level best so my girlfriends could drool a little drool over him, too.

I am determined not to ask anyone for instructions, feeling that by doing so it might appear as if I were angling for attention I have no right to receive. I am sooo not Hollywood. At some DILS meetings, I am often one of the only women there who has absolutely no connection to the entertainment business. When they ask me what my occupation is in "the industry," I say "audience." Me, I think it's funny. They just retort by saying, "Then who are you married to?" Right. I'm married to Kyle Embers, CFO of a major insurance company. REAL Hollywood job there, too. We're like rare fruit perpetually out of season here in LA; popcorn buyers in a land of popcorn makers.

My strategy works, as Claudia, with the help of the men in black, informs me — for the men in black do not speak, they only act — that Momma Lana and I actually do get to stroll the carpet, albeit in between the guests of honor. I suppose this is to build excitement for the crowd, as they couldn't possibly survive the excitement of star after star after star. This makes me a walking, talking commercial break — the opportunity for folks to get up from their seats and take a pee. And here I thought I had no purpose in this town. Nonetheless, everyone still stares and snaps pictures of us, all of us no names, Gabriella included, who's here because she did legal work on the film. With her, the attention still comes naturally, being an ex-model and all. But for me, it's hilarious and exhilarating hearing voices in the crowd saying, "Who's she? Is she famous? Is she somebody?" I can't wait to get home to tell my folks all about it. They'll either die laughing or just plain die.

Julia and Darla go right ahead of us and when Julia reaches the main press area, her name is announced and her reception is akin to that given the stars of the film. She smiles demurely and her fans demand from her a wave, which she manages to get up the courage to give. Then I notice Julia nervously looking into the crowd, actually more like through the crowd, and setting her eyes on what could be the hottest guy alive. I can only assume that this living god must be Jason. Holy cow!

I watch her and feel all the pangs of emotion we've gone through together. All these months stewing over our MILs, only for her to discover that her real problem was her manipulative, opportunistic husband. And to discover it only a few days ago, right before this. The irony. How he longed to get the kind of love Julia is getting right now. There must be a few thousand teenage girls here, most of which will never get in to see the movie this evening, but still they are here, just to catch a glimpse of their literary heroine, to wave their copies of her books at her, begging her for an autograph.

Her MIL, Darla, discreetly steps away from her in order for Jules to have her moment. And what a moment it is. I, too, stay in place a few yards behind her, unable to take my eyes off of her. Did I make the right decision? I glance over at Momma Lana, who is also enthralled by this entire spectacle. If she had continued her standoffish behavior towards me, we wouldn't be together here this night. In her eyes I can see honest, sincere awe and happiness. This really *is* cool. Being on stable positive ground with my MIL brings lots of good benefits, this being only one of many, and a rather superficial one at that. For as much as her behavior was hurting me, she was hurting herself as well. Ironic, as this woman went through so much being married to an alcoholic who died far too young. Self-destructive behavior; it comes in many forms. Some addicts get hypnotherapy, too. Maybe there is some sort of moral imperative at work here after all.

When Julia is finished her interviews and poses, she moves along and we do as well. Lana sidles up to me and whispers in my ear, "Do I step away from you when we reach that area up ahead?"

I look at her funny and then get the reference. Me, I would have said it as a joke, but Lana, she's not joking. "No, Mom; that's only for the celebrities. I'm exactly like you. We're both guests — good ol' ticket holders. Members of the audience. We were simply lucky enough to get invitations to attend. Other than that, we're both just like all those people with the cameras and the autograph books."

She smiles blissfully and continues to walk with me. "Yes, but still, I've never felt more like a queen in my life."

"Me, too."

* * *

The movie itself was pretty good. It's not one of those movies you need to think about days after, but then again, I didn't expect it to be. Lots of special effects, lots of over-the-top romance, lots of swoons from the teen girls in the audience, some of which managed to cop a ticket because one of their parents was involved in the production or knew someone. The two leads will most definitely be gracing movie magazines for the next few months, being hyped as the "next big thing(s)." For them, it must be nice. For Julia, this certainly seals her personal fame and fortune, and I for one couldn't be happier for her. She's one of those people for whom you just want to see good things happen. Some critics will certainly turn up their noses at such commercial fare, but from the look of the movie and the look of the crowd outside the theater, this thing is going to make mucho buckos. I expect the sequel will begin filming sometime tomorrow.

One good thing for Julia is probably none of the multitude of interview shows she will be appearing on will ask about her love life. Bless Mark's little heart for being a nobody as opposed to a celebrity. As we rise from our seats once the theater lights come back on, I grab Julia and give her a big, soulful hug. "Listen," I whisper in her ear, "As hard as it may be, try to enjoy all this. These moments are fleeting and you don't want to look back on this twenty years from now and wish you had this night to live over again." I feel her tears dampening my exposed shoulder.

"I know. I know."

"Besides, what a great time in your life to be on the open market again. Time to go man shopping!" She laughs, but deep down I know that's not her philosophy at all. As it was, Mark hooked onto her when she was semi-famous and look how that turned out. I'm so glad I met Kyle when my company was just a geeky start-up with big dreams and empty pockets, with people like me taking home stock options instead of paychecks.

"Forget men and just take me vibrator shopping tomorrow," she says, then quickly slaps her hand over her mouth. "Oh my God; I hope Darla didn't hear that," she giggles.

"Hey, it would be an easier transition for her, getting used to you moving from Mark to a couple of "D" batteries instead of some new guy. I see the way she looks at you and I get the impression she hopes to remain on the scene for a while."

"Really?"

"Yes, really. I think she likes you. A lot. Kind of like Momma Lana with me, only without the need for a trance."

Julia turns her head to catch a glimpse of Darla, who is indeed looking at her with motherly pride. "Yeah, it's nice; she's been real nice. I think I can trust her. Trust is going to be a big issue for me for quite a while."

"Trust that you've got your Sisters to back you up in whatever you do."

"Thanks, Kat."

As we stride out of the theater, Darla suddenly shouts, "There they are!" and we all turn to look. Just as she promised, a crowd of at least a hundred or so middle-aged women are all clumped together, awaiting the next showing of the movie, holding up signs saying, "JULIA!" in big letters. "See, I told you. I know every one of them and every one of them has read your book; some of their own volition, some because I twisted their arms until they did. I must have purchased at least forty copies myself just to hand out to the ones who cried poverty."

Julia's head swivels towards Darla and her face wordlessly expresses poignancy and then joy—true, unmitigated joy for the first time this evening. Darla had told her the truth, had always been telling her the truth. Unlike the rest of us DILS, Julia Rader always had a loving, wonderful MIL. Good for her! I look to my left and see Mr. Hottie aka Jason walking toward Julia, and I have to correct myself. Julia was very happy when she found out Darla was being honest about her new fan club. However, true, pure joy barely describes the look on Julia's face when she and her lost love lock eyes for the second time this evening. You could damn near see the sparks fly.

Chapter Twenty-Five

"What are we getting all gussied up for again?"

"Claudia is calling it an 'after — after — after party,' Momma Lana."

"My! How many of these parties are there going to be? I've never seen anything like it. There was the party after the premier, then the 'after party' after the premier…"

"And now there's the after-after-after party. I believe this should be it. Until Julia's next film, which won't be for at least another year or so," I reply.

The excitement tonight has, in some ways, less to do with there being a party and as with the fact it's a DILS bash where we have been encouraged to bring our spouses and our MILs without letting them know what organization is sponsoring the shindig. "Why the hell would we want to do this, Claudia?" I asked when she secretively sprung it on us the night of the premier.

"It'll be fun. Tonight there are only a few of us here, but we're a nice, big group and everyone wanted in on helping to celebrate Julia's big success. Especially now since everyone wants to show her some support."

"But that doesn't explain spouses and MILs. We're playing with fire."

"But that's the exciting part. Fire is one of mankind's greatest inventions. Where would we be without it?" Sometimes Claudia is like Confucius in Versace. Or should I say, "confusing"? But from what I've learned over the past few months, there is usually a method to her madness.

"Just be sure not to spill the beans if your MIL — or even your spouse—asks how we all know each other. Just say it's via one degree of separation — the common denominator being Julia's film. It'll work because it's the truth. Most of the girls are either in the industry or married to it, and the rest of us know Julia through DILS, which is another way of saying we know her socially. Really, Kat, you must have more of a sense of adventure! Imagine the fun of being in a big room full of people you've heard so much about, yet never met. It'll be like a book coming to life."

The locale is an LA hotspot, the sort of place where Momma Lana would normally be completely out of her element, but Claudia has rented the entire place out for the evening so it's only us DILS and our guests. Dress is fancy, yet not as formal as the premier. For me, it was an excuse to quickly pick up a metallic Christian Cota mini, diamond accents, and embellished Giuseppe Zanotti booties, while for Momma Lana I grabbed a more sedate yet stunning white Dolce & Gabbana suit with a gray corset top. Kyle, I simply toss into a black suit sans tie, splooge some product into his hair, muss him up a little, and voila! My man looks hot enough to be our escort for the evening.

The men in black are out in full force again, but we're on the list so they let us in, while passersby skulk around, trying to figure out who and what the party is for and why they haven't been invited. Inside, the music is thumping, yet kept to a dull roar so we can chat without screaming.

I look around the club and here are all my Sisters, my support group during my times of trial and tribulation with Momma Lana. They've all heard my Momma Lana Ding Dong stories and suddenly that's what frightens the hell out of me. I can just imagine any one of them walking up to her and saying, "So this is the monster, huh?" But they don't. Perhaps it's the détente caused by all of us being in the same boat. The first rule of DILS is no one talks about DILS. The second rule of DILS is no one talks about DILS.

Kyle has Lana on one arm and me on the other and unlike past days, he no longer looks like the rope in a game of tug-of-war, stretched beyond recognition and obviously in pain. For a moment, I feel sorry for him. I look beyond my own past pain and instead imagine his. Of course I wanted him to choose me over her. I'm a woman dammit, and we're competitive creatures, even if we try to project that we're not. But here he is with both his favorite ladies on his arms and he looks so happy and so confident I want to jump his bones right in front of everyone. A person with inner peace is sexy.

As Claudia promised, it's a voyeuristic thrill seeing so many of the men and women I've only heard about in stories. There's Amber with her MIL, the one she had to use Gabriella's private dick on in order to discover she was sleeping with both her father-in-law as well as his brother. Confronted with that, she turned tail and stopped putting Amber down around her husband. Today, they're actually quite civil together. Funny what a little blackmail can do.

And there's Audrey, who tried just about everything to get along better with her MIL, only to discover the woman was nearly stone deaf. Whereas most people would say, "What?" or "Huh?" this lady tried to make sense of what little she heard and reacted to it. Unfortunately, she was instinctually paranoid and always assumed she was being insulted. Poor Audrey never knew why everything she said was taken the wrong way. It would be funny were it not so sad. Yes, there are a million stories in the red carpet city, and no two are quite alike.

On premier night I wore a long gown but tonight I opted for a mini, something I would have never dared wear when in the company of Old Lana. "Dress like that and people will think my son married a street walker." For years now I've had to lengthen my skirts just to avoid the dirty looks and nasty comments. Who would blame me for wanting to show a little skin tonight as a form of expressing my newfound freedom? And Lana? Not a peep from her.

I look around and most all the other girls have opted for shorter skirts as well. I see Julia and give her the biggest hug I can.

"How are you holding up?" I ask.

She nods with a closed mouth smile. "Better. A little better every day, every hour." She looks like she wants to say more but emotion and confusion block the path from her brain to her mouth.

"You're in a room full of people who love you."

Again she nods. "Yeah, I was thinking the same thing," she says as she scans the room. "Not many people are this lucky. I have a lot to be thankful for."

"Trying to convince me or convince yourself?"

"Me. Ever since I confronted Mark I feel like I'm naked and standing on the ledge outside a 30th story window and I can't get back inside. Shaky. Shaky and untethered. Exposed. Part of me wants to jump and hit the ground; end it all. The rest of me wants to somehow get back to safety."

"Maybe what you need is little distraction to take your mind off Mark. Perhaps in the form of a devastatingly good-looking guy named Jason," I say with a sly smile.

"I nearly melted into the floor when I saw him at my premiere. Just the mere sight of him gets me pre-orgasmic. And sadly, I've never even come close to seeing his "O" face." Julia's mouth is in the shape of an O as she pretends to have a mini-gasm. We both start laughing. "For real, Kat. We've never even reached first base if you don't count the time he accidently touched my breast when reaching across me. Pathetic!" Julia smirks. "Oh well, at least we are still friends. He should be showing up anytime now sans his wife. Apparently, she had some all-girls getaway that she just couldn't miss. How sad for me." Julia and I throw our hands up in the air to simulate a cheering crowd.

"Still palling around with Darla?"

"Yep. She's here somewhere. She's my date again. Oh, there she is," she says, pointing, "talking to your Lana again. Those two really hit it off."

"And to think a few weeks ago we would have assumed they were off plotting our demise."

Julia ponders while staring into her glass, swishing her champagne around. "That's still a sore point, unfortunately. When I look at Darla, part of me actually wishes it were true. I look back on how badly it made me feel and realize in many ways I felt better then than I do now. There's a finality to my situation now. But during the time I was unaware of it, I loved a lot of it. I loved being with him. I loved… him. And I thought he loved me. The delusion was the best part of it. Then I woke up to the hangover."

Stella Diomare suddenly appears to our right, "Girls, this is Aaron, my husband." *Wow*, I think. Rich and handsome, just as she said. This dude could easily be cast as the next James Bond. Now I know why Stella felt insecure about her looks around this guy. We *all* would. There is this crazy yin and yang to life itself. Even when we get what we want, it often makes us more miserable than when we were without it. If you're poor, you don't have to frenetically lock the doors to your house when you leave. The same goes with men and relationships. Marry a guy like Aaron Diomare and even if you look like you stepped off the cover of Cosmo, you'd still feel you had to lock that bad boy up or else.

Stella makes chit-chat with Julia, and I find myself gazing around the room. There's my Kyle, grabbing some hors d'oeuvres, trying not to look too ravenous. It's cute and so is he. He's hot and still makes my heart jump a beat when I see him across a room. I know him. It sounds so simple, but I know him and in knowing him I know all the unique things about him no one else in this room will ever know, and those are the things that fill my soul with love.

And a few feet from him is his mother, for whom he grabs an extra shrimp cocktail, dripping some sauce upon his sleeve which she sees and tries to help him dab clean, just as I would were I standing there. Therein may be the link between DILS and MILs. They raise little boys and we get them as men, but in some ways both parties still see the little boy inside and it becomes like two mothers fighting over custody of the same child. I love dabbing cocktail sauce off his sleeve and so does she. This should make us teammates, but instead, it once made us rivals.

Maybe this relationship I have now with Lana is the thing I'm paranoid of losing. It feels so good, even with its over-the-top flaws, but I've seen what life could be without it and I simply couldn't live that way again. And so I resign myself to being so happy I'm miserable, miserable it could all be taken away somehow, maybe even by me if I were to get too morally righteous and insist that Stella "reverse the curse."

Lost in my own thoughts and uncouthly ignoring Stella and Julia's discussion, I'm the first to notice another party waiting to be recognized. "Ashley!" I yelp. Standing before me is something out of a porno awards show in Vegas. Ashley is a circus of boobs and thighs with nothing more than a few strands of red string covering the nasty parts. Sheesh! Between that, the platinum blond hair and size XXXL lips, I think she'll be arrested by LA Vice the moment she leaves the premises.

"Hi, how're you doing?" she asks, teetering on her nine-foot high fuck-me pumps. Since last I saw her she must have exchanged her implants for some new inflatables. The sight of her brings all other conversation to a halt and even secure Stella must be staring down husband Aaron's trouser front to see if he's pitching a tent. But Ashley's no dummy. She knows the effect she's having and she's smiling about it, although with all the collagen in her lips it's hard to tell what that mouth of hers is doing.

"Wow," I say impulsively, until I realize I have to follow that up with something, anything, or else be construed as being very, very rude. "You look… hot."

"Thanks. I don't get out to clubs much anymore so this is a treat," Ashley says, as she molests the rim of her wine glass with her purple-tipped index finger. I'm sure there isn't a man here who doesn't agree with the "treat" part, and most would be more than willing to become her "trick."

"Stella, we have to talk," she says, and just then I notice something quite odd. Ashley has brought along a man, but he can't possibly be her husband. Ashley is in her twenties and looks like she stepped out of the inside of Hustler magazine. The guy next to her is... well, "homely" would be a kind. I think he's got hair plugs but the closer I look — which is a gastronomical challenge — the more apparent it becomes he's simply got hair coming out of all sorts of places with no uniformity whatsoever. A hunk here, a dollop there, a whole lot of skin in between and as I look at it, most of that naked scalp is flaking off onto the shoulders of his black jacket. Ewwwww! There's even hair growing out of his ears — more, in fact, than from the majority of his skull. He's about six inches shorter than Ashley, although with the heels she's wearing this may be nothing more than an optical illusion. To top it all off, he's got a nose only a mother could love on payday and no chin whatsoever.

She does not introduce him, which leads to even greater confusion. Stella, Julia, and Aaron are talking to Ashley, each alternately attempting to catch a glimpse of her nipples as if to say, "Aha! Caught you peeping!" or avoid being hit and thus knocked out by her Teutonic tits if she turns too quickly. No one but me has seen the troll alongside her. I'm trying my hardest to get past his first layer. I want to speak with him so I can understand who he is, what he's doing with Ashley, and how these two fit together.

I overhear Ashley attempting, less discreetly than any of us would like, to press her case with Stella as to when she might be able to schedule "an 'appointment' for my mother-in-law." I look around and see not only the troll, but an older "mother troll" alongside him. The mother troll is every bit as homely as the troll, but once one gets past the initial revulsion, it's plain to see both of them look welcoming and are well-dressed, although quaintly so, like some pleasant inbred British royalty.

I'm the only one to notice these two folks alongside Ashley, and their presence is driving me crazy. Having been locked out of the conversation for a few minutes, I can't take the suspense anymore. "Hraragh!" I say, clearing my throat far too loudly, like a lawnmower with tuberculosis. Everyone stops dead in their tracks. "So, Ashley, who have we here?" I say, looking at baby troll and mother troll with wide eyes. A wave of confusion crosses the faces of Stella and Julia, while poor Aaron's eyes remain glued to Ashley, still hearing the siren's call of "boobies, boobies, boobies."

"Uh, yeah, this is Marshall and his mother, Lee Ann," Ashley says with no enthusiasm whatsoever.

Marshall. Marshall. Where have I heard that name before? Is that her brother? Her gardener? Her podiatrist? Her... and then it hits me. "This is your husband?!" I say with far too much surprise, so much so that to cover up I quickly begin coughing spastically and Aaron looks like he's going over the Heimlich Maneuver in his head, hoping he remembers how to do it correctly if it falls to him to save my life.

"Yes," replies Ashley, no sense of pride in her voice,

although my hacking drowns her out somewhat, so much so that Julia repeats the question.

"Did you say husband?" I look at Julia and she's thinking exactly what I've been thinking and she, too, realizes she's said it in a far more insulting way than she intended, so she quickly guzzles the entire remnants of her champagne glass since I've already cornered the market on coughing and choking to death.

"Yes," replies Ashley again, although this time her lifeboat-sized lips are pursed in pique.

There's an awkward pause as I search back into my memory from all those DILS meetings I've attended over the past few months, all those confessions we made to one another. Ashley. Ashley. There is so much I remember about her story — the husband whose wealthy father died, the trust fund, the terrible MIL who wouldn't let him have the money that was rightfully his. But what else; what else? *When I first saw Marshall, I just went "Wow!" My knees buckled. I just knew he was my soul mate.* That was it. Julia must have come up with it at the same time. Knees buckled?! Knees buckled?! From what, him swinging a nightstick at them in order to keep her from running away screaming, "It's alive! It's alive!"? This is the kind of guy who gets chased by local townsfolk carrying pitchforks and torches. What the hell is going on here?

"You're a dentist, right?" I ask, almost regrettably, for fear I've got this whole thing wrong and I've just busted her for picking this guy up at some "rich ugly guy convention" on her way over here, but no, he answers in the affirmative, with a smile that shows despite everything else, he actually has a very nice set of straight, white teeth. Since Ashley has not seen fit to introduce her, I add, "And is this your mother?" to which he also pleads guilt. She, too, smiles, and there are those perfect teeth again.

I haven't been listening, but apparently Stella has managed to stave off Ashley's pleadings and has left our conversation circle, dragging Aaron away as dreams of giant jugs dance in his head, leaving Julia and I alone with Ashley and her trollmate. "I've heard a lot about your movie. Are you pleased with the adaptation?" asks Ashley's husband in a very sincere manner.

"If we'd been invited to the premier, we'd know firsthand," Ashley interjects, her voice sharpened with steel.

"Uh, yeah, I think it came out all right. As to the premier, well… the theater only holds so many people and I had access to a limited number of tickets. Sorry. Hardly anyone here tonight went, which is why they're throwing me this thing," Julia shrugs, impishly and uncomfortably.

"Yes, the movie was quite good," and I regret jumping in to break the uncomfortable silence, for in doing so I've just admitted I was one of the lucky ones to have attended the premier, while Ashley was left out. "You know, if you're interested, Claudia will be announcing soon that next Friday, when the movie opens wide, we're all going." Up until a few days ago I had no idea what "open wide" meant, not being in the biz and all, and poor Marshall the dentist probably associates it with what he tells his patients every day. "The plan is to dress down — jeans for everybody, Julia included — and sneak into the back row in order to gauge the reaction of the crowd. It should be a hoot. Y'all should come." A hoot. Y'all. A bad habit of mine is whenever I get nervous I sound more and more like I never left Carolina. *Yeah, and then afterwards we can go out back, smoke a butt, and have ourselves a dang bar-b-que!*

"Jeans, huh?" Ashley scoffs, unimpressed by something as un-chic as rubbing elbows with the great unwashed.

"Yes, you all should come. Marshall, Lee Ann, I'd love to have you there. I'm trying to get as much feedback from as big a cross-section of people as possible. They're about to start shooting the sequel and if there's anything that really didn't work in the first film, I hope we can fix it before it's too late on the second," says Julia. She and I are spending more time focusing our attention on Ashley's husband and MIL because they aren't giving us the stink-eye, unlike Ashley who seems to always be doing it. Which gets me to thinking...

"So, Lee Ann, do you and Ashley get out together much? Mother-daughter sort of things?" It's a bit forward, I know, considering our group's joint attempt at secrecy and discretion, but an idea just popped into my head and once that happens I'm pretty damn impulsive.

Plain Jane Lee Ann, with her rat's nest of curly silver and black hair that looks like an untamed, untrimmed shrub, drops her eyes in sadness. "No," is all she says, almost in a whisper.

"Well, you really should join us. Do you like movies?" I ask with mounting enthusiasm. As I do, I can almost feel Ashley's eyes boring into my skull.

"Yes. Movies are nice. I like a good love story," Lee Ann replies.

"Julia's movie has love in it," I exclaim, still in my cheerleader mode. "Most people wouldn't classify it exclusively as a love story, but there's a young boy and a young girl and they fall in love. That's pretty much the centerpiece of the film; wouldn't you agree, Julia?"

"Yeah, can't argue with that," Julia says, along for the ride on whatever adventure I'm taking everyone on.

"What about you, Marshall? What sort of movies do you like? Love stories, too?" I ask.

"Well," he begins, chortling nervously into his fist, "I'm more of an art film aficionado. Just last week I attended a Man Ray festival. It was scintillating. *Emak-Bakia, Return to Reason,* all those great Dadaist works."

"Boooo-ring," sing-songs Ashley, rolling her eyes. Marshall hangs his head in hurt. I feel sorry for him, much as I always do for nerds, a group to which I feel a sisterly kinship. There's nothing worse than being made fun of for being intelligent and well-read.

"With all apologies to my friend Julia, I don't think her film would be considered art house fare, but still, it has an interesting fantasy element and what's more, you get to see it with the novelist. Think of the questions you'll have. I mean, imagine being able to sit next to Man Ray."

"He's dead," Marshall replies, but nicely so as not to hurt my feelings. "But I understand what you mean. It could be interesting."

"I wanted to be photographed on the red carpet," says Ashley, who is not letting this one go. "Who knows who might have seen me?" she says with a leer; rather inappropriately, considering her husband and MIL are standing right there and I don't detect even a hint of good humor to her quip. Marshall and Lee Ann look down at their feet.

Breaking the silence, Marshall says to Ashley, "Honey, I could use a drink. Can I get you something?"

"Gray Goose cosmo," she replies vacantly as she scans the room, not meeting his gaze at all.

"Mother?" he asks.

"Is it a cash bar or an open bar?" Ashley interjects harshly.

"Open," answers Julia.

"In that case, take orders for everybody," Ashley directs. Sheepishly he does. Julia volunteers to go along with him, figuring there's no way the poor guy could possible bring all those drinks back alone.

So rude! I knew Ashley acted this was around us, but if she joined DILS because she wanted a closer relationship with her MIL… And what about her husband? I'm flummoxed. As soon as our drinks come back I pull an excuse out of the sky in order to drift away from this group and Julia does the same without cue. Great minds think alike.

"Can you believe…" we say in unison, then laugh. "No, really," I say. "What the hell is her problem?"

"And where did she pick those two up? *That's* her soul mate? I mean, far be it from me to criticize someone who can love a man for something other than his looks…" she says.

"But wait a minute," I add. "All she does is complain about his lack of money. She's never said a word about him being sooooo unattractive. And anyone can see they don't have any sort of bond together. What do they have in common? He likes art films. She reads the *National Enquirer*."

"He must be hung down to the ground."

"I wouldn't care if he were hung from here to Seattle. Would *you* sleep with him?" As if on cue, we look over and can't help but notice Marshall with his finger knuckle-deep inside his left nostril.

"Ewwrgh!" Julia spews, shaking her head and sticking out her tongue at the mere thought.

"There's something mighty wrong here. She's hot, he's not, she's dim, he's bright, and she complains there's no money."

"Opposites attract?" Julia peeps.

"They do not attract! You were just with them. There is absolutely no chemistry there. Listen, we met Aaron and Stella. Aaron is hot; Stella knows she is not, but look how well they get along. She's great; we both know that. And she's not bad looking; she's just not Cover Girl glamorous like his past relationships."

"So it's the money," says Julia. "You've heard her at meetings. 'We have no money because my nasty MIL is holding onto Marshall's trust fund like the last lifeboat on the Titanic.' There it is. She married him for his money, but she can't get a hold of it quite yet, so she's pissed. Simple."

"So she gets Stella to hypnotize the MIL and wham, bam, boom — she gets a load of dough. Is that right? Is that what we're all about?"

Julia looks deep in thought. "DILS exists because girls like us want a better relationship with our MILs, and via that, a better relationship with our husbands. We each got married for our own idiosyncratic reasons. Except Ashley's seems less noble than most."

My mind is going a mile a minute. I strongly object to something, but I can't quite put my finger on it. "The moment we started in with lawyers, private detectives, and hypnotism, we all crossed a line. We didn't feel badly about it because it got us to where we wanted to be, but in Ashley's case…"

"Yeah, I know what you mean. It's one step too far. But

what do we do about it?"

"I don't know," I reply. "I just don't know."

Just as Julia is about to respond, she is startled by a warm hand on her shoulder. Jason is standing right behind us. She slowly twirls around to face him like a ballerina in a music box. He leans down and gives her the most tender, sensual cheek kiss I have ever seen. My knees almost buckle from the proximity of the heat. Remembering what Julia had told me about Jason's wife looking like she just stepped out of a magazine advertisement, I must say that Jason does as well. He must be about six-two with sandy blonde hair, and deep-set sparkly blue eyes. He is wearing an expensive, tailored button-down shirt with a pair of well-fitted dress pants. He has a cool, understated, sophisticated look about him with a little bit of sexy college jock thrown in for fun. And from what Julia has told me, he is not just yummy to look at. This guy has a good head on his brawny shoulders as well. Apparently, he was offered both an academic and sports scholarship by one of the top universities in the country. He played college rugby, worked, and managed to carry a 3.8 GPA. He definitely seems like a rare find.

It's a bit hard to understand how these two ended up in the Friend Zone when I swear that the room temperature has just increased by twenty degrees. After what feels like an eternity, they break from their trance to acknowledge my presence. I didn't mind being ignored at all. In fact, I felt as if I was in the heat of the moment with them.

"Katherine, I would like you to meet my very good friend, Jason," Julia says with a doe-eyed expression. Jason leans in to give me one of those sexy cheek kisses, and I graciously accept. His kiss was nice, but it didn't compare to the one he gave Julia. If that kiss could have talked it would have said something like, "I know this is your cheek but it's all that I can give you since I married someone other than the woman I really love. What I wouldn't do to have these lips of mine all of your body, Julia. But no, your soft cheek must do for now." My kiss was much more basic and didn't have too much to say.

"Jason, it's so nice to meet you. I've heard a lot about you," I say, and immediately start to backtrack. "I mean, I've heard so much about you coming here. Uh…I mean, Julia mentioned to me that you and your wife were coming to her premiere and um, oh yeah, speaking of your wife, where is she?"

Wow, this is getting worse by the second. Me and too much wine make for poor conversation. I'm cutting myself off for the night before I'm the drunk fool who tells everyone about our secret society. By this time, Julia is pressing her face into Jason's shoulder with her hand covering her face. Lucky for me, she is blushing AND giggling like a school girl. Jason has his arm around her now and they are both laughing. From the looks of it, I guess my floundering around with words was a good thing. And I'm sure I haven't been the first one to joke around with them about secret boy/girl crushes they may or may not have on each other. Jason knows Julia is in love with him. And I'd be damned if this boy wasn't just as in love with her. They are both standing within each other's personal space and are in their own *dream world.* I decide to give these lovebirds some alone time and excuse myself. Seeing Jason and Julia together reminds me why I love my hunky love monkey as much as I do. We still have that heat between us.

As the party winds down, Kyle, Nancy, and I look for

Julia to say our farewells. We can't seem to find her and other partiers haven't seen her for quite some time. I decide that Julia will not be offended at all if we don't go hunt her out of her cave to say goodnight. I have a feeling Julia and Jason are connecting on a different level this time. I wonder if we could get Stella to turn this into "Level 4-Love Trumps Morality."

Chapter Twenty-Six

Confession time: I rarely watch movies more than once and was I to pick a film to sit through twice in ten days, it wouldn't normally be "Children of the Forest". But as we said to Ashley and her family, there is a certain coolness to watching a film with the auteur sitting right next to you. That especially rings true for me since Julia and I have become BFFs. Watching each scene, I get a better understanding of how her mind works — or at least I allow myself to imagine so. It also impresses me that someone can think up all this stuff. I usually take it for granted, just like everyone else. We're all critics, every one of us, but when we know someone who took nothing but air and turned it into something tangible, something creative, it makes us realize what charlatans we are for not marveling at what we are surrounded by —the everyday genius we take for granted.

This time I also drag dear Kyle along, although having already sat through it once, I can say with certainty this is not his kind of movie — he's totally not the demographic. Not a single thing gets blown up and no one puts a bullet through anyone's head or a karate chop to their neck. Still, I think the jeans concept did it, as did the idea we'd just be sitting in a dark theater like we always do, instead of making a great big fuss with limos and red carpets. Some guys like the limelight, but Kyle is the inconspicuous type, which is fine by me. I suggested bringing Lana along, too, which is becoming more and more de rigueur in our family setup. Three is no longer a crowd for us. Kyle still expresses amazement, but he doesn't take it much further. Being a man, when things are going right, he doesn't seem to care how and why, just, "May I have some more, please?"

My reasons for bringing along Lana are two-fold. Fold number one is I actually do enjoy her company now, since the dust has finally begun to settle on her obsessive worship of me. Oh, she still feels that way; I guess it's simply reached a point where I've managed to convince her to tone it down a bit. Fold number two is I figure I can sic her on Ashley's MIL in order to help me gather more intel. I am still in a moral quandary about what I'm seeing from Ashley and before I do something stupid — which is often my M.O. — I figure I'll try to learn more about the true nature of her family situation. I still don't have the sort of relationship where I can explain all of this to Lana — it would blow the cover off my having her put into a trance — but I can make suggestions. "Momma Lana, you know the blond in the red that I introduced you to at the after-after-after party?"

"You mean the one who looked like…" I see her struggle for a diplomatic way of saying, " a dockside whore," but she catches herself — part of what makes New Lana, New Lana.

"Yes, I believe we're both thinking of the same girl.

Anyway, she's coming tonight and she's bringing her mother-in-law again, too. I think her mother-in-law is a little shy. She didn't seem to know anyone at the last get-together, so I was wondering, since you two are around the same age, if you might try to make her feel more a part of things."

"Certainly. Thanks for thinking of me," and as she says it, there is such a look of sincerity in her eyes. Please God, may this trance never end.

Every modern woman knows there are jeans, and then there are *jeans*. Kyle slips on his 501s and he's done. Must be nice. For us ladies, there is the constant pressure of, "What's in today? Dark jeans? Light jeans? Faded? Are acid washed coming back? Will they *ever* come back? What about appliqués? And God, don't let anyone accuse what I'm wearing of being 'Mom jeans' or I'll slit my throat!" Designers frequently talk about jeans being "distressed." Actually, it's not the jeans; it's us consumers.

I finally grab my Sevens, aged denim edition, and hope for the best. For Lana, I don't bother suggesting anything. I know she doesn't do the jeans thing anymore, so I tell her to throw on some casual slacks and let's roll.

When we arrive at the theater, half the girls are in sunglasses, even though it's dark as tar out. "It's part of the 'inconspicuous' thing," says Gabriella and I laugh, wishing I'd gotten the memo, although it seems kind of conspicuous to be wearing sunglasses at night.

Normally, I would actually try to avoid Ashley rather than seek her out. The truth is I never really liked her from the start. I found her bitchy, trashy, and only mildly sympathetic even at her most vulnerable. But tonight I'm on a mission, the sort I always get myself into, which usually involves sticking my nose where it has no business being. I do my gratuitous hellos with Julia, Claudia, Gabriella, Stella, and my other closest DILS peeps, then spot her ultra-unnatural bleached blond hair and make a beeline for it.

I guess the ripped jeans look is still in, but there's ripped and then there's… obscene. Ashley's aren't ripped so much in the knee area, which is the typical topography of the style, but in the areas most commonly used for points of entry and exit. Her ass and her hoo-hoo are practically hanging out. Why does she do this? And what sort of man puts up with it? Even if you were a total hoochie when you were single, one should usually opt for dressing a little more conservatively when in a relationship. Once the prey has been bagged, why keep your gun loaded with the safety off? Most men notice and say, "Hey, cut that out." But "dreamboat" Marshall doesn't seem the type. He might *feel* like saying it, but just one look at them together and one gets the distinct impression which of them wears the ripped jeans in the family and it isn't him. The poor schlub looks almost physically abused next to her.

"Ready for the big action?" I ask Ashley in greeting.

"It looks like we're just going to a movie; nothing more," she replies, gazing around looking bored. I forgot she could really care less about the movie and about Julia. The whole thing for her is the opportunity to mix with celebrities and maybe hook up with some rich and lecherous producer, but outside of us DILS people, all that's here are 14-year-old girls in braces, freckles, and ponytails, followed by their moms and babysitters who they try to ditch for that cute boy off in the distance, the one who sits behind them in Sex Ed class and keeps saying, "Yeah, I've done that."

"It's a good film. Really. I mean, look at the crowd," and indeed the place is jammin'.

"Whatever," she sighs dismissively.

"So, Marshall; glad you could come. Do you two hit the town together much?"

The poor guy is a mixture of emotions, from practically spitting all over me out of the sheer excitement of someone actually wanting to have a conversation with him, to looking up at Ashley as if to ask permission to speak. As for the permission, she doesn't even acknowledge she's with him let alone cares what he does, so he says, "No, not really…" his voice tailing off fearfully. "We tend to like different things," he adds in a whisper.

"Have you gotten to know the sorts of things Ashley likes to do? I hear communication is the cornerstone of a good relationship." I, too, try to say this as quietly as possible, although if Ashley catches me I'm prepared to defend myself by inferring I'm just passing along the sorts of things we've gone over in DILS — without mentioning the dreaded "D" word. The first rule of DILS is… But she's still not listening and I get the distinct impression the last thing in the world she would ever think was that I was macking on her man.

"Oh, oh yes," Marshall sputters. "Ashley likes dining out, and vacations, and shopping…"

"Good. Do you go with her? Do you enjoy those things, too?"

The homely little man licks his bottom lip in contemplation, then grabs me gently by the arm and leads me a foot or two away, still nervous about getting caught, but aware that Ashley is more interested in seeing if some A-list star might also be sneaking into this performance as well. "I do, actually, but where we diverge is in the level of opulence. I can afford a weekend in wine country, but Ashley tends to prefer a month in Paris."

I smile. I don't want to make the poor guy feel poor. "Well, maybe once you get your trust fund…"

"My what?" he asks, sincerely confused.

I study his face. "It's just a saying. You know, like 'once your ship comes in;' something like that. 'Once you get your trust fund.' All the kids are saying it."

"They are? I don't get around much," he says, still befuddled but satisfied with my quick recovery explanation. That was close. I'm really not supposed to know that much about him or his annual income.

He's kind of a doofy guy and I can't wrap my head around whether he's playing dumb or he is dumb. Ashley herself is pretty dumb most times, but there's street smart and there's book smart, which means there's also street dumb and book dumb. Ashley is book dumb but street smart; Marshall seems the opposite.

"I hear you're a dentist."

"Yes," he answers, and I can see he wants to say more but there's not much more *to* say, until he stammers, "I don't mean to be rude, but you're…?"

"Married."

"No, no, I mean, I forgot your name."

"Katherine. Kat."

"Kat, I'm sorry I forgot, but you see, I don't really know what I'm doing here. It seems Ashley knows you and all these other people and so Mother and I tagged along because she told us to… *asked* us to… but outside of that, I don't really know what the connection is."

"We're all just…" and I try to come up with something

good; something better, obviously, than Ashley has bothered with. "... Friends of Julia, the author."

"And how does Ashley know Julia?"

This guy gets right to the point of matters. Shit...

"Honestly, I don't know. I think we each know Julia in a slightly different way. What you're looking at here is 'Six Degrees of Julia Rader.' You've got some actresses, some industry people, some people she's played tennis with, whatever. So, dentistry... is it true that fillings used to be made out of mercury? Is this something I should be worried about?"

Marshall takes the bait like a hungry trout and while I could care less about his long-winded answer, I see out of the corner of my eye Lana chatting up Marshall's mother. Good.

"Wow, that's very interesting, Marshall. I never knew that," I say after having not paid a bit of attention to a single thing he said. "So, business must be good, yes?" I press.

"It's okay," he shrugs. "I'm comfortable," he smiles wanly, then starts to look a bit depressed.

"Yeah, the economy's tough on everyone; I know." With this he gives me a knowing nod. "Me, I grew up poor, dirt poor. Back in the swamps of Carolina. We went out most nights and had to shoot our own food or starve." I have this problem with laying things on a little too thick and the truth is, while my family isn't rich by any means, if Dad told me to shoot my dinner, I'd take the gun and rob the local grocery store. "What about you?"

"Oh, no, I never shot and ate an animal," Marshall replies.

"That's not what I meant. I mean, how were things for

you growing up?"

"Fine."

He's giving me nothing. "Did you struggle or was it easy? I suppose it's a struggle for everybody, but in different ways. For me, it was financial. How about you?"

"I was a bit shy growing up. I was never good at sports…"

I want to shake him and say, "One look at you and I can tell you're shy and weren't good at sports. You also probably never had a date except with your right hand and a tub full of margarine. Give me your tax returns! I want to know about the money! Where the fuck is the money?"

"What did your dad do?" I ask.

"He… he was in business."

"Did you go to public school or private?"

"Public."

"Swimming pool or no swimming pool?"

"We had a pool."

"In-ground or above-ground?"

"Above ground — why are you asking me all these questions?" I've got him quivering like he's in a police interrogation room.

"I'm just the curious type. Oh look, the line's moving. Time to go in. I'm so enjoying our conversation. We'll have to sit near one another." As much as this invitation may have tickled him before, right now he looks like he wants to soil his briefs.

On the way in, I grab Julia. "Jules, there's something very fishy about Ashley."

"You just noticed that?"

"No, I mean fishier than what we already know. I don't even think her husband has family money."

246

Julia purses her lips and thinks. "Maybe he really is hung like a stallion."

"That can't be it!" I sputter. "If she's only with the guy for great sex, you don't come to DILS meetings and talk about family money. And furthermore, how would someone like Ashley ever discover he was hung like a mule when he looks like that? Just look at him. Is Ashley so deep of a person that she fell in love with his personality? Let's face the hard cold fact that she wouldn't open the package when the wrapping looks like The Swamp Monster."

"Perplexing," she agrees.

I catch up to Kyle and Momma Lana. "Momma Lana, I saw you talking to that woman I pointed out."

"Oh yes; Lee Ann. Sweet woman. Very nice."

"So… what's her story?" I ask.

"Well," and Lana hunches over a little as if to invite me into a private huddle. The only problem is, I'm about a foot taller than her so when she hunches down I practically have to get on my hands and knees in prayer. "I don't think she and her daughter-in-law get along very well at all."

"My!" I say, like a surprised Southern belle.

"Yes, really! You know how she seems kind of shy at first? Once you get her talking, she's quite peppy. The thing is, when she's around her daughter-in-law, she says she feels… oh, what's the right word… *overwhelmed*. Seems that blond girl with the big breasts is sort of overbearing. Bullies her a lot."

"Let me get this straight," I say. "The *MIL* says the *DIL* is the bully?"

Lana looks at me funny. "Katherine, what are you talking about? I don't understand you."

"I said, 'The MIL…'" Oh shit. "Oops. I'm sorry. I'm

using jargon. Don't you just hate when people do that? Sort of leaves you out of the conversation; am I right?"

Lana still looks confused. "MILs, DILs—are we talking about pickles?"

"No, like I said — sorry, my bad. Just continue."

"That's the headline, I guess. Lee Ann thinks she's a gold-digger." She pauses. "This blond girl isn't a good friend of yours, is she? I wouldn't want to be insulting."

"No, heck, you and me; we're fine. No problem at all. Do you get the impression Lee Ann is loaded? 'Cause I heard Lee Ann is holding up the blond and her husband by hoarding money her son has rightfully inherited."

Lana puts on a serious look of contemplation. "I don't know. Why is this important?"

To this, I have no answer. Part of the answer is I'm your average, everyday busybody, but past that, everything having to do with DILS is tugging at my personal ethical code. The nicer Lana is to me, the guiltier I feel for how I tricked her into becoming that way.

"It's kind of hard to explain, Momma Lana. It's just that... did you ever see a family where the people in it should be getting along but they're not? Let's say it's because one of those people has become a tyrant."

"Oy, I should tell you sometime about my mother-in-law," says Lana without a hint of irony. "Nothing I could ever do was good enough. Talk about a tyrant."

"Yeah, something like that. I know it's not right to meddle in other people's affairs, but still, when you see someone taking advantage of someone else and that other person feels powerless..."

"I know what you mean, dear," says Lana. "Something I've always noticed about you. You pull for the underdog.

Kyle told me that about you shortly after you two met. I thought, 'What a nice thing.' It's not the sort of thing a boy brings up about a girl right off the bat. Usually it's how she looks, what she does, where she's from, where she went to school, what her parents do. Kyle told me all that, too, but it was the other stuff that made me understand you were 'the one.' It's a good trait."

I'm touched. "Well, that being said, could you help me out with something else then?"

"What?"

"Sit next to Lee Ann and during the previews and try to sneak into the conversation that I'm a gold-digger, too."

"What?! That's ridiculous. In a million years I will never see as much money as you've made. No one would believe me."

"Lee Ann doesn't know me from Adam. Since she already brought the subject up, empathize with her by saying you have the same problem. People love that. Then see what she says. I'm looking for details. I may be able to help her out, but we can't tell her that just yet."

Lana stews. "All right; if this is for a higher purpose and not just for gossiping's sake."

"That's the spirit. Thanks."

In the theater, I plop down between Kyle and Julia, carrying on two distinctly different conversations. With Kyle, I pull him in towards Julia and I have the creator of the "Dream Song" series explain to a thirty-one-year-old guy what the hell all the fuss is about. As she spins tales about the business process that passes for a creative process in Hollywood, Kyle is as intrigued as most of us civilians.

Conversation number two is quieter and I try to keep Kyle out of it.

"I have a terrible suspicion."

"What?" asks Julia.

"I think Ashley has been playing all of us."

"What are you going to do about it?" she asks.

"Make certain of it. Then rat her out."

"You can't do that," she replies.

"Jules, if anyone should understand moral imperatives, it's you. It would be like… it would be like someone going to a sexaholics meeting just to get laid. And speaking of getting laid, where's Jason?" I inquisitively ask Julia.

"He had a meeting," Julia whispers back.

"Did you sleep with him last night?" I ask, skipping the foreplay and getting right to the point.

"Yes." Julia says quickly, unable to wipe the silly grin off her face.

"I knew it! You little glow ball," I respond, as I playfully punch Julia's arm. "I want all the dirty details later.

Julia looks smugger than I've ever seen her look, more than when she was on the red carpet being screamed at by adoring fans.

Chapter Twenty-Seven

After the movie, I catch up with Lana. "What did you find out?"

"It's funny you should ask. Lee Ann and I got to talking about her daughter-in-law. Seems Lee Ann's really been looking for someone to unload her troubles on. You know, there ought to be some sort of organization for women like her who have troubles with their daughters-in-law…"

I nearly choke. "Yeah, that sounds like an excellent idea. You've had a lot of experience with 12-step programs. Maybe you could figure something out; get something going."

A light bulb goes off over Lana's head. "Yes, maybe I'll do that some day. Although I really don't know much about it firsthand. You're such a dear to me."

My guilt rages. "Thanks. So anyway, you were saying…"

"It killed me to lie and say you were only after my money, but I did as you said and you were right; it got her tongue loosened up right quick. Would you believe…" Lana actually starts to get choked up, "… Lee Ann is *not* a wealthy woman. I mean, not the kind of money you and your friend Julia have, anyway. Her husband gave her a comfortable life, but that's about it — maybe just a little better than Kyle's father gave me."

"You got her to say all this?" I ask.

"Like I told you, honey; she was so ready to unload, I thought she'd explode. Anyway, her son, Marshall, he's a dentist, but he's kind of a meeskite."

"He's a bar-b-que sauce?"

Lana looks at me funny. "No, sweetie; meeskite is Yiddish for 'homely.' I think you're thinking of 'mesquite.' So as I was saying, when he came home with, well let's face it, a sexy girl like Ashley, he couldn't get over himself and Lee Ann was simply happy that he was happy. The problem is, when something looks too good to be true... you know, I actually felt that way about you for a time. You're such a dream. I can't believe how lucky my Kyle is to have you."

I blush. At first, whenever Lana spewed these compliments on me, I couldn't really appreciate them because I felt they were completely trance-induced. Then I talked to The Big Sisters — Stella, Gabriella, and Claudia—and they said, "Remember the overriding concept. Hypnosis cannot make someone feel differently than they really do. When she gushes over you, it's because she really feels that way." Now I can't help but feel good about these things.

Lana continues, "I think this Ashley girl thought there was more money lying around somewhere than there really was. Or else she was just using Marshall as a stepping stone; I don't know. Lee Ann thinks she used to do dirty movies."

"No!"

"Yes! And from what Lee Ann says, they don't pay all

that well. I always wondered about that."

I'm trying to picture Ashley doing porn — a strange thought to consider about anyone one knows from real life. "Why would you wonder about what porn pays?"

"I don't know," Lana shrugs. "I'm a lonely old woman. I have lots of time on my hands to think about a lot of things. That's the only good thing about one's golden years — lots of thinking time. Like, when people envision the future, they always show pictures of jetpacks and flying cars. I've lived a nice, long life and I've seen a lot of things, but every decade they show me these same pictures of jetpacks and flying cars and every decade ends and still — no jetpacks, no flying cars. I'm feeling shortchanged."

"Anyway, Ashley the Underpaid Porn Star marries Marshall the Meeskite for his money…"

"But there isn't that much money. And she spends like a drunken sailor…"

"Why do people always bring up drunken sailors? People talk about spending money like drunken sailors; running around like drunken sailors… In my entire life, I've never even met a drunken sailor," I say.

"I grew up in a city that used to have a major seaport. I've seen a lot of drunken sailors and everything they say about them is true. Anyway…"

"Sorry. Continue."

Lana takes a deep breath in order to rev up her engines again. "So this Ashley lady goes through Marshall's money like… whatever sort of person goes through money quickly… and then she starts in on Marshall's mother's money. Lee Ann, the poor dear, doesn't know at first what the money's for; she's just a mother who loves her son, so she gives it to him. And gives it to him. He says he needs new office equipment, then a bigger office, then he has to redo his office. Finally, she comes over to his office one day and the place hasn't changed a bit. Not only that, he's down to a skeleton staff and there's an inch of dust all over everything. His wife, Ashley, bilked him out of everything and she still wants more.

"Lee Ann tries to confront her, but this Ashley, she's a mean one. She blasts her and tells her she feels Marshall deceived her, that he led her to believe he could provide for her better and that constitutes fraud and deception. She's threatening lawsuits and divorce lawyers, the works. Meanwhile, poor Marshall, the schlub, he still loves her. Well, I don't know if it's love; it's probably more like lust, but men, they often can't tell the difference. He's down on his hands and knees asking Ashley to stay and he's also down on his hands and knees asking his mother for more money. Lee Ann starts dipping into her savings — very reluctantly, I might add. But now…" Lana starts to get all weepy on me again, but she has me on the edge of my seat.

"Yes, yes, so what's up now?"

"All Lee Ann has left is her home. It's a nice home, she says. But this home is the home her late husband bought them. It has so many memories for her. When you're a widow, memories are important, they really are. I pray to God each night neither Kyle nor you ever have to feel that sense of loss. Lee Ann knows someday she's going to have to give it up — it's too darn big for her all by herself. But she's not ready to do that right now, and especially not just to give the proceeds to Ashley so she can go get more of those transplants."

"I think you mean 'implants,' Momma Lana."

"Transplants, implants, it's all the same to me; what do

I know? I say go with what God gave you. Lee Ann wants her home because it's her home, and even if she were to sell it, she doesn't want to give all the money to Ashley Big Boobs."

My chest is heaving. For me, DILS was a godsend. But in the hands of a woman like Ashley, it's "the dark side." Every good thing it offers, she's managed to twist around for her own, hoggish selfishness.

"You look blue," says Lana.

"I am." I collect myself. "I just want you to know; I would never do anything bad to you, Momma Lana. I'm not perfect; I know that. I do some crazy things sometimes. But I would never do anything to hurt you or Kyle. I love Kyle and…" and what I'm about to say, I've never actually said before. The newness of it is not unlike the newness of saying it to a new and true lover, and in that same spirit, I really mean it. "…I love you."

"I love you, too, Katherine."

Chapter Twenty-Eight

I get off the elevator in Stella's building and find Ashley, Lee Ann, and Marshall sitting in her waiting room. Lee Ann looks up at me with eyes that tell me she thinks I'm as satanic as Ashley, but then I realize it's because I told Momma Lana to tell her that I was, so I forgive her. Me, what I really see is a beaten woman about to endure the final insult in her life's journey — to have her free will taken away from her, and it kills me.

"Kat, what are you doing here?" asks Ashley, genuinely surprised.

"I need something," I say, as I brush past her and go straight into Stella's office. Inside, Stella has the lights turned down low and is with another patient, a woman.

"Kat!" she says. The woman sitting across from her turns her head, snapping out of whatever trance or semi-trance she was about to be put under or was in the midst of. I immediately feel like I've thrown up inside a patient on an operating table. "Kat, what are you doing barging in here? Can't you see I'm with a patient?" I've never seen Stella pissed before, but she is and I deserve it.

"Excuse me, but this is an emergency."

"Will you excuse me please?" she says to her patient, who is too surprised to say anything pro or con. Stella grabs my upper arm and leads me into a powder room.

"What on earth could you be thinking?"

"I have to save the planet."

"What?"

"I know, I'm prone to hyperbole, but hear me out. Ashley is in the waiting room with her MIL and she's a fraud. She's been making everything up about her MIL. Ashley is playing the system. She's using us all to bilk her husband and her MIL out of all their money. You've got to stop it."

Stella, who is a no-nonsense person to begin with, gives me her most serious look. "Kat, you just ran right into my office while I was with a patient. Not cool. Not cool at all. The sort of work I do here is very delicate. You don't know what I could have been working on with her. You don't know anything."

"I know that you can't hypnotize Ashley's MIL. You just can't."

Stella takes a deep breath. "Kat, I don't lose my temper easily, but you're pushing it; you really are."

"But if I don't do this, it wouldn't be right. I know things."

"Kat, what you don't know is protocol. You never barge into a doctor's office without an appointment while she's seeing another patient."

"I get that. I'm sorry. I tried calling. I left messages. You never returned them."

"I pick up my calls at the end of the day and I return them all."

"That would have been too late," I reply.

"Lastly—and this is a big one — you don't meddle in other people's business. Ashley is Ashley and you are you. I don't discuss your situation with her, and I don't discuss hers with you. Do we understand each other?"

"But we're Sisters."

"Kat, I'm a doctor first, a Sister second."

"That's a bit hypocritical." As soon as I say it, I see I've verbally slapped Stella in the face — hard.

"Excuse me, but you're way out of line," she replies.

"What you do; what we do as a sisterhood…"

She cuts me off. "Katherine, leave. Now. I mean it. I have a patient in the chair and another one in my waiting room. *My* waiting room. *My* office. *My* rules. When I start having to answer to you for everything I do, let me know, but until then, that's the way it is. Now leave. I mean it. Leave now and don't stop to chatter in the waiting room. It's not your place."

I look at her, but I'm been knocked off my high horse for the moment. If you knew you could stop a disaster from happening, would you? Isn't that one of those classic moral and ethical questions they put into icebreaker party games? Sure, if I were Marshall the Meeskite, I would love to be in bed every night with a porn star like Ashley — if that's indeed what she does or did — but at what cost? Does it give him the right to ruin his own life? Even if it does, if he makes that decision of his own free will, what about his mother?

Stella's eyes bore a hole through me as I back down and back away. Like a kid in a dunce cap, I slither by Stella's patient and out into the waiting room, wordlessly, not saying anything to Stella or to her patient.

In the waiting room, things are not much better. Ashley has her arms folded over her chest — no small feat considering how high up that puts her arms. "Did you have an appointment?" she asks curtly.

"No," I quiver, still stressed from my confrontation and embarrassment in front of Stella.

"So you just waltzed on past us without knocking; without an appointment? Jumping ahead of us? How rude!" Ashley continues.

"I'm sorry," I mumble. "I shouldn't have done that," I say as I bow my head unconsciously. I look up at Lee Ann and she's still giving me the stink eye. Marshall looks embarrassed for me, sad soul that he is. He's smiling and all I can think is, "You're such a fool. In this world, women who look like her don't fall in love with men who look like you" and I feel sorry for him again. Maybe he is a nice guy, and maybe if we lived in a world where people got to know one another facelessly at first, Ashley — or better still, a nice girl — would have met his personality first and his face and body last and by then she'd have been hooked. But no. He's in a world of deception in which he hasn't a clue. And me, I'm just too late.

* * *

The great thing about being friends with a writer is you can almost always expect them to be home. Working from home must be nice, I suppose, although Julia has complained to me that sometimes it feels like she's in a minimum security prison. She's disciplined herself to write a certain number of words per day, every day, sort of like a workout fanatic. The only difference is that a workout takes x amount of time and what Julia does takes up pretty much the majority of her day. Still, she says that's how all the prolific writers do it, so I respect her dedication.

"C'mon in," she says as she greets me at the door. I follow her into one of her living rooms — she must have half a dozen of them. She probably has names for each one — not names like "Buck" and "Sammy," but names like, "The Blue Room," "The Play Room," "The Parlor." Once I'm seated, it reoccurs to me that, for her, they're also all known as "The Sex Room." I jump up quickly from my seat.

"Did you do it on this chair, too?" I ask.

"Uh huh," she answers languidly. "That was a very good afternoon."

"Now I don't want to sit here."

"If that's how you feel, you're just going to have to stand."

I grimace in envy. "Must be nice."

"Wrong tense. Must have *been* nice. But it was also all a lie, so the niceness is merely visceral. What you have with Kyle; now that's real."

"Yeah, but still, at the time you were doing it all over the Taj Mahal here, I was simply leading a normal, mundane sex life. A few times a week. In a bed. At night. Lights usually off."

"I guess we can agree to disagree, or merely agree to envy one another. Oh, and if you're going to refuse to sit anywhere we did it, we can't go outside, either," she giggles.

"You tramp! Can't people see? You've got neighbors. People own telescopes."

"That was part of the allure. Listen, sit yourself down. It's not like we don't have a cleaning lady. I'm not gross, you know."

Slowly, I sit, but after a few seconds I lean over and sniff the fabric.

"Stop that! Now even I'm getting grossed out."

"Okay, fine." I don't know where to begin, so I just do. "I busted into Ashley's session with Stella."

"No!"

"Yes."

"What happened?" Julia asks.

"I got thrown out."

"Did Ashley hear anything? Did you two get into it?"

"No. Ashley seems blissfully unaware of my suspicions. Furthermore, I failed in my endeavors."

Julia sits across from me, curling her legs up underneath her. For a moment or two she says nothing. "You could be wrong, you know."

I mull that one over.

"No, really. We all took Ashley's side because we got to know her and we heard her talk about it week in and week out. Then you and your MIL spoke to Ashley's MIL once or twice and suddenly you've completely taken *her* side. I know you've never been crazy about Ashley. Neither am I. But still…"

"You make a good point," I say with a sigh. "Wow, that really makes me feel like an ass."

"It's true, you know. Not that you're an ass, but that you could have it all wrong." Julia grabs her knees, pulling them up under her chin like a little spider monkey. "You don't have a smoking gun here. It may be very convoluted, but maybe Marshall didn't cop to the trust fund because he thinks it's none of your damn business. He just met you. Why would he let you audit his books while we stood waiting to see a movie?"

She's right. And wrong. "The best and worst thing in the world is to go with your gut. In my gut, I just have a feeling that Ashley's no good."

Julia shifts now and stretches out her legs as well as her arms, lying almost sideways on her chair. Due to the power of suggestion, I somehow manage to envision her naked, doing the nasty with her ex, in exactly that position on that very piece of furniture. Why did she have to tell me about her and her furniture? TMI! "Kat, you did what you could. Given the circumstance, you couldn't have done more or better. What happens now, happens. It's out of your hands."

"The thing I worry about more is the way Stella looked at me when I burst in. I know that the moment she finishes with Ashley's MIL, she'll be on the phone with Claudia and Gabriella. Once she rats me out — and she has every right to — I'm going to get drummed out of the corps. I can't have that. For the past few months, you guys have been my salvation. That's why I've kept on going to meetings even though things between me and Momma Lana Ding Dong are good now. I go because I like the people and I like the energy. I haven't felt that since being in a sorority at college. I miss it; I miss my girlfriends."

Julia gets up and walks towards me, her body language indicating she's coming in for a sisterly hug. "No matter happens with the others, we'll still friends."

As she is just about to put her arms around me, I put my hand out. "Fine. Thanks. But I can't hug you now."

"Why?"

"'Cause I'm in one of your 'sex chairs' and you've got a faraway look in your eyes. I love you but I'm not acting as a surrogate for your ex."

Julia laughs out loud. "Ah, you have me all figured out. See, on that chair he sat just like that. And then I got on top of him like this…"

"Stop! I almost forgot. You aren't having sex-filled flashbacks of you and Mark. You did the dirty with Jason last night. Now dish!" I say laughing.

Julia laughs out loud. "Ah, you have me all figured out. After all these years of apparently two-way sexual temptation, Jason and I purged ourselves of every ounce of built-up sexual tension we had. We made love, we had raw sex, he took me to places Mark never could and I did the same for him. My imagination didn't come close to what the reality of making love to him would be like. I used my body and mouth in ways I never thought I would have the guts to do. It was animalistic and went on for hours and hours and hours…"

"You need to save this for the next DILS meeting."

Julia isn't smiling anymore, and I can see she is struggling with something.

"I can't wait until the next meeting. It will be too late." Her voice begins to tremble.

"Too late for what, Jules. I'm lost."

Sounding so distressed and desperate, Julia begins spilling her heart out. "I know Jason is married, and I should feel guilty for what we did. I have never been a mistress or condone adultery, but I don't feel bad for it at all. No regrets. He should have been mine but it was my fault for acting too much like a buddy rather than a potential mate. She won because I wasn't playing the same game. Besides her looks, she is a bit of a snob. I should have been confident enough to show him what a poor match they were together. Kat, have you ever heard the song by Cheap Trick, *I Want You To Want Me?*"

Clearly, this was a rhetorical question because she continued speaking without coming up for air.

"That's been my theme song about Jason all these years. The song I sing at the top of my lungs when no one is around." Julia is now standing up, singing this song like a drunk on Karaoke night.

"I want you to want me.
I need you to need me.
I'd love you to love me.
I'm beggin' you to beg me.
I want you to want me.
I need you to need me.
I'd love you to love me.
I'll shine up the old brown shoes, put on a brand-new shirt.
I'll get home early from work if you say that you love me."

At this point, I think my once poised pixie might be suffering from Female Hysteria. Julia sits down next to me and grabs both of my hands in hers. Her eyes are wide like a wild woman. "I need Stella to hypnotize Jason before he leaves to go back home," Julia says bluntly.

"Jules, I don't know how to put this without hurting your feelings. You were with a man who used you to get famous. It was fake love. Now you want Stella to hypnotize Jason to *make* him love you. I mean, I can see he already loves you. It's written all over his face, but he is obviously in love with his wife too. You said it yourself, from the photos you have seen his social network page and the bits of dirt you get here and there from mutual friends, they are the perfect couple." I anxiously await for Julia to respond in hopes that I was not too harsh. "Do you want that on your conscience?"

"That's just it, Kat." Julia is now calm and controlled, which is a major departure from her bout of craziness a few minutes prior. "I *thought* they were the perfect couple. Jason and I have always flirted shamelessly with one another. We've done it in front of our co-workers, at tradeshows, and at parties. But we did it in a way that kept it light. No one took us seriously. We would get the occasional 'go get a room already' comment, but nothing more. Then he met the other one and that part of our friendship naturally fizzled out. I didn't fight it because I didn't think I was good enough for him on a physical level. She won because I gave up."

I open my mouth to respond but Julia half-jokingly puts her tiny index finger to my mouth suggesting I keep quiet. Point taken.

Julia continues, "After Jason and I spent the night together, I starting thinking about what Stella said about hypnotism. She can't make people do something they don't want to do. However, if there is part of the person's brain that is feeling something either positive or negative, then she can tap into it and cultivate the idea. Therefore, if Jason was completely happy and satisfied with his wife, then he would have left my room. I don't want Stella to hypnotize Jason to love me. Last night proved he already has those other type of feelings for me. I want her to make him NOT love *her* anymore. I know it sounds awful, but I don't want to play fair this time."

Since joining the DILS, I am the last person who should dictate what is morally right from wrong and will back my friend up with whatever she decides to do.

"Love is love, Jules." I wanted my mother-in-law's love and you want Jason's love. How can I fight that logic?" I say.

"Do you think Stella will agree to do it?" Julia asks almost nervously.

Having recently had an ethical tongue-lashing from Stella, I would be terrified to even broach this subject with her. "It can't hurt to ask," I respond trying not to sound so doubtful.

Chapter Twenty-Nine

A few days later, my phone rings at work. "Kat, you're not going to believe this," says Julia.

"I'm listening."

"Claudia just called. We're all invited over to Ashley's."

"Huh?"

"'We' as in she specifically asked me to call you."

I ponder this for a moment. "She didn't call or e-mail me herself? She just made you the messenger?"

"Well, its good, isn't it? You're invited, right?"

"Yeah, but to me it means I'm still in the doghouse. Why are we going over to Ashley's? What's the dress code?" In DILS, you *always* need to ask what to wear. It would not surprise me if someday Claudia were to say, "Didn't you get the memo to bring along your SCUBA gear?" You gotta keep up with her.

"Casual. Something you wouldn't mind getting a little dust on, she said."

The mind reels. "Are we burying a body?"

Julia cracks up. "Anything's possible. But yeah; dust was definitely mentioned. And you. You and dust."

"Uh, okay," I reply, for lack of a better response. Going to Ashley's? Why the hell for? We've never been there before. The paranoid inside of me begins to grow. We're headed to Ashley's so Stella and Claudia can show off the new, improved, and hypnotized Lee Ann, just to rub my nose in the fact I was wrong and Ashley got exactly what she wanted, which is… what we all joined DILS for. Right? Wrong. If I'm right and Ashley is a shallow gold-digger, then DILS is nothing more than a cult where people join up just to learn how to take advantage of others — sort of like auto repair school.

"See you Saturday at 10AM," Julia says pleasantly and hangs up.

I'm befuddled and morally torn, but to simply choose not to go would kill my sense of curiosity. Okay, I'm in. I may hate it, it may be one of the worst days of my life, but I'm going in, hell or high water.

* * *

Dressed for dust or dirt-biking, I pull up to Ashley's address. It's a nice place. Big and most likely expensive, yet not anywhere near as eye-popping as Claudia's place, Julia's place, or even my place, for that matter. But it's definitely not a shack. I ring the doorbell and Ashley answers.

"Hi Kat, how are you? So glad you could come." She's smiling. I've never really seen her smile. It scares me. Claudia did mention "getting dusty." Maybe Ashley really did do in her MIL — and her husband, too — and we're all there like a coven of witches to burn and bury the bodies. Nice.

Ashley continues the mind-fuck by pulling me in for a

hug. Note: hugging someone with super large fake breasts is less fun than one would think. The pure physics of the act causes you to have your pelvis pulled forward, while your upper body is pushed back, which can cause whiplash or disc compression. As Ashley releases me, I can't help but look at what she's wearing. It's… it's… decent. I mean, she's actually covered. The last time I saw her like this was at our first DILS meeting, where I suppose she was trying to put on a better impression. She's got on a pair of jeans sans sexy gaping holes, and she's wearing a t-shirt with a crew neck — and the shirt is large enough so her mammaries don't look like they're going to explode out of it. If I didn't know better, I'd think she was going to a church picnic. Do bleached blond ex-porn stars have their own church? Their own religion?

"C'mon in," she says, and I do, although the impetus to quickly turn, go back into my car, and peel out in horror does cross my mind. A smiling, wholesome-looking Ashley will do that to you.

I go inside and the place looks like a tag sale. Check that — the place *is* a tag sale. The entire Great Room is filled with boxes and boxes of shoes, dresses, jewelry, crap of all sorts, and my girls are placing tags on everything, while some are trying things on and setting things aside.

"Kat, c'mon in! Better move quickly or all the good things will be gone," says Claudia.

I scrunch up my face and try to figure out what the hell is going on here. Gabriella grabs my arm and pulls me deeper into the mass of merchandise. "Okay, tell me what's happening here," I finally manage to get out.

"Ashley is unloading her overage," says Gabriella, and for a second I think this must mean she's about to pull out her implants, which would be very bloody and gross.

"Yeah, I've simply got too much in the closet. Too much everywhere. So I thought I'd invite you girls over to see if there's anything you'd like to put dibs on. I've been quite the spend-a-holic over the years and I'm crippling poor Marshall with my wicked ways," Ashley says with a smile, that damn smile again, albeit a smile with very nice, straight white teeth. Marshall the dentist has been good for something.

"Now, I don't want anyone to look at this as charity. Ashley and her husband are not destitute and we don't want them to feel that way, nor do we want to be afraid of feeling like vultures, either. This is a win-win. We're helping her out, she's helping us out, and what doesn't sell today will go to second-hand shops all over Los Angeles. And what doesn't sell there, she'll take back and bring to a good charity. Ashley doesn't have to do this; she *wants* to do this," says Claudia with a smile. "We're very proud of her."

I'm listening — I'm not believing, but I'm listening, and then I become seduced by something… the come-hither sight, sound, and smell of fashion. I look around and I see Hermes bags, Manolo Blahnik boots, Balenciaga wallets, Annick Goutal perfumes. My breath becomes short. My head begins to spin. Senseless sounds imitating words come out of my mouth.

As I attempt to control myself, the women around me are in the same percolating lather, grabbing things, picking things up, asking, begging, "How much for this? And this? What do you want for this?"

I pat myself down and find my own wallet. "Do you take plastic?" I say to Ashley, and everyone laughs.

"We've all asked that same question. We're trying things on and putting dibs on what we want most. Then we're taking turns making ATM runs," says Julia.

I have never been to an actual orgy, but this is the closest thing to one I have ever experienced. Unlike mad-dash sample sales, we are all quite civil, for we are Sisters and this is a private home, so we do not get into tugs of war or hair-pulling battles. We even attempt to help one another out. "Oh, this would look good on you. It's not my color." The giving, the taking, the hands and bodies everywhere, the silent pacts made to insure mutual satisfaction for all; yes, this must be what a Roman orgy feels like.

As I move to the hypnotic rhythm of fashion, I bump into a new body, one I hadn't focused on before, but then again, who's looking at bodies or faces when there is jewelry to be tried on. "Hello, Kat. Glad to see you came."

Oh yes, I came. I came and I'm coming again. And again. And… "Stella?"

Of course it's Stella; I'd know that voice anywhere. It snaps me out of my trance — no pun intended — and brings me back to reality. "Can I see you a moment? Privately?" she asks.

I'm sober now. I follow Stella out of the main room. Ashley passes us by, carrying a new armload full of tops and belts and I am almost drawn back away from where I was headed, but I correct my course and am back among the living again, as opposed to the shopping. As I gaze longingly back at the newest pile of booty, I once again see Ashley's face and it still has that damn smile plastered upon it. Her husband, Marshall, races up to her and quickly grabs half her load from her, helping her. She gladly allows him to assist, brushing a loose strand of blond hair from her face and thanking him, then placing a kiss upon his lips. Coming in from what must be the kitchen is Lee Ann, Ashley's MIL, toting a tray full of snacks. Ashley lays down what's left in her arms and, mimicking Marshall's actions, runs up to Lee Ann and helps her out. They smile at one another — no kisses, but nice, sincere smiles.

By now I'm in the dining room, alone with Stella. She stuffs both her hands in the back pockets of her jeans and looks at me, waiting for me to collect myself from this sensory overload. She remains quiet, letting me get in the first word.

"You hypnotized Ashley."

"Yep."

"And not Lee Ann."

"Yep."

I say nothing. Instead, I play it all out in my mind and yes, it all falls into place now. "I was right," I say quietly, not haughty or proud, but simply matter-of-fact.

"You figured out the family situation correctly. The thing is, so did we; we meaning Claudia, Gabriella, and I. That's what we do. It's not that we're better or smarter or anything else than you or anyone else in this place. We've just been doing it longer and, most importantly, we trust one another. We know better than to go it alone. That's what a sisterhood is. That's what keeps us from acting impulsively. When we talk together, we keep each other in check. I suppose other groups of people might do that and actually make things worse, like inciting one another to riot, but that's not how we roll."

"A sisterhood," I repeat thoughtfully. "You mentioned once before that you worried sometimes about playing God. Is this how you keep from doing that?"

"That's exactly how I keep it from happening. We all play a role. Claudia met Ashley first. She had the first inclination things were not as they seemed. Gabriella's been tracking the family for weeks now. She knew long before you said anything that Ashley was the bully who was bilking her husband and her MIL out of everything they had. The last thing of any value left was Lee Ann's home. Ashley never came right out and said it, but she was hoping we could help her latch onto that, too. Sell it out from under her and pocket the change. But as you can see, that won't be happening now. And a lot of what she used the money for, Marshall and Lee Ann will be getting back, one way or another. They'll be living within their means from now on, or at least that's the plan."

"Her and Marshall. Does she love him?" I ask.

"In a way. He's a nice guy. Homely, yes, but then again, some might say the same about me."

"But you're not…"

"I'm not fishing for compliments, Kat. I know who I am. I'm also happy to report — swearing on the lives of my children — I did not and have never hypnotized my husband. The point is, Marshall is nice and he's been very nice to Ashley all along. Obviously, with the passage of time, some of that invaded her psyche. She's felt what it is to be truly loved. Maybe he's no Playgirl centerfold, but he'll never treat her badly and he'll never leave her, so she's got a pretty good thing. Part of her mind knows that. It's just that now she's actually in touch with it."

"And you say this *isn't* playing God?"

Stella snickers. "I told you; it's a team effort. I guess you could call us 'The Goddesses.'"

"I like that," I reply.

273

"Kat, you have a good soul and a brilliant mind. A little — a lot — impulsive, but with us around you, we could smooth out those wild edges. I hope you'll forgive me for blasting you in my office the other day. We'd love for you to stay; to continue to be part of the Daughter-in-law Society."

"Wow, sure. Thanks. Does this mean I get to be a Goddess, too?" I joke.

"Goddess-in-Training. We'll work you in. Maybe this time next year if you live up to expectations, we can offer you full Goddess-ship."

We both laugh, then hug. Now that I am comfortably back in her good graces, can't resist asking her about Julia and Jason. "Stella, can I ask you one more question?" I regret the words before they even catch air. Even in the short time Stella has known me, she's got my number. She doesn't respond but her expression tells me to go ahead and ask the question she already knows is coming. "I know I am not supposed to ask you about your clients or what you do behind your office doors, but I want you to know that I am all for you working your magic on Jason. Whether it is right or wrong, no one is more deserving of it than Julia." Stella hasn't stormed off so I continue to ramble. "I mean, I don't even know if Julia has asked you yet, and I haven't had time to ask her about it with all this Ashley stuff going on. Anyway, if she didn't say anything, please don't mention that I said anything to you. And if she did ask, then I hope you will help her." I hold my breath and wait for Stella to either respond or beat me to a pulp.

"Sometimes, you have to let nature takes its course. Whatever is meant to be will be," says Stella with an unreadable smile. "I have to leave for an appointment now

Kat. I will see you very soon." She gives me a quick hug and leaves me there trying to unscramble the meaning of what she just said. I guess I will find out soon enough anyway.

Chapter Thirty

Ashley and Lana could not be farther apart in size or taste, but jewelry tends to be more universal and I found a bracelet that really caught my eye. I even stopped by my house for a little gift box, some wrapping and a bow and now I am here, walking up the sidewalk to Lana's door, unannounced but hopeful.

"Katherine, what brings you here?"

Over the course of my marriage, I have never appeared before her like this. I'd dreamed of it a few times, envisioning confronting her outside of Kyle's sight and earshot. But never would I have dreamed I'd be here willingly and enthusiastically bearing gifts.

Without a word, I stick my arm out like a little girl, handing Lana my pretty, decorated box. "Surprise!"

"What's this for? Come in, come in, come in." I follow her into her living room, but we don't sit; we're still too caught up in the moment.

"Why are you giving me a gift? It's not my birthday."

"I know. It's just… it's a long story, but the short version is I was out shopping, I saw this, and I thought of you."

She doesn't open it. All she does is put her arms around me. Soon I feel her weeping. "What's the matter?"

"I'm sorry."

"What?"

"I said I'm sorry. I never treated you right."

I don't know what to say. All this time, ever since the hypnosis, I was under the impression Lana was in complete denial of how she acted towards me all those years. She remembers? She knows now? I don't get it. I wish Stella were here to interpret.

"What do you mean?" I ask, although I know exactly what she means. I just want to hear how she perceives it.

"Sit down," and I do. "Katherine, I'm an overprotective mother. Kyle's father, he was a mean drunk. He was a fine man when he was sober. That's most all of what Kyle knows because I shielded him from the worst of it. It was a lifelong struggle. I never wanted Kyle or his brothers to know how bad it was. Children should be allowed to be children. Boys should think highly of their father, and there was a lot there to admire. But the drink…" she shakes her head at the memories.

"I took the overprotectiveness too far. I realize that now. Once I started protecting the boys from their father, I started protecting them from everyone who could hurt them. Not just hurt them physically, but ruin their souls. A wife can do that. She's so important in a man's life.

"I thought you were a dream when Kyle brought you around. But still, I worried. It was a pattern for me. I was so afraid you would hurt him that I began to hurt you first. I never should have done that. I'm sorry. I can't believe after all I said to you over the years you're here now, giving me a gift for no good reason."

This time it's me reaching over to hug her. "I'm sorry, too. I'm sorry we never had this conversation before. I should have tried to tell you how much I love Kyle and how I would never ever hurt him."

Lana's body shakes against mine. "You didn't have to. I already knew. Deep in my heart I always knew; I just couldn't break the pattern. But you broke the spell. Thank you. Thank you."

I hold her for a while and tears are rolling down my cheeks as well. I want to tell her about DILS. I want to tell her about Stella and the trance. But sometimes it doesn't matter what road brings you to your destination, it's whether or not you get there. Many years ago I left my own parents in North Carolina and never looked back. I did it with their blessing and encouragement. Yet like everyone else, I wanted it all. I wanted the career and the adventure, but I also wanted this. I wanted family. Kyle and I, we're lovers and friends, but it takes more than two to make a family. Holding onto my Momma Lana, I feel I'm finally home.